ECLIPSE

To Sam

WELCOME TO TRINITY

2 4 MAY 2025

--] ENTRY/176BRIDGE

THANKS FOR READING!

Phil .

Front cover designed by Getcovers

ECLIPSE

Entanglement Book III

Phil Oddy

Part One

CHAPTER 1

CANNON
THE MIDDLE SEA
ONCE UPON A TIME

Cannon spat on the deck. He hated the way the salt coated his tongue, the way it made it swell and stick to his cheek and the roof of his mouth. He hated the salt, and he hated the sea it was whipped from. He hated this boat.

Was it a boat? Or was it a ship? It didn't matter to him. The boat, or the ship, didn't care if he knew what it was or how to operate it.

Sail it?

He looked up at the vast sheets above him, flapping in the wind. Sails, the boat had sails. You probably sailed it.

You would, if it wasn't perfectly capable of sailing itself.

Cannon spat again, gripped the spoked wheel and spun it. It ran freely. It shouldn't do that, it should be attached to something. A mechanism, something connected, ultimately, to a rudder that could steer them across the sea.

It was just for show, a decorative flourish. Like the sails which, despite the way they rumbled and billowed and

3

snapped in the wind, were not actually pushing the good ship *Dukey Run* towards the horizon.

That was helpful, in a sense, because the wind would often drop. It wasn't a problem for them. They were never becalmed, never stuck. Perpetual motion, always moving, day after night after day...

But it didn't make for an interesting voyage. Nothing needed doing, so nothing got done. Most of the crew - passengers, Cannon felt that a crew should be taking a more active role in proceedings - stayed below deck. It was only Cannon who seemed interested in the strange circumstances they found themselves in. It was only Cannon who seemed to care.

Cannon spat once more. Maybe they cared, just not enough to put up with the salt. Cannon thought that might be a smart position to take.

It didn't make any difference, anyway, whether he cared or not, whether he knew the plan or not. It wasn't his role, not his place, to understand. He was there for one job and one job only.

He was the Human Cannonball. He was there to perform. But chance would be a fine thing.

He had to wait. He couldn't even practice on the ship, not if he didn't want to get left behind. It was fine for Bonzo, or for Strongman, or for the Flying Squirrels. They could while away the interminable hours going through the motions, polishing their routines.

He supposed he could practise his landings. He looked up into the rigging. The Squirrels were up there now, meaning that he wasn't as alone on deck as he thought he'd been. He watched as they swung and twirled and dropped, defying gravity high above the deck.

He hoped they hadn't seen him lurking down here, hadn't

seen him spitting on the deck. That would not leave a good impression, and Cannon hoped to leave a good impression with at least one of the Spectacular Squirrel Sisters.

He looked back down at the sea, away from the glare of the sun in the bright blue sky, which was making his eyes water. The reflection on the water wasn't a lot better. The dazzling light made him scrunch up his cheeks.

There was a shriek from the sky, and his head snapped upwards, expecting to see the tumbling form of a Squirrel, anguish on the face of the sister who failed to catch her. There were no nets. It was going to be a hard landing. Even that was better than landing in the water and being left behind.

But no one was falling, no one had been dropped. All three sisters were huddled together in the crow's nest, staring ahead of the ship, and the swell beyond.

'What is it?' shouted Cannon. 'Is there something wrong?'

Tabitha, the smallest Squirrel, pointed. Cannon ran to starboard and tried to follow the line of her arm to where she was pointing. There was nothing.

He looked again, eyes scanning the surface of the water, searching for something, although he didn't know what. Something fallen from the ship? Or from another vessel?

He saw it. In slow motion, as the wave fell, and the ship rose on the next one, he watched as a head hovered into view, then was lost again.

Once more, the head reappeared and disappeared, but this time Cannon saw arms waving, flailing. Maybe drowning. Cannon started to shout, very loudly.

The bobbing person was in front of them, so they hadn't come from the *Dukey Run*. He looked around frantically for another ship, but there was nothing. No ships, no land, nothing but the wild, wide expanse of the Middle Sea.

It was impossible that they were there. If they were there, it was impossible that they were alive. Yet they *were* there and they *were* alive. Cannon could see the evidence with his own eyes.

He didn't have a moment to lose. They weren't in control of the ship. They couldn't slow it down, or bring it around, or manoeuvre close to the person in any way, even if such a thing was possible in a ship of this size without pushing them under the waves and finishing them off in a way that the ocean hadn't managed.

They needed to be brought on board quickly, before it was too late. Cannon couldn't do it on his own. He needed help.

His fellow passengers responded quickly to the alarm he raised. He was surprised and gratified by that. Ropes were thrown, and lifebelts, and despite Cannon's worst fears, the owner of the head in the sea managed to cling on and let Strongman drag them closer to the ship.

A raft was dropped. A human chain, made primarily of Sensational Simian Brothers, who had just the right combination of core strength and flexibility, was extended. They brought him onboard, where he was wrapped in sacks and laid on the deck. At some point he'd lost consciousness, but they still found him to have breath and a pulse and they all felt pretty pleased with themselves for their heroic rescue.

It was rare, on this voyage, to have anything to do, let alone something that required them to pull together and work as a team. As a *crew*.

Alejandro, the Ringmaster, stepped forward at this point, as he was nominally their leader. He rummaged in the man's pockets, pulling out a plastic card that, at the press of a small button, projected a holographic image that looked enough like the man, without the after-effects of prolonged exposure to freezing salt-water.

'Estrel Beck,' read the Ringmaster out loud.

At the sound of his name, the man's eyes flicked open. He let out a faint gasp.

'Estrel Beck,' repeated the Ringmaster, bending close to the man to talk directly to him, making eye contact and flashing his winning smile. 'Welcome, Mr Estrel Beck, to Alejandro's Floating Circus.'

CHAPTER 2

Dawn was breaking. Applicant Lek was perched on the corner ledge where the outside wall of the keep met the courtyard perimeter. Somewhere, someone was ringing a bell.

Lek suspected that it was for him, so he had been attempting to ignore it. He wasn't sure how long it had been ringing for now. Quite a while, he considered.

As an Applicant to the Trinity Brotherhood, Lek was supposed to pay attention to bells. He knew he should react, that his long-term prospects within the Brotherhood might be better served by doing what was expected of him.

He could hear the noise of the Acolytes gathering in the courtyard for morning routines, voices raising, sticks clacking against each other by way of warm-up sparring. Someone would probably spot him soon. He should get on.

Might as well answer that bell.

When he went and checked the board, it turned out to be

Onu Castor's bell, which actually made Lek feel a little guilty. Lek had no time for most of the monks in the Citadel, and certainly none for the Acolytes, who all thought they were so much better than they were. He made an exception for Onu Castor, who always had time for Lek, which was all Lek really asked.

The Brothers' rooms were at the back of the castle, down several very long, dusty corridors - havens for spiders and slithery things that slipped back into the shadow when Lek swung his pocket torch at them. By the time Lek was banging on Onu Castor's door, it was some twenty minutes later. He really did feel quite bad about it all now.

The door swung open without a sound. Inside was dark and filled with smoke. The familiar aroma of moss and butter snaked around him. Lek found that smell comforting. He thought that, one day, if he ever was accepted into the Brotherhood, he'd like to spend his days shrouded in darkness, smoking a pipe filled with butter.

He smiled to himself and stepped inside.

'Onu?' he called.

He stood still for a moment, on the threshold, to let his eyes adjust to the light. Eventually, he could make out a figure sat on the bench that ran along the far wall. He waited for it to notice him.

'Well, don't just stand there!' said an ancient voice. 'Come closer. I can't see a thing at the best of times and I can't be doing with you lurking in the dark!'

'You called?'

Lek moved further into the room and closed the door behind him.

'Hours ago,' replied Onu Castor. 'I've sobered up now. Can't remember what I wanted. It was probably another drink, but I'm making do with the contents of this instead.'

He waved his pipe. It was long, at least as long as Lek's arm. Thick smoke curled from the bowl.

'So… should I go?' asked Lek.

Whilst he was confident that Onu Castor liked him, Lek thought it best not to overstay his welcome with someone whose temper was legendary and who could have him cast out from the Citadel on a whim.

Onu Castor laughed with a body shaking intensity. The sound of it rumbled from him and Lek was sure he could feel the vibrations come up from the floor through his feet. From the stone floor.

He obviously couldn't, but maybe this meant that he could relax. Somewhat. It was unlikely that he'd angered the old monk.

'Is there anything else I can do?' he checked. 'For you?'

Onu Castor shook his head.

'Sit down.'

He waved at the bench on which he perched. Lek sat down next to the old monk and tried to make himself comfortable. He was keen to know what the old man wanted. Usually, he helped by fetching intoxicating drinks or clearing used trays of crockery and glassware. This felt different. He'd never asked him to sit down before.

'If I can…?'

'You've been here some time, have you not, boy? You're, what, twenty-four? Twenty-five?'

'Twenty-nine years, Onu.'

It was getting late for him. He knew this. Plenty of Applicants submitted to the Trial younger than he was now. Some were Brothers by his age. He hadn't got as far as making up his mind about whether this really was the path for him.

'What are you doing here?' Onu Castor asked.

It was a fair question, but Lek bristled at the suggestion that he might be wasting anyone's time, least of all his own.

'I am an Applicant. I am training to be an Acolyte in the Brotherhood. One day I hope to be accepted as a Brother such as…'

'I don't think you believe that any more than I do.'

Lek had nothing to say. He was right, though.

This was it, then? Was this the end of the road? This was the moment that it all came crashing down and he found himself cast onto the street with no home and no prospects?

He supposed it couldn't have lasted forever. Maybe if he'd tried, just that bit harder, to believe. In anything.

Maybe he could work in the kitchens. For money. There weren't many paid positions down there. Applicants like him did most of the work, but maybe there was something he could do? He had a good relationship with Chef. He was always complaining about how useless the new Applicants were.

'And yet you are still here. You should submit to the Trial.'

Lek leaned back in surprise. This was not what he had expected the old man to say. What was this? A show of faith where he himself had none? A validation of…

'Don't get me wrong,' continued the monk, cutting off Lek's train of thought for the second time. 'You would be a terrible, ill-disciplined Acolyte, and an unpious, troublesome Brother…'

He paused, placed his pipe between his back teeth, and grinned.

'…but you wouldn't be the only one.'

This seemed to be a joke, rather than an admonishment, so Lek laughed. He still wasn't sure what he was being told to do. Onu Castor didn't seem to have a lot of faith in him, but he had definitely said that he should submit to the Trial.

'Thank you,' Lek said.

It seemed the safest thing to say.

'Right, now go away.'

Lek was taken aback. He had expected more. Instructions, guidance, some kind of plan of action. This was quite an abrupt stop.

'Is that it?'

'For now,' confirmed Onu Castor. 'I would like you to come back, however. Tomorrow, as the sun sets, if you please. And next time, I don't want to have to ring a bell until it sends me deaf before I get your attention. Now, begone!'

He snapped his fingers on this last utterance. Lek could have sworn he saw blue sparks fly from his fingertips. He hurriedly got up from the bench and bolted for the door.

CHAPTER 3

The Citadel Library was a vast building filled, as one might expect, with towering bookcases which created dusty aisles where the Brotherhood's Readers could lurk. Here they spent their long, candlelit days teasing meaning from the pages of the cryptic texts of the Library's books.

Each book in the Library was the result of an Applicant's Trial. Their return, with the pages that they collected in the course of their quest, marked the point at which they became Acolytes to the Brotherhood. The contents of their finds - which usually took the form of abstract marks, diagrams and arcane symbols - were meticulously copied at thirty-two times the size of the original, then illustrated, decorated and bound in ancient leather.

They never talked about where the pages came from, or what it took to collect them. Some said the paper was made of what remained of the Tree itself, but that wasn't a widely held belief anymore.

Regardless of how they were collected, once a book was transcribed and accepted into the Library - a process that typically took more than ten years - its compiler would attain the rank of Brother and become a fully fledged monk. From that point, it was the Reader's job to make sense of what had been found, while the monk was allowed to retreat into contemplation, meditation and feasting.

Haezle Muñoz was a Reader. She had been a Reader since her late teens and now, on the cusp of her thirtieth birthday, she had finally been allocated her own book from which she was expected to add to the total wealth of knowledge possessed by the Order of the Brotherhood.

The Citadel, and its Library, was an important part of Trinity's heritage, and Haezle was proud to uphold its traditions. It was interesting work, even if she was sceptical of the more mystical aspects of the belief that surrounded her. She worked hard, took her task seriously, and was never happier than when she had a puzzle to solve.

It wasn't, however, her book that she lifted from the shelf now and dropped onto the table. It landed with a thump that gave away the lack of control she'd had over the heavy tome. She glanced around nervously. She got enough grief from the mostly male Readers about her perceived deficiencies without dropping books on the desk.

No one was looking. She'd got away with that one. She tucked her chestnut hair back behind her ears, smoothed down her robe and, thus composed, turned back to the young Authority Cadet who remained standing patiently by her table. He'd asked very nicely if he could see one of the books and she didn't want to disappoint him.

Unlike most of the books in the Library, this one wasn't dusty. Isaak had been working through it only that morning. If he hadn't been, they'd still be coughing their way through the cloud it would have kicked up.

'So,' she said, lifting the thick cover and folding it over. 'This is the Book of Moors. It was compiled by Onu Walsam over sixty years ago. We're still learning from it, even today.'

The Cadet nodded, peering at the page that Haezle had revealed.

'I don't recognise the script.'

'That's what we're here for, the Readers. We try to interpret the writing. The symbols, the markings, the *words*, hopefully, only emerge after lengthy study.'

'And what does this one say?'

'Ah...'

Haezle felt embarrassed. She wasn't sure why, she wouldn't be expected to understand the Book of Moors. She'd never studied it. She wasn't convinced that Isaak understood as much of it as he claimed. But this stranger expected her to understand it and she felt regret that she didn't.

That's just professional pride. Pull yourself together, Haezle. He's not here to arrest you.

Haezle had learned to be wary of Authority. It was a matter of survival for people like her. Her job gave her a layer of respectability, a layer of belonging, but underneath she was a Commons girl and that never went away.

This Cadet seemed different, though. He seemed genuinely interested, without an agenda.

Careful, Haezle. That's how they get you...

'This isn't my book,' she confessed. 'My friend Isaak studies this one.'

'So where's your book?'

He asked it gently, warmly, with actual interest. That made Haezle sad, because she couldn't show him.

'My book isn't here, not today,' she said. 'It's been taken back to its Brother... Onu Lek. The one who compiled it. I had some questions…'

She stopped. The Book of Keyes was definitely in Onu Lek's quarters, waiting for his thoughts on the questions she'd raised. It felt like an excuse, though. The Cadet looked disappointed.

'That's a shame,' he said.

'There are plenty of others I could show you, if you like,' she offered eagerly. 'The Book of Leif, that's a beautiful one. Let me…'

She slipped out from behind the desk and disappeared in between two tall racks of shelving.

'It's OK,' called the Cadet. 'I don't mind. I… Come back?'

Haezle's heart skipped, and she cursed it for that. What was she even trying to do? Why was she trying so hard to keep him around?

There was something about him. It wasn't a romantic attraction, she was certain of that, but she had a strange sense that this man was important, that it was important that they get to know each other.

That wasn't like her. She didn't believe in "strange senses". He was just a nice guy, interested in her work. It was OK to want to impress him.

She stuck her head out from between the shelves. He smiled at her, motioned for her to come back to the desk. Unable to help herself, Haezle obeyed, silently cursing the confusing emotions that were running through her at that moment.

'Tell me about the books,' he said. 'Generally, it's the Acolytes who, what, *"compile"* them?'

'Not quite…'

Haezle returned to her position behind the desk and closed the Book of Moors, running her hand over the intricate carvings that adorned its cover. 'It's compiling the books that earns them their place as an Acolyte in the Brotherhood.'

'Ah, I see. That's what's known as the Trial, right?'

'It is. If they complete the trial, they become an Acolyte on their return.'

'And if they don't complete the Trial?'

'Then they probably haven't returned,' said Haezle grimly. 'We're not allowed to know what the Trial entails. There are rumours, strange stories about portals and doorways to other places, but whatever the truth, you submit to it. That's what they say, "I submit to the Trial". "He submitted to the Trial". I don't think it's something anyone does lightly. Not everyone comes back.'

'And I thought getting a promotion to Junior Oficier was tough.'

'Is that the same sort of thing?' asked Haezle.

The Cadet's laughed response was a little harsh, she thought. She had no no more reason for her to understand the rituals and customs of Authority than he had to understand those of the Citadel.

'No,' he said. 'It's much more about putting in your hours on menial duties, cultivating relationships with Senior Oficiers and immersing yourself in the prevailing drinking culture… Then it just kind of happens.'

'Mysterious…'

'You'd be surprised. I'm still very much at the menial duties stage, although I'm already working on my drinking habit.'

'It's wise to get some training in early.'

'Some might say. The books are enormous, though, aren't they? Do they have to carry them around while they compile them?'

'Oh no,' Haezle laughed. 'The compiled books are much smaller. The Acolyte gets to keep those. These are transcriptions. The books are written up, decorated, embellished so that they are in a format fit for their surroundings…'

The Cadet looked up and around, as if taking in the sheer scale of the library he was standing in for the first time. Haezle followed his eyes. It was impressive. Rows and rows of shelving banked up on stages that formed steps as high as the roof. Every single one of them stacked with books.

'I see. And do you do that, too? The Readers?'

'No. There are Writers whose job it is to…'

'Of course there are. Welcome to Trinity…'

The interruption was so affably delivered that Haezle didn't mind.

'These are the ones we read. If there are any oddities, or contradictions in the text, we can ask the Brother to compare with their copy.'

'Like with your Book of…?'

'Keyes, yes. It's a bit of a complicated system, but it's a very ancient one. There are many, many books, and some of Trinity's most important discoveries have started with insights from within their pages. Now, I'm not sure, personally, if I hold that these are the words of the Creator themselves, but there's definitely something in the…'

'Some of those are really high,' the policeman observed, still staring upwards at the towering shelves. 'How do you get the books down from there?'

'We don't really need those any more,' she said, sadly.

'How come?'

'They're the books of monks who have passed. We study every book for the lifetime of its compiler. And then, out of respect, we stop. We believe every book contains something of them. Not their soul, exactly, but… something of their essence.'

'Sounds nasty,' chuckled the Cadet.

There was a chime from his hip. He pulled out his Com and checked the display.

'I'm sorry,' he said, 'I've got to go.'

Haezle's heart dropped a little, but she hid her disappointment behind the Book of Moors, which she lifted onto its side, preparing to heave it back onto the shelf.

'Good luck with the Mayor,' she said.

'It's not the Mayor,' replied the Cadet. 'It's one of the Candidates. The outsider. Chaguartay?'

'Ah, Chaguartay,' she agreed. 'I hear good things about him.'

'I don't think we've been talking to the same people. But each to their own.'

Haezle's heart dropped a little further. She'd only been trying to make conversation and now she'd made him think less of her.

'Well, good luck anyway,' she said quietly.

'I'll let you know how it goes. I'll see you again.'

'You might,' she said. 'Maybe I'll have my book back by then.'

'I'd like to see it.'

Haezle watched him turn away as she cradled the Book of Moors in her arms.

'I don't know your name,' she called.

'I thought you'd never ask.' He turned back and pulled out his Authority token. 'My name's Simeon. Simeon Lagrange.'

'It's nice to meet you, Cadet Lagrange.'

'Likewise, Haezle the Reader. I find all this fascinating, you know. My job is all about facts and evidence and this is... this is something else. Something... and I hope you won't take offence at this... magical?'

Haezle laughed, although she took offence a little.

'It's not so different, Cadet Lagrange. Insight. That all either of us is looking for. Our investigations are quite different, but our goal is the same. Don't you think?'

Lagrange said nothing, just nodded firmly in what Haezle thought was agreement, before turning once more and leaving the library.

CHAPTER 4

I leave the library and walk out into the sunshine. The courtyard is empty now. Before I went in, it was filled with Acolytes running through their drills, the clack-clack of wood on wood substituting for the steel of an actual weapon.

I wonder if they'd really be able to fight, if the training they put them through genuinely prepares them for hand to hand combat, or if it's all just for show, an elaborate dance for purely ceremonial purposes.

Not that there's anything wrong with ceremony, or tradition, or symbolism. It's not for me, but I see it everywhere, especially here.

That's why I wandered into the Library. I want to understand. Everything. I want to understand everything. But I particularly want to understand what motivates people and for these people it's not money, or power, or sex, or addiction, or anything of the things I'm used to.

From what I know of Stam Chaguartay, he doesn't

23

understand it either. He certainly doesn't like it. I could tell that much as we passed through the Citadel gates. His platform is progress and I'm pretty sure that his idea of progress doesn't involve monks and their ancient knowledge. I'm pretty sure it doesn't involve books.

I might be a grumpy old man, well before my time, but I am irritated by this assignment. I do not know what we're doing here. I don't even know if monks vote. I assume they can, but whether they exercise that right? It seems a bit earthly, a bit too mundane.

Unlike those books. That library was something else. Away from the noise and the dirt that the Acolyte training kicked up, it was an oasis. I'm glad I checked it out. I liked the books, the idea of them as much as the books themselves.

I also liked Haezle.

It's funny. I think I'm usually quite good at figuring out what other people think of me, but I've just walked away from that conversation without a clue about her. I was trying to flirt, and she seemed friendly enough, but she was a bit on edge. As enigmatic as her books.

She seemed pretty dedicated to her calling. It would probably never work. I enjoyed talking to her, though. I should come back. Another time, off duty…

Hang on, where the fuck is Mortimer?

Tom Mortimer is my partner on this assignment. He was supposed to meet me back here, in front of the Superious's residence. I'd gone to the library, and he'd gone for a piss, or to get coffee, or maybe both. Now I'm back, having taken longer than I intended. Plenty longer than it takes to take a leak and grab a drink.

This is not unusual behaviour. Tom Mortimer is a prize pain in my arse. I look around for him. Of course, he's nowhere to be seen.

A figure skulks along the far side of the courtyard, his head down, his feet scuffing the ground in a way that must be filling those sandals with tiny stones at every step. He's wearing the grey robes, which makes him an Applicant, I think.

'Hey!' I shout.

The Applicant stops in his tracks, almost jumps on the spot. He looks around frantically, until he's satisfied that it's only me here, and therefore only me that could have shouted at him. His shoulders slump back down again and he resumes his shuffle, only this time across the courtyard, crossing to my side.

What happened to respect for the law? See… grumpy old man.

Eventually he reaches me. His voice is so quiet I have to strain to hear him.

'Can I help you?' he asks.

'Have you seen another Authority agent? Dressed the same as me, this uniform.'

I gesture to my own clothing, the dress uniform that I hate. It's all stiff blue collars and shiny buttons. We don't usually wear uniforms in Authority. It's just as well, I wouldn't be able to stick it.

But we're on public duty. Security for mayoral Candidates, like Mr Chaguartay. Mr Chaguartay, who decided that today was the perfect day to visit the Citadel for a very long lunch with the Superious, for some reason I can't quite fathom.

At least, *I'm* on public duty. Fuck knows where Mortimer has got to.

The shuffling Applicant doesn't seem to know where Mortimer is, either. He's put on a very thoughtful face and is doing a passable impression of someone thinking very hard, but he's not fooling anyone, least of all me.

'It's fine,' I grumble, waving him away. 'If you see him, he's probably lost. Point him back in my direction.'

'Yes, yes…' The Applicant nods his head and bows in a way with a deference that makes me uncomfortable.

He turns in the opposite direction to where he was heading before I called him over and shuffles away to the door of the Library, through which he slips.

Strange chap, I think. They're all strange chaps.

I take my Com out of my pocket and call Mortimer. It auto-answers in hologram mode, which is a horrible way to have your Com set up. The holograms are a new feature and they don't work properly. I now have a flickering sprite sat on top of my Com. Makes my eyes go funny as I try to figure out where he is and what he's doing.

Fortunately, he isn't on the toilet, but he seems to be standing in some kind of queue.

'Tom,' I say, as quietly as I can.

He must have the volume up because he leaps several feet out of his own skin, with an involuntary yelp that must make the rest of the queue turn around and stare at him. The hologram only extends to the back of the man in front of him, but that guy definitely does.

'Idiot. It's Sim. Where are you? You've been ages.'

I see the hologram Mortimer try to put his finger to his ear, but then realise that he's holding two cups of coffee and doesn't have a free hand. His earpiece must be playing up. Also latest tech. Which also doesn't work properly.

'I know, I'm sorry,' he says in that whiny voice he has. 'I got myself a coffee, but then I thought maybe you'd want one so I came back to queue again…'

It was good of him to think of me, but I'm not bothered about a coffee. I could have saved him some time.

'…and then I had two, but I thought maybe I should get one for him, you know, the Candidate…?'

Mortimer has trouble pronouncing Chaguartay's name and

so he avoids it, lest people think he's being racist. That he knows this, and still hasn't bothered to learn it, suggests to me he should be worried because he is, in fact, racist.

'So you went back to queue a third time?' I don't wait for him to answer. 'Get back here. Chaguartay's due any moment and he's just had seven courses for lunch. If he wanted coffee, I'm sure he's already had it.'

'You're right, Sim, I'm sorry, I'll be right back…'

I see the hologram turn and push his way out of the queue. The paper cups don't seem properly covered, so he winces at regular intervals as he spills hot coffee on himself. He doesn't hang up, so I do.

There is no way that man is ever going to make Oficier grade. There's a chance he's not going to make it to the end of this assignment.

CHAPTER 5

ESTREL
THE NORTHERN EXPOSURE
NOW

It was different this time.

Last time I did it, the previous occasion I jumped back in time, I didn't remember what had happened to me. I could barely speak, couldn't have told you what my story was. It took me hours to piece it all back together.

Maybe I was getting used to it. This was the earliest I'd ever been to Trinity, but maybe the jump hadn't been as big. Maybe that had a bearing. I didn't understand enough about what I was doing to know either way.

Not that I was actually in Trinity now. I'd appeared in a similar spot to the one I'd jumped to last time, high in the hills around the city, looking down on the walls and the murk below. It might even have been the same scar, but there were too many that looked too alike for me to have any certainty about that.

The point was, this time, I remembered. This time I knew. Who I was, where I was, why I was there…

If he'd done this right, then this was a few months before I left, which in itself was about two weeks before I arrived the first time. The timeline was confusing. The timeline was always confusing. That was before I even thought about the fact that where I'd come from…

What? I wanted to say that it didn't exist, but it did. I was just there. I'd met…

No, I wasn't ready for that. I took a mental run up at it. I'd been in Research, following Evie White. She was up to something, but not something I knew about, from my original timeline. This was something new. She was trying to change things, but I didn't understand how.

Then there had been another one, another version of her, from my future. She said she'd come back to stop me. She'd built a machine, one that she said would protect her from any paradox she created so she could do what she liked.

I'd wavered. I'd thought about using it for my own ends, using it to stop her. That had been the moment, the moment I should have stopped her, but I hesitated. Then it had all fallen apart.

I shot at her, but Lagrange got in the way.

Dear Creator, I killed him.

All this time, we had wondered what had happened to him. It was me all along.

But was it? When that bullet hit, it gave Evie the paradox she needed to start her machine. Was that new, or had that always happened?

I didn't understand. Those three words were becoming a mantra.

Regardless, she'd tricked me. I fell for it. I think she tricked us all. Then Lek had pulled the emergency stop cord, metaphorically speaking, and taken me out of there into…

Well, into nowhere. He'd taken me "outside time", so he'd

said, although I still wasn't sure what that meant, not really. He said I'd been there before, although I didn't remember it. I'd lived a lot of lives I couldn't remember.

I'd seen them.

The other lives.

The other versions of me, they'd all appeared at that point. I thought they'd come to help. They seemed to say that they'd come to help, but I don't think that's what it was at all. I don't think they had anywhere else to go.

The way Lek explained it, I think Venn's theory was wrong. Incomplete, at least. I think he always knew this, which was rich given that he'd encouraged me, maybe even persuaded me, to make that first jump, to go back in time and instigate the time loop that would enable me to stop Evie White before she destroyed Trinity and everything and everybody we loved.

My heart swelled in my chest, filling the cavity, pressing against my ribs. It was a metaphorical swelling, but a physical pain.

Mouse.

She'd been there, in the lab, in Research. I hadn't been able to talk to her; I hadn't been able to hold her, but just seeing her had been more than I could have asked for.

She didn't know who I was. She couldn't have. She hadn't met me yet.

Now I wanted to go and find her. I didn't care that she wouldn't know who I was. I didn't care that she wouldn't understand why I pulled up a stool at the bar in Eamer's and ordered a beer like we'd known each other in another life.

It wasn't fair; I knew that. I wouldn't be able to stop myself from using everything I knew, everything I'd got from her, to make her fall in love with me again. Not again. It hadn't happened yet. Not for her.

It wouldn't be manipulation, would it? It had already

happened once, for me. We were happy in my past. She would be happy in our future. *And if we met now, if she loved me now…* With what I knew, we could get out. We could escape before it all went wrong.

Before she died.

I couldn't do it before, but I could do it now. Evie's machine. *Continuity*. It made it possible, cleared the way. No paradox, no foul.

Apart from the universe exploding, if I did. Lek had been very clear on that topic. I couldn't do it, anyway. At all. It *wasn't* fair. I wasn't the same man I'd been before.

Lek had explained it. All the people who appeared, all the different versions of me, were all part of me. That was where Venn had got it wrong. She thought the loop was like rubbing out a mistake and trying again. I could iterate forever, until I got it right, until I solved the loop. Then that timeline would be the one that survived. No one would know that any of the others ever existed.

That wasn't how it worked, though. Every loop I split in two, peeling off part of myself and the world I existed in and sending it back for the next try, while a fragment of who I was carried on. The existence of the other Estrels had changed me. I wasn't the same man.

I hadn't been able to put the time loop into action, but Evie Chaguartay, the version who came from my future, had come from a place where I had. Aborting the plan, which we did after I shot Lagrange, should have erased the time loop. I never created it so none of those other Estrels should have been created. It had happened anyway. That was the effect of the machine.

The machine was the problem, but the effect of the machine was part of the solution. The fact that there were so many of us, that was what Lek was going to use to put things straight.

I didn't know the full extent of the plan, there hadn't been time for explanations but I knew what I was here to do.

I had to get a message to Lek. Time was of the essence.

Clouds rolled overhead as I ran down the hillside. In the distance there was a rumble of thunder, static fizzed in the air. I couldn't hear anything but the echoes of an elephant's screams.

CHAPTER 6

CANNON

Estrel Beck slept for five days and nights while a storm raged across the Middle Sea. It made little difference to the ship, which ploughed on across the water, buffeted by the rage all around them.

For all of that time, Cannon was a frequent visitor. He would bring water, bread and soup, stew, simple things that he thought might nourish and heal the man after his ordeal.

But every time he found Beck asleep, and he left his trays and retreated to his own quarters in the cabin next door, or escaped back onto deck for as long as the storm would allow. As far as he knew, no one else visited. No one else cared about the man they'd rescued from the sea. It was almost as if no one else remembered.

It was almost dawn on the fifth night when loud bangs and pained yelps woke Cannon from his sleep. He scrambled from his bunk and dashed into Beck's cabin to find the man in a heap on the floor, entangled in his blankets and unable to stand up.

He looked at Cannon with panic in his eyes. Cannon bent

down and started unwinding the blankets from his legs, a friendly smile on his face.

'You're awake,' he said.

'Where am I?' asked Beck frantically. 'Who are you? Why is the floor moving?'

Cannon realised that the man must have lost some memory, or was struggling to wake from the deep slumber that had taken the best part of a week from him.

'You're on a ship. You were in the sea? Do you remember?'

'I…'

Beck screwed up his eyes and grimaced. He opened them again and stared intently at Cannon, who was still carefully removing the blankets from around him, until his legs were free enough for him to scramble back onto the bed.

'I…No. I was in the sea?'

Cannon nodded, getting up from where he crouched and sitting down on the opposite bunk.

'You were in the sea. We pulled you out. I don't think you would have survived very much longer. It was cold enough in the water, and there's been a storm the last few days.'

As if in response, the *Dukey Run* lurched to port.

'We're still at sea?'

Cannon regained his balance, righted himself from where he'd fallen onto the bunk.

'We're still at sea,' he confirmed. 'You're on a ship.'

'Yeah, you said… I…'

Beck screwed up his face. Cannon wasn't sure if he was in pain or trying to think very hard.

'Mr Beck.' He reached out a hand and placed it on Beck's arm. 'Maybe you should eat and drink something. You've been out for days, you must be feeling very weak. Perhaps when your strength returns…?'

'Call me Estrel,' said Estrel. 'Mr Beck is my father and I

generally try not to think about him.'

'As you wish, Estrel,' Cannon grinned. 'My name is Cannon. And I didn't mean to dredge up unpleasant memories. I don't need to know any more. We all have our pasts we're trying to escape.'

'You too?' Estrel rubbed his neck.

'Why do you think I ran away and joined the circus?' asked Cannon.

Estrel looked confused at this statement.

'I thought you said we were on a ship?'

'We are on a ship,' Cannon confirmed for the third time. 'The *Dukey Run*…'

'But you said the circus? Was that before you ran away to sea?' Estrel looked at Cannon with an expression of deep sympathy. 'That's a lot of running.'

'I'm still in the circus. It's not just my name that is Cannon. It's the act, my performance.'

Cannon waited for Estrel to ask the obvious question. He said nothing. Cannon appreciated the consideration.

'This is a circus? This ship?' Estrel asked a different question.

'Yes,' Cannon said. 'Alejandro's Floating Circus. This ship is carrying the Floating Circus across the Middle Sea. We are expected, soon, in…'

'In Trinity?' finished Estrel.

'Yes. How do you know?'

'I…' Estrel began, then faltered. 'I don't know. I don't know how I know, but it does mean something. I heard something, remember something… just not very clearly. I've heard of the Floating Circus, too.'

'You should have. It was the first thing Alejandro - our Ringmaster - said to you when we pulled you aboard.'

'No,' said Estrel, getting excited. 'It's not that. It's from before. Before I came here. Before I was in the sea. There's something I'm supposed to remember. Something I'm supposed to do.'

'What is it?' asked Cannon, eagerly.

'I have no idea,' replied Estrel, deflated. 'It's gone. I know I knew something, but I don't know what it is now.'

'The circus, though. You think it's something to do with the circus?'

'I thought so. But now I don't know. It's all fog, there's nothing clear.'

'You said something about before, before you were in the sea. Where did you come from?'

'I don't know. I don't know that either…'

Tears of frustration filled Estrel's eyes. Cannon was certain that whatever he was trying to remember, it would not come from pushing. Estrel had shown him consideration. He would do the same in return.

'It will come.' He tried to reassure the other man. 'It just needs more time. You've been through a lot.'

'I've been through…' Estrel put his head in his hands. 'I don't know what I've been through.'

'You were in the sea. Whatever came before that, it probably wasn't the best situation, given where you ended up. Whatever it was, that dip alone would be enough to knock someone sideways.'

'I know but…'

'I don't think that you're going to get anywhere like this. You need to get out of here. The storm is passing. Come for a walk on the deck with me. We'll leave this topic alone; it will still be here when we get back. The elephant in the room.'

Estrel dropped his hands. His eyes cleared as quickly as they'd filled.

'Elephant, you say?' he said, his voice faint as if his mind was far away. 'That reminds me of something…'

CHAPTER 7

LEK

As the sun set behind the Northern Exposure, darkness took hold of the streets and swallowed the light. In the stone corridors of the Citadel, this brought with it a chill that was not noticeable in any other part of the city.

The air in Trinity was generally described as thick. Thick with the noise and heat of several millions of lives, thick with the scents of the same. It was thick with a toxin that seeped from your skin and made it slick. You sweated Trinity.

Not so in the frozen heart of the Citadel. Lek pulled up the hood of his robe and hurried. He was on time. It was now *"tomorrow, as the sun sets"* and would be for the next half hour, but he didn't really trust his ability not to get lost or sidetracked in the short distance he had left to cover. The sooner he got there, the better.

When he did, Lek's knock was strong and resonant, belying his trepidation. This was important. He was submitting to be an Acolyte. He was committing to the Brotherhood. This was it. He would never leave the Citadel. His life was mapped out from here.

He hadn't chosen it, hadn't decided that this was what he wanted, but that wasn't the way these things worked. As an Applicant, you'd already been called once. It was the sort of thing that you needed to get used to.

The door swung open. The light inside was ice blue. A gust of air blasted him and he realised it didn't just *look* cold.

Whatever was producing the light, it *was* cold, the icy blast making his teeth ache. He could see his breath, and felt the moisture crystallise on the hairs on his upper lip.

This was unexpected. Cautiously, he took a step inside.

'Onu?' he called into the cold, empty space.

There was no reply. Lek took a few more steps into the room. He could tell, before he looked, that it was empty. Not just empty of people, although Onu Castor was nowhere to be seen, but empty of anything.

All of Onu Castor's items of furniture – which were mostly bookcases – were gone. There were no bookcases, but also no drapes, no filthy rugs, no candles, or inkwells, or pipes. The only light was the blue ice that he'd seen from the doorway and, now that he had made his way into the main sitting room, he could see where that was coming from.

Lek shielded his eyes as he looked into the corner of the room. The light was coming from an object on the floor, the only object remaining in the room. It was an open book.

It wasn't huge, or leather bound. It didn't look like any of the grand collection from the Library that Lek recognised from his many visits to bring the Readers tea and, sometimes, something stronger. But he recognised what it was instantly.

It wasn't just a book. It was Onu Castor's book, compiled by him during his own Trial. The Book of Ness. Small, unprepossessing, battered and torn, but the Book of Ness all the same. The original.

The book was lying open on the floor, and from it shone a

bright blue light. Lek took a step closer, but was hit with another icy blast that made him stagger backwards.

'What the…?' he exclaimed.

'What are you doing here?'

The voice filled his head. He didn't hear it; it was there already, the words a memory before he realised that the moment had passed. The memories sounded like Onu Castor.

'Onu?' he asked, out loud, because he didn't know how else to put out his words.

Was there anyone there to hear them?

'Why are you here?' asked the voice of Onu Castor, although that may have been days ago, for all Lek knew.

'I came, like you asked,' said Lek.

It felt inadequate, both the words that he said and how he said them. Faced with sheer, unbridled power, he felt so weak.

'You should not have come,' said Castor.

'You told me to come. "*Tomorrow, as the sun sets*",' protested Lek. 'It's tomorrow now. I did as you asked.'

'You should not do as I asked,' said Castor. 'You do not have to do as I say. You are devoted to the path now.'

'I…'

Lek had a bad feeling that he'd done something wrong. This was feeling very much like a test. A test that he was failing.

'You submitted to the Trial,' declared Castor.

There it was. Lek's shoulders slumped.

'No,' he confessed. 'I wasn't sure if…'

What wasn't he sure of? If he was really allowed? If Castor had meant it? What was he scared of? Doing it wrong?

Well, yes, of course.

He was scared of doing the Trial wrong, failing in the quest, not making it back with a compiled book. That was before he considered his fears that, even if he did all of those things, he wouldn't make it as an Acolyte, would never see his book transcribed, would never hear himself called "Onu".

It was all of those things. All of those things terrified him, and that terror had conspired to root him to the spot, stay his hand, prevent him from taking the first step. It wasn't even that hard. It was a marking on a piece of paper, that was all that was required.

Nailed to the wall of the dining hall, that notice would declare his submission and instantly raise him from his status of lowly Applicant. Not yet an Acolyte, but no longer an Applicant.

Didn't he want that?

'You should have submitted to the Trial. The Trial sets you on the path to devotion. Those who are devoted need not heed commands. That is why we have Applicants.'

It had been a test.

He had failed.

'I'm sorry.'

Lek was surprised to find that he was crying. For so long, he'd been uncertain, not knowing whether this was a path he wanted to take, whether this was a commitment he was ready for. He was waiting to be called.

Now he realised that this was all wrong. He'd already committed, he'd already begun on the path. He'd had many chances to step off already, and he hadn't. He had thought that this was because of apathy, or laziness. Now he realised that he'd already made the choice.

But he'd failed at the first real hurdle.

'I'm sorry!' His voice rose to a wail as he fell to his knees. 'I don't know why I didn't do it. I don't know what it is, just a voice in my head. My mind tells me I can't, I won't. It just gets in my way. If I could ignore that, the voice, the feeling, I know I can do it. I know I want to do it. I want to do it. I thought you were going to tell me how, but…'

There were too many words coming out too fast. He wasn't making sense. He was trying to clarify, to justify his lack of action, but he could see that all he was doing was digging a bigger and bigger hole for Onu Castor to bury him in.

'I have little interest in your excuses.'

Again, the voice of Onu Castor appeared in his memories. This was it. It was all over now, surely. He resigned himself to his fate.

'You will submit this evening…'

Lek looked up. He was still kneeling in an empty room, apart from the book, which was still bathing him in the blue light. But, it seemed, he wasn't alone.

'Good,' said Onu Castor. 'Stand up, take the step. I am pleased that you have chosen the path of devotion. It is important.'

'I understand,' said Lek.

He had a second chance. He doubted he would get a third.

CHAPTER 8

HAEZLE

'I don't understand,' said Haezle. 'What was the blue light?'

She was sitting on the floor at Onu Lek's feet. The pipe he held was very much like the one he'd described in his previous story, about the day Onu Castor had told him to submit to the Trial. The aroma of the tobacco was also very similar. Moss and butter.

As she understood it, Onu Lek had taken Onu Castor's rooms shortly after his death. He was a Brother by that time. The Book of Keyes, the book that he had compiled during his Trial, had been transcribed in record time, so it had been a rapid promotion.

The shortest ever time spent as an Acolyte, so they said. That was part of the legend that surrounded Onu Lek. It was, it appeared, a legend that was largely built on his own telling of the stories about his life, and Haezle had heard most of them.

She doubted that many of them were true.

A pang of guilt stung Haezle. That wasn't a gracious thought. Here she was, in the presence of one of the most revered Brothers ever to live in the Citadel, and she was thinking blasphemous, unworthy thoughts.

She scolded herself, then resumed listening. If Onu Lek, in his wisdom, wanted to use his own life story to make some kind of esoteric point, then, well, that was his right.

But she had her own questions, and they were nothing to do with any of this. They were awkward questions for one of the most senior members of the Brotherhood. She'd asked them in the proper way, through recognised channels, and heard nothing.

She had work to do, and a lack of answers was impacting her ability to do it. So she'd come to get the answers herself. So far, all she'd done was sit on the floor and listen to stories. They were interesting stories, masterfully told. She could see why Onu Lek carried the mystique and respect of most everyone in the Citadel in the way that he did.

That wasn't helpful to her, though. And she wasn't certain she believed what she was being told.

She glanced at the young man sat next to her. She wasn't sure what to make of him. She couldn't get a handle on how old he was meant to be. He carried scars, but they were fresh. His calluses were not yet fully formed and hardened. It seemed he'd not had an easy time of it of late, but she expected things had been pretty soft for him up to that point.

Which point?

Haezle had no idea. She'd only just met him. He was the other reason she was here, though.

She'd been finishing putting away the Book of Moors, after she'd shown it to the nice Authority man. This new stranger had stumbled into the library, dressed in Applicant robes, but so obviously not an Applicant to anybody with the slightest knowledge of Citadel etiquette.

'This one's green,' she heard somebody mutter.

But that wasn't it. He wasn't just inexperienced. He was clueless. Like he'd been picked up from another time and place and dropped into Trinity, in strange clothes, in a strange building, and he was trying to figure out where he was and what he was supposed to be doing.

From the look of him, that was not going well. Haezle felt a pang of sympathy. She wiped the spine of the Book of Moors with a soft cloth, made sure it was clean and free of fingerprints, so that Isaak would never know she'd been messing with his book, then stuffed the cloth up her sleeve and rushed over to the newcomer.

'Hello.' She spoke in firm but hushed tones. This was, after all, a library. 'Can I help? Are you looking for somebody?'

The not-Acolyte's eyes had widened, saucers gazing at her in shock and confusion and relief and gratitude.

'I'm not meant to be here,' he whispered.

'That much is clear.' Haezle smiled, steering him away from the main concourse and between some racks of shelves, away from curious and disapproving stares. 'Come with me and we'll see if we can get you back on track.'

'Thank you,' mumbled the man, 'but I don't think that's going to be easy. I'm not meant to be *here*. I'm not meant to be *now*.'

Haezle nodded reassuringly. She wondered where this one had come from, how he'd got through the front gate, but she was used to dealing with tweak-heads and space-cowboys who had wandered into somewhere they weren't supposed to be. Growing up in the Commons, it had been a necessary survival skill to develop.

He moved steadily, though. She couldn't feel a tremor through her arms as she put it around his shoulders. There was no sway to his gait, no turning of the ankles, nothing to suggest he was physically compromised by anything chemical.

Did that mean she had to take his words seriously?

No. She didn't have time for that. She just needed to get him sat down, figure out where he was meant to be, and send him on his way. Or find a Guardian to help him on his way.

He was agitated, flicking his head back and forth, his eyes darting everywhere, taking in the library. To be fair, that wasn't a quick thing to do. Haezle needed to calm him enough to leave him and reasonably expect him to still be in the same place when she returned with some help.

She pulled over a chair that was wedged between two bookcases and got him to sit. She crouched until his face was level with his.

'Just wait here for a moment. My name is Haezle…'

She didn't get any further than that before his reaction stopped her in her tracks. His eyes grew wide again, even wider because they hadn't completely recovered from the last time.

'Haezle?' he repeated. 'Haezle Muñoz? You're Haezle Muñoz?'

He was standing now. Haezle straightened up, tried to sit him back down. She couldn't imagine how he knew her name, but she was certain that he wasn't well. She needed help; she wasn't equipped to deal with this.

'Do I know you?'

She didn't think she did, but how else did he know her name? She was not expecting the answer.

'You're Haezle Muñoz! You're who I've come to find!' he'd exclaimed. 'My name is Estrel Beck. I need you to take me to the Book of Keyes. Everything depends on it!'

CHAPTER 9

LAGRANGE

Mortimer is basically an overgrown child. I expected him to be better at this than he apparently is. It would be understandable, if I thought he also viewed this activity as not being part of our jobs and therefore, in the nicest possible way, beneath us. But I just think he doesn't know how to talk to kids.

We're babysitting, to be clear. Apparently, Chaguartay's lunchtime summit with the Superious has moved on to… I don't know what's left. Cigars? Whatever, they're still at it.

Someone was looking after his daughter. I don't know who that was. The nanny, or tutor, or nurse, or whoever, looked harassed and in a hurry and didn't really stop to explain. She just brought the child to the anteroom, where Mortimer and I were waiting to collect the Candidate, and left her.

'Daddy will be along soon,' she'd said to the child, who couldn't have been older than six, boosting her onto the deeply cushioned chair and placing a straw boater on her head and a dainty floral handbag on her lap.

The little girl had said nothing. She'd just smiled and nodded. It wasn't a proper smile, more of a tightening of her lips that showed acknowledgement but didn't betray her or hint about how she actually felt about any of this.

I recognised that smile. Her father does it. It's a politician's smile. Not a campaigning politician, that is all beaming and teeth and fake bonhomie. This was the smile of a negotiating politician, one keeping their cards close to their chest. A politician in competition determined that this was a game they were going to win.

I feel sorry for this little girl, sucked into playing these games so soon, so early. She is being shaped by her environment. I hope that one day she breaks free. I hope that one day she'll know enough to want to.

The woman bustles off, and I look at Mortimer. He doesn't move. I dart my eyes toward the girl, but he just shrugs and looks blankly in response. I don't want to have this conversation out loud, within earshot. How bad would that make her feel?

But Mortimer doesn't appear to want to have the conversation at all. Or he doesn't understand what I want to say.

The little girl sits in the chair, her hands in her lap clutching the bag. She looks patient. She looks calm. But that's no way for a small child to spend their time. I do not know how much longer Chaguartay is going to be. I can't bear to watch her sit there playing grown up.

Double checking that my gun is secure and tucked under my jacket, I take a few paces towards her and drop to my knee. On her level, I can see the quiver in her lip, the lines of worry etched on her forehead.

'Hello,' I say, in my least threatening and most approachable tone. I don't know how unthreatening that really is, but I can only work with what I've got. 'My name is Simeon. Sim. You can call me Sim.'

The little girl half-smiles. This is a vast improvement on the tight lip thing, though. The half is because I am a strange man who has started to talk to her out of the blue. It is entirely correct that she should be wary of that. The smile, though, is genuine.

'Hello Sim,' she says shyly.

'It's very nice to meet you.' I hold out my hand. 'What's your name?'

'Evandra Mallory Acorsi Chaguartay.' She takes my hand, primly, and squeezes it with surprising force. 'My daddy is going to be the Mayor of Trinity, you know…'

So now Evandra Chaguartay and I are best friends. There is running and chasing and hiding and giggles. She has that boundless energy that is only possessed by the very young.

I do not, and so now we're sitting on chairs. She's kicking her legs and fidgeting and my chest is heaving while the blood drums a march through my head.

'Now it's time for you to hide, Sim,' she demands.

I don't think I can move. I catch my breath for long enough to get a few words out.

'In a minute,' I gasp, looking around for something to distract her while I remember how to breathe normally..

I stick a hand in my pocket and pull out my Authority token. I flick it through my fingers. Up and down and over and under. Evandra's eyes are transfixed. I flick the chunky plastic card back the other way.

She smiles. I repeat the trick. She keeps on smiling. I flick the card faster, back and forth, back and forth, until I palm it and make it disappear.

Evandra gasps. I grin. My grandfather taught me that one. I show her my empty hand, then reach behind her ear and produce the token. She gasps again.

Hearing it this time, I don't discern surprise and wonder. I hear shock and disapproval. I look at her face. She's frowning. I screwed up.

'I don't like magic,' she scolds. 'Daddy says that religion is believing in magic. He says that it's exactly as real.'

I don't altogether disagree with her father, but I'm taken aback by the chill in her tone, and the adult way she speaks the words. It's like her personality has flipped in a moment.

'I wouldn't let the Brothers hear you talking like that. They might get upset.'

I drop my voice, lean in, try to create a conspiratorial bond between us. It doesn't work. She folds her arms and turns her head away. I sit back. I've lost her.

At that moment, the heavy wooden doors on the opposite side of the room swing open, and two Acolytes emerge, heads bowed. They slowly push the doors until they are fully open, at which point they stand and hold them, to prevent their work from being undone.

A wide, burly figure appears in the open doorway. The slick of oil that holds flat what is left of his hair shines brightly, reflecting the overhead light. He pauses, takes in the room, grunts.

Mortimer and I scramble to our feet. This is our charge. Candidate Chaguartay is our responsibility once again. I can't wait for today to be over.

'Evie, come here,' he rumbles.

Evandra jumps from her seat, grabbing her hat and bag, and skips across to her father. She stands with her hands behind her back, looking up at the big man. It's not with affection, or with respect. It's a duty. She's standing to attention. It's very odd.

Chaguartay nods and trundles out of the room. Mortimer falls in ahead of him and his daughter. I take up the rear.

So I'm facing the doorway as the two Acolytes swing the

doors closed again. So I see who is still sitting inside, at the table with the Superious at the head. He's swilling brandy.

And I recognise him. I know him well. I have no idea what he's doing here. It's a long way from hijacking transport coming from the docks, a long way from filling warehouses with stolen goods. It's a long way from protection rackets and punishment beatings and contract kills.

Eamer, it seems, is going places. He looks to be on the up.

CHAPTER 10

ESTREL

I still had the pass that Venn had given me, and so I accessed the city through Research. It was becoming a familiar route for me. I was even starting to get a sense of my direction while I was down there. This time I didn't have anyone to guide me - no Jo Jo, no Venn, no Lek - and despite that, I only had to retrace my steps four times.

No Black Knights encountered, either, so no need to duck and hide to avoid difficult questions about my business. Research was rarely a hive of activity, but it seemed particularly quiet that night.

As I emerged from the drain cover which was somewhere south of the Citadel, if I'd not screwed up, it was the early hours of the morning. That could be a dark time on the streets of Trinity but, even with that considered, I could tell that something was wrong. A rumble of violence seemed to reverberate in the air, crackling with imminent danger. I couldn't tell where it was coming from, not at first.

I moved quickly. I remembered this as a quiet area, a friendly area, even. It was residential, far from Docklands, out of the centre, clear of the usual flashpoints. But something had happened here.

A wave of destruction had swept these streets. I passed walls daubed in paint, a strange symbol I only vaguely recognised repeatedly painted over the usual *"Fuck Chaguartay"* graffiti. At one corner, buildings were missing chunks of masonry, crumbling into the road.

On the main TransWay, paper littered the ground. Flyers and pamphlets, bearing the same strange symbol - a circle with a sword across the middle - were scattered over a basting of urine and petrol.

At every corner I approached, I could feel the tension. Every empty street I turned into, I felt it dissipate, but the noise I could hear in the distance - shouts and horns and sirens - told me I couldn't relax, that trouble was only a street away. The trick was going to be to avoid that street.

A loud crack and muffled boom somewhere behind me made me jump. Already on edge and primed for flight, I took off, breaking into a sprint. Something made me take the steps up to the PedWay. It could have been a terrible call. If the trouble I was trying to avoid was above me, I could easily have found myself trapped.

But I was reacting, not thinking. I was relieved that it worked out. There was no one on the PedWay, but from up there I could see what I was afraid of, a large knot of people moving up the TransWay, not far ahead.

I couldn't tell how many there were. It was a seething wave of bodies flowing against the traffic, traffic that was powerless to fight it. TransPods sat, unable to move as the crowd blocked their way, pushing and pressing, spilling over the roofs when the pressure built up too far.

A speeding TransPod can do a lot of damage to a lone pedestrian who finds themselves in the middle of the

TransWay. Without the speed and ramping up the number of pedestrians, I was watching the tables turn. As a metaphor, I thought that should fill me with hope - the power of people to overcome the machine was what I'd been fighting for. Watching it, I felt nothing but fear.

I felt a presence by my side. I pulled my gaze away from the mob. It was moving away, and I was up high. I thought I was safe for the time being.

I recognised the person next to me. He wouldn't recognise me, though. He hadn't met me yet. We were standing at a point between the overhead lights, so I thought maybe it was the way the shadows were cast, but as I looked at him and my eyes adjusted and his features took shape, I realised he looked younger than I expected.

Sami's face was rounder, his jaw less set. The Sami I remembered most recently was ten years older, in his early twenties and Resistance hardened. But our first meeting was only a few months away, and I didn't remember him ever looking this soft.

He was never innocent, raised as he was by the streets of Trinity, but he looked so young. There was no way this was a boy of thirteen.

'What's happening?' I pointed at the mob as they disappeared into the darkness ahead.

'Don't you know?' scoffed Sami, his voice high and clear. 'Where you been?'

'Indulge me. It's been a long day. Let's say I know nothing. What can you tell me?'

Sami grinned. This was usually the point at which he'd discuss payment. Every piece of information had its price.

I took out my Com and flashed it over his wrist. I expected to hear the confirmatory beep, but nothing connected. I tried again.

'What you doing, Mister?' asked Sami, confused. 'You trying to buy me? What are you after? You a pervert?'

'I was trying to pay you for information,' I sighed. 'I have no interest in you, not like that. Where's your wristband?'

'I ain't got no wristband,' he spluttered. 'You'd pay me? To tell you that?'

Oh shit. This was one of those situations. I didn't think I was actually about to create a paradox, at least not a big one. Sami was likely to turn snitch regardless, he had the nose for it, but it happening at my suggestion wasn't ideal. At a minimum, I was about to do something that was going to shape my own future.

But if I didn't, would someone else? Or would my inaction cause even larger ripples? Had it always happened like this?

I was kind of committed now. I had to try to extract myself from this situation as carefully as possible, and tread carefully from now on.

And hope the universe doesn't explode…

'I'd pay you to tell me many things,' I said, eventually. 'I think many people would. You've got a keen pair of eyes and an ear to the ground. I bet you have a lot of valuable secrets.'

'We met before?' Sami screwed up his face in a familiar grimace of suspicion.

'In a sense, yes. Don't worry about it, Sami.'

He didn't seem to know what to do with that, but he turned away from me and looked out again along the TransWay.

'Well, maybe you've helped me out there,' he mused, 'so you can have this one as a freebie. Especially as everyone knows about the Clippers…'

'The Clippers?'

That wasn't right, that couldn't be right. Lek had miscalculated, sent me back too far. That was why Sami seemed so young. That was why I didn't encounter any Black

Knights in Research. It was too early. They hadn't begun to infiltrate down there yet.

That was why a violent mob was rampaging around the city. I was three years too early. The Clippers were abroad, unconstrained by any thoughts for the repercussions of their actions because, as far as they were concerned, the end was nigh.

I looked up at the sky and noted the position of the moon. I hadn't seen that before. We could only be days away from the eclipse.

I needed to find Lek.

CHAPTER 11

CANNON

Cannon and Estrel spent most of their time together. There wasn't a lot else to do on board, and there was nowhere to escape. It wasn't a problem for Cannon. He enjoyed having someone new to talk to, but as time went on, he found it harder and harder to engage the newcomer.

The more Estrel remembered about who he was and where he'd come from, the less he wanted to reveal. This behaviour wasn't building the bond between them that Cannon had hoped for. It didn't make for easy conversation.

He was pleased when the clown, Bonzo, had pulled up a barrel on deck. Usually, Bonzo's cod-psychological pontification was too much for Cannon. This was a clown who enjoyed the sound of his own voice. But today, it was a useful distraction from the yawning silence that had developed around Estrel.

'…The tears of a clown, of course,' said Bonzo. 'It's a cliché. But things only become clichés because they're very, very true. You wouldn't do the job, dress up like this if you weren't trying to hide your face, hide your eyes, hide your tears….'

Bonzo leant back and folded his arms, waiting for a reaction. He didn't get one. Cannon had heard this speech several times before, and Estrel seemed buried in his own thoughts.

None of that mattered to Bonzo. He could wait. The group sat in silence again.

Alejandro's Floating Circus had rolled into Cannon's town one week and turned its central green into a bustling encampment filled with magic, mayhem, and manure. The local children had flocked, dragging their wary parents behind them to marvel, gasp and cheer before exchanging copious credits from those same parents' wallets on popcorn and candyfloss and cheap plastic toys that would be broken, discarded and forgotten before the weekend was out. Sooner, if their parents could prize the tat from their sleeping fists in the middle of the night.

Cannon had been working all weekend, and had missed it all. He was disappointed about that, because the poster had looked amazing. It still looked amazing as he stood, admiring it, even as it peeled from the telegraph pole by the bus stop, promising eclectic delights.

He couldn't remember when he'd decided to join, but he had, in an uncharacteristic move that surprised him as much as it would have surprised the friends and family members he'd left behind without so much as a word. Just a few months ago. It seemed so much longer than that.

Maybe it had been. Things got a little fuzzy when he thought too hard about it.

'It's convenient.' Bonzo was holding court again. 'Everyone pities the clown, well, everyone who isn't laughing, or scared out of their skins, does… We cut a sad figure, performing solo, even in groups we're constantly tripping each other up or hitting each other with stuff. Being a clown is a lonely life. Pity, ridicule, fear. No-one wants to come near a clown. Which suits us fine. It's the best way to keep our secrets.'

Bonzo leaned forward again, looking for the glimmer of curiosity in Estrel's eye. He found none. Bonzo shook his head sadly. He was wasted on this one.

He turned and looked out to sea.

'It's good to be sailing again,' he sighed. 'I feel most adrift when I am landlocked.'

'Where are we headed?' asked Estrel, suddenly.

Cannon snapped out of his memories. Surely they'd discussed this? He couldn't believe it hadn't come up.

'Trinity.'

Cannon furrowed his brow. They'd definitely discussed this. Hadn't they? Now he was trying to think about it, Cannon couldn't remember anything that they'd talked about.

'Trinity,' nodded Bonzo. 'Big lights! Big city! This will be a prestige performance. Lots of money in the city!'

Estrel laughed.

'Good luck with that,' he said. 'This setup feels a little frivolous for the Trinity I remember. It has problems.'

'We are an award-winning distraction!' declared Bonzo.

Estrel laughed again.

'Well, like I said, good luck. Anyway, maybe I'm wrong. Maybe it's not like that right now.'

He looked directly at Cannon and asked a question that made no sense.

'I forgot to ask. When am I?'

Cannon was sure he had misheard, so he answered the question he thought had been asked.

'You're at sea,' he explained again, not sure why this wasn't obvious. 'The Middle Sea. We're on our way to…'

'No.' Estrel was firm in his response. 'When. What time is this? What year?'

Cannon looked at him. He understood all the words, even got the sense of the question, but he couldn't find an answer. The question seemed abstract, meaningless, like something from a parable.

That was time, wasn't it? Meaningless, abstract, something we tell ourselves, like a story, to make sense of the chaos that is happening.

"For five days and nights…"

"As time went on…"

Those were just things you said, turns of phrase so that you didn't go mad with the noise of everything that happened.

Like "before". There wasn't a "before" he joined the circus. It didn't matter what he remembered.

Alejandro's Floating Circus. He'd imagined a boat the size of a field, floating serenely down rivers, while trapezes flew out from the giant big top pitched in on the deck, the artistes shooting out over the water before being pulled back inside by the backswing of their apparatus. In his mind's eye, it was magical.

The reality was disappointingly different. That was usually the case. But the reality was real. It was now. His memories didn't count. There was no before.

He remembered standing and marvelling at the giant sculpture at the edge of the green. The big top was being dismantled beyond it, deflating like a disappointing, stripy soufflé. Cannon had wandered from the bus stop and stood in the shadow of the giant elephant effigy that reared up on its hind legs and towered over each visitor as they passed through the turnstiles.

The elephant itself was jet black, with a dramatic halo made of glass jewels of every colour. It cascaded down the creature's back to its glittering trident tail, which it held proudly, raised to the sky. It carried, or was possibly trying to shake off, a golden howdah, and intricately woven tapestries were draped across its flanks, depicting abstract geometric patterns that, if you looked at them from a particular angle, seemed at the same time to hint at something not entirely wholesome.

'Elephant,' said a gruff voice by his shoulder.

He jerked his head around to see the circus strongman, all loincloth and bulging pectorals, standing just behind him.

'You like?' asked Strongman.

'Y-y-yes,' Cannon stammered, taken aback by the sheer scale of the human being talking to him. It was like talking to a mountain. An exceptionally well sculpted and alarmingly glistening mountain, but a mountain nonetheless. 'V-very impressive.'

Cannon swallowed hard. Strongman said nothing. Cannon worried that he'd offended the man mountain.

'The elephant,' he clarified. 'It's a very impressive elephant.'

Still, Strongman said nothing. Now Cannon worried he hadn't offended him the first time, but he had done so the second time.

'You, also...' he began, trying to dig himself out of the hole that he was certain he'd got himself into.

At this point, Strongman nodded.

'Oh thank The Creator,' breathed Cannon in relief.

'Twenty credits.'

Cannon turned the other way to see the clown he now knew as Bonzo standing a shoe length away from him. Even though it was one of Bonzo's shoe lengths, he was uncomfortably close.

'Is it? That's very cheap for... what's it made of?'

'Idiot,' said the clown, holding out his hand before repeating: 'Twenty credits.'

'What for?' Cannon asked, backing away.

'Magic,' replied the clown. 'I'll show you a trick.'

'It's fine,' Cannon remembered stammering. 'I think I should be going.'

Even as he said this, he could feel the solid sausage fingers of the strongman closing around his skinny arms.

'I take,' said Strongman, as Cannon heard the beep of twenty credits being transferred from his wallet. 'Is easy.'

'You should lock your Com,' observed the clown.

'Now you own elephant,' said Strongman, releasing him and walking away.

That was how he'd joined the circus. He remembered now. He hadn't had any other choice.

CHAPTER 12

LEK

Lek awaited further instructions. This turned out to be another misstep in his series of mistakes.

'Why are you still here?' asked Onu Castor.

Embarrassed, Lek muttered something and excused himself.

An unease followed him down the cold, stone corridor to the dining hall, but he marked his name on the declaration anyway and submitted to the Trial. There seemed little reason to hang around after that. He had a vague sense that he needed to prepare for a Trial; it didn't sound like it was going to be easy, but he had little notion of what to expect and in some senses, hadn't he been waiting - and therefore preparing - for this for far too long, anyway?

In a semi-trance, Lek laboured up the spiral steps to the Western Tower, where Pietro was waiting for him. One uninformative briefing later, Pietro pulled down a scroll from the pile on the shelf and rolled it out onto the desk in front of him. He anchored one end with a half-empty mug and the other with an apple. He picked up his sandwich and took a large bite.

Lek peered at the map. It was sketchy. Rough lines criss-crossed in slightly varying shades of grey-black. It looked like it had developed over the decades, with many people adding and altering and crossing out what had been there before. The margins were filled with scribbles, words and numbers and symbols at every angle.

'It's a work in progress,' said Pietro, through a mouthful of bread and ham. 'It's kind of the nature of the beast.'

'Everyone who does the Trial adds to this?' Lek stared at the map, trying to figure out how to memorise something so densely complicated.

'Everyone who completes the Trial,' Pietro corrected him. 'If you don't come back… well, maybe your input wasn't really useful, anyway.'

'It's the people who never came back that I really want to hear from,' countered Lek. 'It would be very helpful to have "don't go here" marked in big letters anywhere I'm likely to drown.'

The map was of the Catacombs. The Trial took place entirely in the Catacombs. The Catacombs were formed when the original basements of the Citadel had collapsed, the result of subsidence caused by unstable foundations and a high water table.

As a result, large sections of the Catacombs were treacherous and impassable. It was easy to get trapped down there, and once you were trapped, the chances were that you would not find your way back out. The problem was, no one knew which parts those were.

Lek tried to note some of the more blank areas of the canvas.

'But I can't take it with me?'

He knew the answer to this. Of course he did. He knew the

rules of the Trial. No maps, no support. You were completely on your own.

Pietro laughed, then wiped soggy crumbs from the corner of the map, where they'd landed from his open mouth, taking several Acolytes-worth of accumulated knowledge with them.

'That's disgusting,' said Lek.

Pietro shrugged, then grinned. Lek observed he had something in his teeth.

'Good luck.'

Lek stared until his eyes pricked. He closed them and tried to picture what he had been staring at. There was nothing. He opened them again. Still, nothing.

'If I promise to come back, can I take it with me?'

'You can't promise that. You don't know what's in store for you.'

'I'd have a lot better chance of coming back if I could take the map with me.'

Pietro shrugged.

'A lot better chance,' he agreed. 'But that's not enough for me.'

He picked up the apple and took a bite, letting the map roll up again. Lek looked up in desperation.

'Is that all I get?' he asked.

'Sorry, I don't make the rules. Not that there are rules, not really.'

He pulled a face and spat his mouthful into his hand, before dropping it, along with the rest of the apple, into a small wastebasket by his foot.

'That wasn't nice,' he said, by way of explanation. 'Really mealy. Tasted of mud.'

Lek ignored him. He felt he was being goaded. He would not rise to it.

'So, do I just get going?' he asked instead.

'Yep.' Pietro pulled a rolled cigarette from behind his ear. 'Off you go. No time like the present.'

'There's no fanfare, no starting pistol?'

'Not usually. You got a match?'

Lek didn't, but that didn't matter because Pietro pulled one out of the pocket of his robe. Sticking the cigarette between his teeth, he struck the match on the edge of the desk.

'Tell you what,' he said, as best he could whilst keeping the cigarette in place. 'I'll light this, then that's your signal to start. Like a smoke signal, like when they're choosing a new Superious.'

It was the custom, in the Citadel, when the Devotional Council who sat to select a Superious had reached a consensus, that a fire was lit and the smoke emerging from the ancient chimney in the centre of the city was taken as a sign that the decision had been made.

At least, it was understood that was the custom. No one could remember the last time a new Superious had needed to be selected. The current incumbent had outlived all of his peers and none of the current members of the Devotional Council had ever had to meet.

So Lek hadn't seen those smoke signals, no one had, but he suspected they were a lot more impressive than the one now floating upwards from Pietro's bottom lip.

He hooked a messenger bag from the rack by the door and threw it over his head. He was going to need something to carry his pages in. The leather was stiff and dug into his shoulder. It also smelled as if someone had recently used it as a jockstrap.

Ignoring all of this, because he was trying to maintain what dignity he had remaining, he turned and left without another word.

Lek's Trial had begun.

CHAPTER 13

HAEZLE

Onu Lek had gone to retrieve his book. Haezle had never seen the original, only the copy which, to her mind, was the shoddiest reproduction she'd ever come across.

Haezle had taken on the Book of Keyes from its previous Reader, a man named Korfe who had a reputation as a cantankerous drunk and had died mid-page, sat at the very table that was now Haezle's, reading the very book that was now Haezle's.

Haezle had requested a new stool when she started, but every nick and notch on the table's surface caused a slight shudder from the thought of both the man who had created it, and the fate that had befallen him.

Before she had been allocated her own book, Haezle had seen - if not actually opened - a wide selection of the Library's collection, mostly peering over Isaak's shoulder, or helping some of the more elderly Readers return their heavy works to the shelves. The Book of Keyes stood out from all the other books, and not for the best reasons.

The text was faint and lacked much of the illustration and illumination that other books contained. The pages were thinner, and more ragged around the edges. It seemed to have been copied in a hurry, and then barely cared for after that. It made sense, given Onu Lek's rapid ascent, but Haezle didn't know why they'd been in such a rush.

It made her job harder. She needed five candles where most Readers could manage with three. She had to lean until her face was inches from the page to catch the indentations of the symbols etched there, because the ink had faded to nothing. She regularly finished a day's work with a splitting headache that no quantities of herbs, alcohol, or narcotics could soothe. Consuming those things rarely made for a productive next day, either.

It was when she turned a page to be confronted by two completely blank spaces - without a scratch or a dent to indicate that there had ever been anything written upon them - that she'd finally raised the issue to Guardian Whiteley. Miss Whiteley had referred the matter upwards, but then had heard nothing every time Haezle had asked.

Now, finally, she might get her answer from the source. If the pages in Onu Lek's book were, indeed, blank, then she would accept it and return to the Library to cook up an explanation for that fact. The idiosyncrasies of the Library's works were such that it wouldn't be a complete surprise.

If they weren't... *well, what would that mean? Accident? Conspiracy?*

Onu Lek hadn't returned, and seemed to be taking his time to locate the book. Occasionally there would be the thump of something falling, or the clatter of an upset plate. There were also a lot of grunts and grumbles, none of which suggested a lot of progress towards recovering anything.

Haezle folded her hands and glanced across at the newcomer, Estrel. He seemed happy to wait. Given the urgency with which he'd dragged her to see Onu Lek, she thought he'd be as impatient as she was.

'He never explained the blue light,' she said, making conversation.

This seemed to perk Estrel up. He smiled and turned his body until he was facing her. His arm slipped out from under the robes he was wearing. He appeared to have camouflage fatigues underneath his Applicant garb.

'I don't think he actually knows,' he said. 'Not yet.'

'Not yet?' asked Haezle. 'What does that mean?'

`It means that he will, but he doesn't at this moment in time,' explained Estrel.

'I fucking guessed that,' muttered Haezle, frustrated. 'But what does it *mean*? How do you know?'

'I know him,' said Estrel. 'In the future.'

'Well, that doesn't make any sense,' Haezle objected. 'How can you…?'

She looked at the man's face. There wasn't a twitch, no hint of a smile. He was serious.

She knew some of the wilder theories that had emerged from the texts in the Library, of course. She knew the rumours about portals to foreign places, deep in the Catacombs, that formed part of every Applicant's trial. Some said that they also led to other times. She'd always dismissed it.

She had found nothing so bizarre in the Book of Keyes, not yet. Some Readers, however, and their respective Brothers, believed that they were on their way to unlocking the secrets of the universe. Possibly including time itself. The Book of Arcon, the Book of Chessar, the Book of Stay; all of them were purported to mention the possibility that we weren't anchored to the present.

Haezle also wouldn't rule out egotistical Readers keen to make a name for themselves, to get ahead by flattering their Brothers with false veneration. The Brotherhood was a religious order, after all. It was amazing how much bullshit could be dressed up as faith.

'If you know him, "in the future"…' she began, slowly. Whatever her personal beliefs, she needed to examine this.

'Then I'm not from around here,' he finished.

'No, quite. You said something like that…'

There was a silence. Haezle's mind was racing. She had so many questions. He didn't seem to be in a rush to answer many of them.

'So, what about the blue light?' she asked.

What did he want with the Book of Keyes? What did that mean for Onu Lek? What did that mean for her? Haezle found a box in her mind to lock those questions in for the time being. The blue light seemed like the safest subject for now. The truth about the man claiming to be from the future could wait. Whether he was telling the truth or not, it suggested he had an agenda. She should be on her guard.

'Well, I don't completely know how it works, but…' Estrel backtracked. 'The Book of Ness, you know what it means, right? You know what they found?'

'It's vague,' said Haezle.

She didn't really know what she meant by that. They were all fucking vague. Books and books of symbols and diagrams that meant nothing other than the interpretation placed upon them by the Reader tasked with trying to understand them.

She could feel the box she'd only just locked cracking open.

'Yeah, well, OK.' Estrel had the grace to look awkward. 'It's still pretty vague, but Lek has been trying things. Experimenting.'

'But it's not his book!' exclaimed Haezle.

There was no rule against it, but the Citadel wasn't the most collaborative place. That belief about the books containing part of a Brother's soul ran deep, and it was unusual for the monks to show any interest in anyone else's book. They liked to behave as if they had no interest in whatever wisdom any of their peers brought to the table.

She was also pretty sure that they all had a burning desire to know. They were just too scared to admit it openly. Haezle was sure it happened, late at night, in private rooms; hidden secrets buried under shame. It shouldn't be that surprising, particularly for Onu Lek. He always found a way of doing what he wanted.

'Things are… different in the future,' explained Estrel, without explaining anything. 'And there's a problem with the Book of Keyes.'

'So it's real? It's permanent?' asked Haezle, thinking about what she'd discovered, the blank pages.

Estrel looked confused for a moment, then caught up.

'Oh, yes,' he agreed. 'That's right. You're definitely onto something. But that's not what I meant. It's missing. Lek's copy. In the future. It goes missing.'

'Missing?' asked Haezle, horrified. 'The Book of Keyes?'

She didn't know that any book had ever gone missing. They were sacred things. Most monks would rather die than let theirs out of their sight. That made it hard to lose one.

Although, wasn't that what Onu Lek had already done? It seemed to be taking a long time for him to return with the book. He was evidently struggling to find it. Wasn't that the very definition of having lost it?

Was this when it happened? Was she witnessing history taking place, right here, right now?

She'd asked Onu Lek to examine it. Now he'd lost it. Was it her fault?

'Yes,' confirmed Estrel. 'No one really knows when or how… Lek was trying to find his book by examining other books. He thought they might, in some way, be related to each other but…'

'You've still not found the Book of Keyes?'

'We haven't. He hasn't,' Estrel confirmed. 'But…'

'But…?' Haezle raised her eyebrows. 'But he did find something else?'

'The blue light,' said Estrel. 'He was amazed. He said he remembered it, had always remembered it, from when he was an Applicant, from when he was first convinced to submit to the Trial…'

'In the story he just told us, yes,' agreed Haezle. 'What does it mean?'

'Mean?' asked Estrel. 'I'm not sure… I don't know what it means, but I know what it does. Lek used it to get me here.'

'What do you mean, to get you here? From your time?'

Estrel scratched his head.

'I wasn't really in my time,' he said. 'I wasn't really anywhere, I don't think. I got taken somewhere, and Lek was there, but so were lots of other people.'

'Lots of other people?' asked Haezle. 'Who? Monks?'

'No, not monks,' said Estrel. 'There aren't any monks where I come from…'

That confused Haezle.

'But Onu Lek…?'

'He's not called Onu Lek any more. It's just Lek. And this isn't important. None of the people were monks, or Clerics, or… They were all me.'

'All you?'

'All me. All different versions of me, pulled from their own timelines.'

'But Onu Lek was there too?'

'Yes. He was.'

Estrel stopped talking. Haezle wanted to shake him. She couldn't let him stop there. This was mind-blowing, unbelievable, but there was something inside her that felt like pieces were starting to fall into place. The mystique around Onu Lek, the blank pages in his book, the fact that this Estrel knew who she was… She wouldn't go as far to say that this story was the only explanation, or even a very plausible one, but it was *an* explanation. An explanation that she was inexplicably drawn to.

'The blue light,' Haezle reminded him. She needed to understand, but she didn't quite have the full picture yet. But she felt something. Underneath her world-weary scepticism, there was something inside her. She felt… excited?

'The blue light,' Estrel nodded. 'Yes. Of course. Well, I knew what it was as soon as I saw it, but I didn't know what it meant. Lek, my Lek, had been close, I knew that, but this version must have made a breakthrough. He did it to someone else…'

'Someone else?'

'Another me, then, you know what I mean…'

Estrel seemed frustrated. Haezle realised she was interrupting and decided to keep her mouth shut. This *was* exciting, though.

'He pushed him,' said Estrel. 'Just stepped forward and pushed him. Then he disappeared, in a flash of light.'

'Blue light?' asked Haezle.

'Blue light,' Estrel confirmed. 'He vanished, and then there was a flash of blue light.'

'Where do you think he went?' asked Haezle.

She desperately hoped for the answer she wanted. Estrel didn't disappoint.

'Back in time,' said Estrel. 'He travelled in time. Just like I did.'

'So, what, he sent you all back in time to different points? Why?'

'I don't know,' said Estrel.

'You know why you're here. You came to find me.'

'I know,' said Estrel. 'I don't know how I knew that. I found myself here, and I just knew. He didn't tell me. I didn't hear him tell anyone else. There wasn't time.'

'Time,' mused Haezle. 'It's all about time…'

'It is,' said a voice from the doorway.

Onu Lek stood holding the Book of Keyes. He patted its cover and plumes of dust rose from the closed pages.

'It's like you've read my book,' he grinned.

CHAPTER 14

LAGRANGE

Strictly speaking, I'm off duty. Evening has fallen and I'm out for a drink. As an Authority Cadet, there's no expectation on me to follow my own leads, to do my own investigations. As a Cadet, there's very much an expectation that I'll keep my head down and do the jobs I'm given.

Therefore, this sort of activity would be frowned upon. But I want to make Oficier, fast. And to become an Oficier, I need to think like an Oficier. And to think like an Oficier, it really helps to act like one.

I find myself a seat in the corner. With the wall behind me, and on either side, I can't be taken by surprise. Nobody can sneak up on me. I just need to keep my wits about me and my eyes straight ahead. This is not my kind of bar. These are not my kind of people. I hate it here.

There are two sorts of bar in Trinity. The other sort, like the Rigger or the Bosun's, the sort where I think I'd feel more comfortable, is generally darker and dingier and smells worse. It doesn't have little menus on the bar. It doesn't serve its beer in bottles. Many would say that those dives are the more dangerous places to drink.

I beg to differ. But I do need to be careful in those sorts of bar, given my job. I work for Authority. It's my job to uphold the law, and the law is kind of optional once you step over the threshold of those sorts of bar. I have to turn a blind eye, which I'm getting very good at. Still…

Tonight I'm here, pretending to be upmarket, feeling uncomfortable and out of my depth. I still can't let my guard down.

I look around. What people don't realise is, the clientèle here aren't much better, not once you dig under their shiny surfaces. A decent percentage of all the wealth in Trinity is currently within my immediate vicinity. You don't get that filthy rich by playing it straight.

I sip at my bottle of beer. The liquid fizzes ineffectually against my tongue, washing my palate clean with its offensive lack of flavour. I'm not even convinced that it's alcoholic. Maybe that's for the best. I could do to keep a clear head.

A group of men in suits stands up from their table, taking their drinks and their forced laughter with them. They can't stand the sight of each other, I can tell, but there are rules to every game.

Winning and losing, success and failure, victory and defeat. Such close cousins, the difference between them is little more than knowing when to follow the rules, and when to break them. I worry, already, that I've broken too many. I'm a Cadet. I should be keeping my head down…

I am keeping my head down. I'm drinking in a safe place.

I hate it here.

I watch the men go. I know what happens behind those doors. It's the same thing that happens in the dive bars. Powerful men play cards. More games, more rules. Lives are at stake. The difference is that, at the docks, they play with their own. Here, in the casino, it's other people's. That's what the rich do. They sit at the top of the pyramid, pulling our strings.

'What'cha doing?'

I need to remember that, just because no one can sneak up on me from behind, I still need to pay attention. I drag myself mentally back into the room. I didn't see her coming.

Kamla sits down opposite me. She glides into her seat. It's really hard to tell when the motion begins and when it ends, so smooth and effortless does she make it appear. But it has ended because now she's sitting in front of me.

She puts a bottle of beer down on the table. In her other hand is something icy and tall, which might be a glass. Vapour drifts from the top of it, swirling around a thin straw, which she places into her mouth.

'Thank you,' I say, indicating the beer. I don't want it, but she doesn't know that.

Kamla takes a long, slow drink from her straw, her pursed lips twitching as the cold liquid passes. She winks at me. I feel something. I can't help myself.

I know she knows the effect she's having. I should be careful. I put my beer down next to the one she brought me.

'You haven't finished that one,' she says, taking the straw out of her mouth and pouting at me.

'What do you want, Kamla?' I ask.

She laughs. It's a delightful sound, unless you're listening carefully. Then it's menacing.

'What do *you* want, Cadet Lagrange?' she counters.

I'm not going to play. I want to. I have done before but… it's complicated.

'Information,' I say.

Kamla's face drops into a stern expression.

'Oh, it's *business* time, is it?' she says.

I think I can sense a hint in her tone that she may be mocking me. I am able to ignore that.

'Eamer,' I say. 'Tell me about Eamer.'

Kamla laughs again, this time genuinely and freely, which is confusing because I don't think I said anything funny.

'What about Eamer?'

'Have you seen him recently?'

'Are you jealous?'

'No,' I say. I resist the urge to ask why I'd be jealous. That would be playing and I'm not doing that. 'But do you know what he's up to?'

'Generally..?' she says, pausing again to sip at her drink. There isn't a lot left in her glass. Her eyes wobble as the alcohol hits.

'Generally is a good start,' I say. I don't yet know what specifics I'm interested in.

'Generally, same as ever,' shrugs Kamla. 'Armed robbery, handling stolen goods, money laundering… I think there's some smuggling going on, I haven't figured out what yet, but it's a safe bet that it's nothing legal. You don't need to smuggle cupcakes.'

'Associates?'

'Nobody you don't already know about. Nobody significant. Nobody new… Where are you going with this, Sim? What have you heard?'

'What do you know about Stam Chaguartay?'

'The rich guy running for Mayor? Nothing other than he's got no chance.'

'Says who? He's very rich. That ought to help.'

'Says everyone. I know nothing about him, Sim. Are we not talking about Eamer any more?'

'We are still talking about Eamer. Why, is there something you can tell me?'

Kamla sighs, obviously frustrated.

'I would happily tell you anything I know Sim. You know that. I like you…'

This doesn't mean anything, and I remind myself about my earlier resolution not to play. Kamla likes a lot of people. But it's intoxicating to be in her circle. I won't deny its allure.

I pick up my beer and take a swig. It's got warm. I put it back down.

'I saw him with Eamer,' I say.

I don't mention the Superious. I'm not sure what to make of that. Do I genuinely believe in a conspiracy that involves all three of them? I don't think I do. The Citadel is wealthy though, and it's Eamer's proximity to wealth that's making me twitchy.

One thing at a time. Kamla hasn't said anything. I don't want to confuse things.

'Chaguartay,' I clarify. 'I saw Chaguartay with Eamer.'

'And..?'

This might not be fruitful. I think my network is deficient, in that my network is basically Kamla. She can tell me a lot about Eamer, she can tell me a lot about his peers, the scum and villainy that lurk down in Docklands. There's a lot of power in that square mile, and she can tell me a lot about that power.

She can also tell me a lot about the men who sit on the other side of that door over there. There's a lot of money in that room, and she can tell me a lot about that money.

Chaguartay is a different kettle of fish. He sits at the intersection of money and power and that is a blind spot for me, as things stand. I have no one on the inside. I don't have anyone on the outside looking in, for that matter.

All I have is Kamla.

'Do you know how he makes his money?' I ask. 'You said

he's very rich.'

'I said he's rich,' she smirks, finishing her drink and cutting off the gurgle from the straw with her tongue. 'You said he's very rich. Maybe I should get to know him better?'

That would solve one of my problems. I think it could create some new ones for Kamla, though.

Kamla puts a hand on my knee. I feel a shock of electricity shoot up my leg. I'm not certain that it's static, not certain that it's real. Other than that I felt it.

Not. Playing.

She makes me want to drink. Drink more. This would all be more simple if I wasn't thinking about it so damned hard.

'He makes things, doesn't he? Owns factories, or something, in Ashuana? Maybe Eamer's discussing some import opportunities?'

'You're suggesting that Eamer's going legit?' I ask.

'I'm suggesting that his money laundering capabilities might be about to level up,' smiles Kamla. 'I don't think I said anything about him going legit. You asked me about Eamer. If I know one thing about him, it's that "going legit" is nowhere on his radar.'

She stands.

'You think too much, Sim. Less thinking, more drinking!'

She picks up the untouched bottle of beer she brought me and places it in my hand, before turning and returning, hips swinging in a way that I feel I am definitely meant to be watching, to the bar.

Chaguartay isn't from Trinity. Maybe he doesn't know what Eamer's business is. Maybe he's not a mastermind here, maybe he's a mark.

I tip up my bottle and give myself permission to forget about it.

CHAPTER 15

ESTREL

I waited until morning to make my next move.

There wasn't really a back way into the Citadel. Maybe, once upon a time, there had been a front, a main entrance that would, by implication, have defined a back. But it had stopped being an important part of Trinity's defences centuries ago and, over those years, additional gates and doorways had punctured its perimeter and no one could agree anymore where that front had ever been.

There was a way in from underneath, which would have been my preference, given that I was trying to keep a low profile and the fewer people knew what I was doing, the better. The fewer people who knew that I existed, the better. Underneath was the way I'd come last time, from Research directly into the Catacombs and in through the Devoted quarters.

But the Catacombs were another level of labyrinth and I only just found my way through Research. I wanted to keep a low profile en route to my destination. I also wanted to actually get there.

Venn could have helped me, and Venn could probably have handled a stranger from her future knocking on the door of her lab, asking for help. She would already have started to piece together her time travel theories, somewhere down there. She'd be the least surprised to meet someone who knew her from the future.

But I'd already done that once, from my perspective, although Venn wouldn't know that yet. What chaos could I wreak by turning up to cause a paradox on top of a paradox? I'd already messed with Sami's origin story, I didn't want to be the one who gave Venn the idea that developed the theory that enabled me to travel in time in the first place.

That wasn't how I'd travelled back, though, not this time. It hadn't been Venn's science; it had been Lek's faith, or magic, or whatever had meant he could just place his hand on my chest and push and that would be enough to send me spinning back through time in a flash of blue light.

It wasn't Venn I needed. I needed Lek, and only Lek would understand. Even if I was three years too early.

So I couldn't come up through the Catacombs because I couldn't get to them, and I couldn't sneak in the back door because there wasn't one. Maybe Mouse would have known a secret alley with a plain door at the end, that would have conveniently been left unlocked and allowed us a way to sneak in through the kitchens, or a storeroom, or something like that. But I wasn't allowed to see Mouse, either. I had to try one of the gates.

I usually used the Eastgate. After I'd moved in with Mouse, it was the closest entrance to her terraced house. My face had been familiar. There was no problem with me coming and going as I pleased. I'd got to know the gatepersons at least well enough to be on nodding terms. It was easy, never a hassle.

There, again, was somebody who didn't know me.

There weren't any actual restrictions on who could pass through the gates into the Citadel. It was certainly easier than trying to get in or out of Trinity itself. But that didn't mean they let just anyone in. They wouldn't need the gatepersons if they did.

At a minimum, they need to be satisfied that you were supposed to be in Trinity, that you hadn't swum underneath the sea walls, or snuck in through Research via one of the access shafts outside the walls, like a Resistance agent.

They need to be satisfied that you weren't actually a Resistance Agent, or that you at least had fake credentials convincing enough that they had plausible deniability.

I had snuck in through Research. I was, kind of, a Resistance Agent, although no one in Resistance would have a clue who I was, yet. Those weren't my primary problems at that moment.

I had a legitimate set of credentials. I had a bona fide Citizen's License token, of course I did. But its issue date was several years in the future and I didn't think the scanner would have accepted it, even if I'd been willing to dodge the inevitable questions that would have come my way.

So I was forced to argue my way through the gate. It wasn't going well. It didn't help that the gateperson didn't seem to know who Lek was. She'd already pretended to look him up on her registry twice.

She had to be pretending, because she'd told me he wasn't there.

'Lek,' I said, for the fifth time.

'Lek who?'

This wasn't the first time she'd asked the question. Her expression hadn't changed throughout our entire interaction, but she must have been frustrated by that point. I knew I was.

'Just Lek,' I insisted. 'That's all he's ever been known as.

Lek. Onu Lek, I believe, back in the day, but just Lek. Always. To everyone.'

"Back in the day" was a phrase that, surely, marked me out as a Trinity resident. "Back in the day" meant before the dissolution of the Brotherhood, but specifically it meant before "that particular family" got their claws into Trinity.

It meant before Chaguartay. No one who wasn't part of the city would understand what that meant. Given what was about to happen, given what I'd lived through, I understood it even better than the jobsworth who was trying to judge whether or not I belonged there.

'And it's not short for anything? It's not Alek, or Abymelek, or Elimalek or something that doesn't begin with "L"?' she asked, not picking up on how my causal usage of Trinity circumlocutions was as good as a Citizen's License that had a sensible issue date attached to it.

'No, it's not short for anything…'

'Only I've looked under "L" and there's nothing under "L".'

I realised this. I also realised that this conversation wasn't going to get any further.

'OK, must be my mistake,' I said, trailing off. I said the last part quietly because I was only saying it to be polite. It was definitely not my mistake.

I thought I might need this woman's help again at some point. It didn't hurt to be polite. At a minimum, I didn't want her to recognise a past version of me, in her future, as the rude guy who insisted she look up some Cleric who didn't exist.

I shouldn't be talking to people who weren't Lek at all. I was a walking paradox hazard.

I briefly contemplated pushing through and making a run for it. There wasn't an actual gate in the Eastgate, but the passage through the walls did narrow significantly and I didn't think I could make it past the gateperson without her taking me down. She looked like she could, and I'd annoyed her enough to make it likely that she would.

I turned and walked back onto the street.

What now?

There wasn't anybody else I could go to for help. I'd already gone way further than I should have done - human-contact-wise - with the Eastgate guard, as well as with Sami. If I was going to talk to anyone else, literally anyone else, I had to be completely confident that it they would not interact with me in any significant way, ever again.

Of all the people who could be of any use to me, which of them would meet that criterion?

I turned and shuffled up the pavement. I didn't pick the direction, because I didn't know where I wanted to go, but I soon realised that I was headed towards Mouse's terrace. I knew that wasn't a good idea, but I couldn't stop my feet from moving. I glanced over my shoulder and checked for oncoming TransPods, before angling out and crossing the TransWay diagonally. It was the most natural thing in the world. I was heading home.

He was waiting for me on the other side of the road.

A cackle came from a figure huddled under a pile of blankets in the doorway of a boarded up shop. It startled me; I jumped into the air as my heart began thumping and the tremor of adrenaline surged through me. Fight fought flight. I found myself rooted to the spot.

'You're not supposed to be here,' the figure said.

'Mm-hm…'

What I really meant was "What?" but I thought I knew exactly what he said. What I needed explaining was why he'd said it, what he knew.

I didn't ask that. I didn't walk away, either. There was

something in the voice, something I was drawn to. I didn't get any closer, though. The stench he emanated was eye-watering.

'You're not supposed to be here,' he said again. 'You don't belong here.'

I turned to face the mound. I struggled to make out much more about the man within. The voice suggested they were old, but that's all I was getting. As far as I could see, they were a bundle of rags.

'Nobody knows, do they?' He cackled again. 'Nobody knows *you*!'

My mouth flapped. It couldn't be possible, but it appeared that this vagrant, whoever they were, knew who I was, knew how I had got there. It seemed that he saw the problems I was facing because of those facts.

'How do you know?' I asked. '*What* do you know?'

An explosion of coughing burst from the blanket mound. It shook with the force of the hacking and retching. From within the folds of the blanket mound, a head emerged. It was dirty and smudged, and bald and wrinkled. I didn't think it was possible to recognise someone from the top of their head, but that was all it took.

'Lek?' I asked, in amazement.

CHAPTER 16

CANNON

Cannon prised an eye open. He immediately regretted it. The light of the sun was too bright, the crust that had built up around his eyelid too stiff and scratchy. The world flooded in with a painful rush that sent his head spinning and his stomach lurching.

He closed his eye again, scrunched up both his eyelids. The pain of his squeezing his swollen eyeballs pushed against the pain that cut through his head and he saw bright lights. He thought, for a moment, that if he squeezed hard enough, he could squeeze out all the pain and he wouldn't hurt anymore.

That was stupid. That wasn't what happened. Instead, Cannon turned his head to one side and vomited.

When he had finished, he rolled the other way. His shoulder and his hip bones dug into the hard surface of the deck, and he groaned as he coaxed his muscles to get him all the way over, away from the pool of bile he had left.

The sun beat down on him. He could feel his skin burning while he lay. His throat was parched, his tongue several sizes too big for his mouth. He thought that if he lay there much longer, he would surely shrivel up like a raisin and die. He wasn't sure that wasn't what he wanted.

He couldn't remember why he was still on deck, why he wasn't in his bunk. He had a feeling there was a lot he didn't remember. A wave of shame and anxiety shot up his spine, burning at the back of his head. He'd said something stupid, done something unforgivable, he was sure of it. He needed to remember, but he also couldn't bear to.

He curled himself into a ball and rolled himself up into a seated position where he stayed for a moment, hugging his knees, keeping himself upright with his heels, until the world stopped spinning and he was certain that he wasn't going to be sick again. When all he could feel was the swaying of the boat on the waves, he rubbed his eyes on his two knees and opened them to let the light in again.

He needed to find Estrel. He didn't *want* to find Estrel but, in that moment, he wasn't entirely sure why. Thinking about Estrel caused him some discomfort. There was something in that thought that wasn't there the day before. It was difficult, and awkward.

He couldn't tell why, but it seemed probable that something had happened between them. Something that Cannon felt responsible for. Something he regretted. Something vague and hazy in the hours that felt like minutes between starting on the barrel of rum and ending up lying on his back on the upper deck.

Cannon had form in this department. He knew he was more than capable of causing such a situation. He had a recollection of surging emotion, intense joy, complete abandon. The sort of thing that was usually a prelude to disaster.

It would not come back to him easily, he could tell that. It was going to sit at the edge of his awareness, burning and burning into him.

He told himself that he would be OK. Experience had proven that, whatever he'd done, it wasn't as bad as he believed it to be. The contrary voice in his head told him it was much, much worse than that.

He tried to tease a memory out from the matted fluff of last night. He remembered the gathering on the deck, which had started quietly enough - just him and Estrel, and Bonzo, and Strongman...

...no, that wasn't right. Strongman hadn't been there. That was a different memory, but...

Then Strongman had arrived anyway. He'd been carrying a Squirrel on each shoulder. The two sisters, Jenny and Tabitha, sat lightly, swinging their legs while the giant carried them as if they weren't there. He'd invited himself into the group by swiping the bottle from Cannon's hand, and the two Squirrel Sisters somersaulted down to nestle beside him as he sat cross-legged on the deck.

They passed the bottle between them, taking their swig and passing it on. The amount that Strongman could gulp easily offset the sisters' tiny mouthfuls. The rum quickly went to their heads, and they recounted, in between gasps of hysterical giggles, the events of earlier in the evening which had resulted in the third sister, Penny, retiring to the Ringmaster's cabin. In lurid detail, and with great imagination, they speculated on what she might be getting up to at that moment. The rest of the party listened in rapt silence.

Cannon had no trouble recalling that part of the night. The detailed descriptions of sexual acts that seemed barely possible, and only just slightly more imaginable, would be something he would look forward to recalling on dark, cold, lonely nights until he suffered his last dark, cold, lonely night.

Three extra mouths meant that the bottle was finished

quickly, though. Bonzo went to find a Candy Butcher from whom he could scrounge a barrel containing more rum. He returned with said Candy Butcher, two contortionists whose names Cannon hadn't yet learned, and the promise of the barrel of rum if Strongman went below to fetch it.

This he duly did and, when it was tapped, the liquor flowed again. Cannon's memories washed away. He remembered, though, the ease with which Estrel inserted himself into the middle of conversations, and the pangs of envy that he felt as he himself slipped back towards the periphery.

'You're awake, then…'

Cannon lifted his sore head and opened his itching eyes. Estrel perched on the gunwale immediately in front of Cannon, his legs over the side. He was swinging them, freely and absentmindedly, in a way that reminded Cannon of the Squirrel Sisters on top of Strongman's shoulders.

He remembered…

'I feel like crap,' he admitted.

Estrel laughed. It was a strange, neutral sound. Cannon couldn't tell if he was being offered sympathy or scorn for his lack of control the previous night.

'It was certainly an interesting night,' pondered Estrel. 'I learned a lot…'

Again, a stab of panic hit Cannon. Those words felt loaded.

He remembered Penny, the third Squirrel Sister, making an appearance, with a fresh bottle from Alejandro's private supply, swiped from his cabinet as he slept off their carnal exertion. The crew had been in no state to appreciate it, but they'd gulped it down, anyway.

'What did I…?' he began, but Estrel cut him off with another, emotionless laugh.

'Don't worry. I don't mean about you. I think I already know everything about you.'

Cannon wasn't sure how he felt about that. It was good, wasn't it, for a friend to know a lot about you? He did want to be Estrel's friend.

He knew next to nothing about Estrel, though. To be fair, Estrel didn't seem to know a lot about himself. Although he'd said he'd learned a lot…

He remembered crying.

'Are you remembering things?' Cannon asked.

'Maybe.' Estrel stared out across the ocean. 'There's a lot that doesn't make sense, though.'

Cannon remembered that he'd been crying, sobs choking him, tears streaming down his face in a way that he didn't believe was possible in real life. Tears like that were reserved for hyperbolic metaphor, only in songs and stories.

'Can I help?'

Estrel turned, a scowl on his face.

'You didn't want to help last night,' he snapped. 'All I wanted to do was find out what was out there…'

He gestured with his arm, indicating the ocean, wide and open and empty, all the way to the horizon.

Cannon remembered, with a sick, sinking feeling on top of the sick, sinking feeling had already been experiencing, why he'd been crying, what had sent him into a blind panic.

'You wanted to fire me out of a cannon,' he said.

'It's your job,' sniffed Estrel.

'It is, but…' Cannon fought back the tears, with some success this time. All that gave him away was the slight tremor as he spoke. 'I need to have somewhere safe to land, somewhere soft, a net… something! You wanted to fire me into the ocean.'

This all made sense, logical sense. Saying it made Cannon feel like he knew his job, like the ins and outs of being a human cannonball were familiar to him. But that wasn't right. He had joined the circus by accident. He had no experience as a human cannonball. That would explain the blind panic, the uncontrollable sobbing. His name might be Cannon, but…

His name was Cannon, right?

'I don't think it's real,' mused Estrel. 'I don't know what it is, but I don't think it's really the ocean.'

'But…' spluttered Cannon. 'That's not any better! If you don't know what it is, how do you know it's safe? How do you know I'd survive? Come to think of it, you nearly drowned in it! Praise The Creator! What is it if it's not the ocean?'

'I don't know!' roared Estrel, leaping from his perch and storming towards Cannon.

Cannon shrunk back, almost falling onto the deck. He'd let his friend down. He should have helped. Then Estrel wouldn't be angry with him.

He remembered…

'Penny?' he quivered. 'Penny went out? I think I remember…'

'Yes! Poor, dear, Penny. Penny, who hardly knew me and owed me nothing. Yet she was willing to go out there, to help, to brave the not-ocean and find out what the hell is going on here! And now?'

Penny had a boat. Penny had *found* a boat? *Stolen* a boat? Penny had acquired a boat, and she had launched from the ship and set out to…

If Estrel still didn't know, then she couldn't have made it back.

It could only have been hours ago. Cannon scrambled to the side of the ship and hauled himself up. He scanned the horizon, searching for something, a sign.

'I thought that was her, over there.' Estrel waved towards the stern. He sounded almost disinterested.

About three ship's lengths away, there was a shape. It was

long and solid and, for a moment, Cannon's heart leapt. It was low in the water. If it was a boat, it has capsized.

'I thought that was her,' sighed Estrel. 'But that's not Penny's boat. It's a log, probably, maybe a dead sea creature. I've been watching for a while. Wherever she's gone, we're not going to find her.'

Without another word, Estrel walked away and disappeared below deck.

Cannon's tears flowed freely. He couldn't stop them, even if he'd wanted to.

CHAPTER 17

LEK

Lek scratched in the dust on the floor of the cellar with the end of his stick. He wasn't sure where he'd got the stick from, but he was pleased now that he had it. He made another marking, a vertical line. It was one of several vertical lines that he had drawn and he was certain that it was the right thing to do, that another vertical line was definitely what came next, but all of a sudden he couldn't remember why.

It must have meant something. He just couldn't remember what it was anymore. That knowledge was lost to him. He'd taken another swig from the bottle in his left hand, and then it had vanished, like a dream he had woken up from. Only last-gulp Lek understood the lines in the dirt on the floor. And last-gulp Lek was no more.

Lek sighed and scratched out the lines. He suspected it had been a plan. He was trying to make a plan. He needed a plan. He needed to find the pages and make the book that would earn him his place as an Acolyte. Onu Castor had put his faith in him, some of it, anyway, and Lek had decided he would not let him down. He just needed to figure out what to do.

He put the bottle to his lips again. Tipping it up, only a dribble of the rich, red nectar reached his lips. He pulled the bottle away and stared at it in disgust, turning it in the light to double check that it really was empty.

It really was. That wasn't a problem. There was plenty more where that came from, but it did mean that he was going to have to stand up. He wasn't sure how that was going to go.

Lek placed the end of his stick between two stone tiles and wiggled it a bit. Satisfied that it wasn't going to slip, he leant on it and tried to use it to lever himself to his feet. Lek became more confident that it would, in fact, take his weight and fully committed to his lean. It snapped.

The world tipped, and Lek found his head bouncing off the unforgiving stone as he fell, face first, to the ground. A clear, bright pain pierced his head. It took a moment for his vision to adjust so that he only saw one of everything there was supposed to be one of. Lek grunted. A staff is what he needed. Not a stick, a staff.

'Not a stick, a staff,' he muttered to himself, pushing up onto his hands and knees. Blood dripped onto the slate from a gash behind his eyebrow. 'Not a stick, a staff. Not a stick, a staff.'

Lek held himself in position, his head hanging, too heavy to hold up. Perspective, if not actual sobriety, seemed to have seeped into the blur of his brain. Maybe the blow to the head had done him some good. He dabbed at it with his sleeve. The bleeding seemed to have stopped. Unless that was the wrong eyebrow.

Lek staggered to his feet. He almost went down again, but steadied himself on a stack of barrels.

He had not started this quest particularly well. He would admit that. He couldn't remember anything from Pietro's map, apart from the parts that were blank. There were three ways out of this cellar - two up, one down - each a set of spiralled steps disappearing into darkness, further into the heart of the Catacombs. Apart from the one he'd come down, and he couldn't remember which one of them that was.

Perhaps he'd come up?

Because of this uncertainty, he'd taken none of them. He'd found a rack of wine and had drunk a bottle while he gathered his courage and made a plan. He'd drunk the second while he'd tried to face down the blind panic he felt and desperately tried to remember his plan.

He had done nothing of use. He had made no progress. The thing was, he knew he wouldn't. He was doing exactly as badly as he knew he was going to. He didn't care about becoming an Acolyte, he never had. He didn't have whatever it took. Dedication, devotion, patience, insight... he had none of those things. Didn't want them, didn't value them.

But he'd allowed himself to be flattered by Onu Castor, who, despite everything he represented being things that Lek viewed with scorn, was a man Lek actually respected. He'd said that Lek could do this. That he should do this. It hadn't made a lot of sense at the time. It really didn't make sense now.

That he was going to fail in this quest was inevitable. The right thing to do would be to go back to Onu Castor and apologise for letting him down, then to leave the Citadel and start the new life he should have embarked upon many years ago.

He didn't know what that looked like, what that meant, but he knew it was what he should do. It was time to stop hiding. It was time to stop running from things and run towards something for once. Whatever that something was.

Whatever it was, it wasn't this. He felt better now that he had a plan. Of course, this could have been the plan he'd formed a bottle ago, the one that he'd forgotten. He should record it, write it down. Somehow.

With a stick in the dust? Was that what he'd been doing? He looked forlornly at the broken half-stick on the floor.

He would just have to remember. Or hope that, because there were no other realistic choices open to him right now, he'd make the same plan again, in the morning, when he'd sobered up.

Because he couldn't go to see Onu Castor like this. He needed a sleep and a wash and some fresh clothes. But first of all, a sleep.

Lek turned to one of the upward staircases, which might have been the one back up to the Citadel's ground floor, and so to his quarters. He wasn't confident he would be able to get back up there, even it was the right one. He had found it difficult enough to stand up a few minutes earlier. Even if it was the right way, and he did make it, he wasn't sure he knew how to find the way back to his bed.

Lek looked at the hard stone flags. If he wasn't going back to bed, then he was going to have to sleep here. It was an unpleasant prospect, but it had less potential for embarrassment than staggering around the Citadel all night, trying to find the room that he'd slept in every night for the last five years. He had form in that. It was hard to live down.

It was going to be a cold, uncomfortable night. Maybe that was what he needed. Maybe that was what he deserved. He was going to hurt in the morning either way.

Getting off to sleep was going to be tough as well. Not just because of the cold, or the discomfort. His mind was whirling with thoughts as he played through the scenario he'd have to face tomorrow.

He needed to figure out what he was going to say to Onu Castor. But he didn't think that was a decision for now. For now, he needed to rest. His mind needed quieting, and there was one surefire way he could think of to achieve that.

He'd already established he was going to hurt in the morning. There was only so much more that it was possible to hurt after that. He turned to the racking on the far wall. It was tempting to say that one more bottle wouldn't do any harm. He knew that wasn't true.

One more bottle would do plenty of harm. It wouldn't even send him to sleep, not in a meaningful, restful way, but he wanted it anyway. He let go of the barrels that were holding him up and lurched towards the rack that held the rest of the wine.

There was something wrong. His vision was blurred, his senses numbed, but he was certain he was facing the right way. There should have been a large rack, wall to wall, floor to ceiling, holding dozens more of bottles of dark, numbing wine. It should have been a short lurch, a desperate grab away, but there was nothing there.

That wasn't entirely true. There was something there, but something unexpected. Unexpected to Lek, but he thought it would be unexpected to anyone, because it definitely hadn't been there a moment ago.

He'd been alone, he was sure of that. If someone else had been down there, he would have noticed them. He wasn't that drunk…

…no, he was absolutely that drunk, but he would have noticed. They would have noticed *him*. That guy, there, the one sat behind the ornately carved, wooden writing desk, that guy would have noticed him, Lek, slumped only a few metres away, drunk and moaning incoherently. He would have said something.

He might not have offered help, Lek might not have accepted it. But he wouldn't have calmly sat there, like he was doing. Even now, he didn't look up. He just kept moving his quill across the page in front of him, scrit-scratching words onto its surface.

Lek stood in silence, considering the man. His head was bowed, but he could see that he had a full, non-tonsured head of hair. He wasn't a monk.

His clothing was unfamiliar to Lek. It was patterned, like an animal hide, and coloured, but in tones so muted that there was almost no point. Splotches of brown, and green, and grey were spread at random across his jacket and his loose, canvas trousers. It was like he was from another place altogether, picked up and dropped into the middle of Trinity, with no explanation, no transition, no context.

And then Lek realised, as the man lifted his head and acknowledged Lek for the first time.

'Ah.'

His voice was clear and clipped, with the trace of an Ashuanan accent lingering. *No, not Ashuana. Somewhere else, but filtered through Ashuana.* He certainly wasn't from Trinity.

'You're here,' he said. 'That's good. I have something for you.'

'F-for me?' Lek managed to stammer. All his plans, all his thoughts about owning up to his failings, and leaving the Citadel, and starting the life he knew he was meant to have… All of them fell away in that moment.

'Yes. I have something very important for you. It will become part of your book.'

'M-my book?' Lek didn't want it. He didn't want this path. He wasn't called. He wasn't supposed to be there, he wasn't the one.

'Yes.' A note of impatience was working its way into the man's tone. 'Your book. Your book of initiation. Lek Benwar, you are to bring my words to the world. My name is Keyes. This is the Book of Keyes.'

CHAPTER 18

HAEZLE

Two copies of the Book of Keyes lay open on the table. Haezle couldn't bring herself to look. She was dreading what she might be about to find out.

The familiarity of the larger book triggered intense attachment in her, imperfect as it was. The smell of the paper, the curve of its pages, the thud as Onu Lek had dropped it onto the table, the crack of the spine as Estrel had hefted it open; she hadn't realised how attached she'd become to it.

It's only a job.

That wasn't true. She was proud to be part of the Citadel, part of the Library. Whilst she harboured some reservations about how meaningful the Readers' work actually was, what they did was the continuation of hundreds of years of tradition, and that meant something.

In a city that was rapidly changing, it meant a lot. For someone like her, who came from where she came from, it meant even more. The excitement she'd felt at the stories of the time travelling stranger standing next to her had dissipated to be replaced by apprehension. This could be it. This could be why he was there.

Haezle's heart broke when she saw the blank page. It shattered when Estrel turned it to find another, and then again, another, and another. He grabbed a handful of pages and turned them all at once. The page he landed on was blank.

'That's not right,' said Haezle, her heart hammering in her chest.

Onu Lek leafed through the original. All the pages were blank. Not a mark remained. Haezle turned away from the table, shaking with sadness and anger and fear.

'I don't understand it,' complained Estrel. He sounded indignant, like it was his future that had been snatched away. 'This is not how it's meant to be.'

'It isn't how it was,' shrugged Onu Lek. 'We can't say what is meant to be.'

Estrel's head snapped up. He scowled at the monk.

'You don't seem very concerned about this?'

It wasn't clear to Haezle whether this was a statement or a question. Estrel's inflection implied it was a question, but it was quite obvious that Onu Lek was unconcerned by the fact that pages of the Book of Keyes seemed, somehow, to now be completely blank.

'I didn't do it,' replied Onu Lek. 'I can't imagine anyone who could have. Maybe the time of these words has passed. Maybe they have served their purpose.'

'No!'

Haezle and Estrel both cried out together, but only Haezle had tears in her eyes. Estrel's reddening face was creased with anger. His eyes flashed with unconcealed frustration. She guessed that the disintegration of the Book of Keyes must have put something of a roadblock in the way of his plans. If the book was worthless now, what had he endured a journey back through time for? If it was for nothing, did he have a way to get back?

That was his loss. Now she felt that, too. A tear rolled down her cheek. She let it fall without trying to wipe it away.

'Are you alright?' asked Onu Lek.

'I'm fine.' The words croaked from her throat in a way that betrayed her.

'Of course,' muttered Estrel, remembering himself, albeit begrudgingly. 'You have lost…'

'We have all lost,' Onu Lek cut in. 'But perhaps that was how it was meant to happen. The creation of these books is mysterious enough - and I say that as one who had submitted to the Trial. Who is to say that they leave this world with any less mystery?'

'But why should they leave?' Haezle complained.

The books didn't leave. That was ridiculous. She had never heard of a book ceasing to exist.

'Ah, but that's where you're wrong,' smiled Onu Lek, seeming to read her mind. 'This has happened before. Books fade, books fall apart, books disappear. Why, Estrel here said that this very book had disappeared, that in his time it was missing. Maybe people in his time got the story wrong, maybe…'

'No!' Estrel was shouting now, the colour that had faded for a moment rising back and rendering his face a shining beacon. 'No! You told me. You told me the book had vanished. Not the words, the book. Why would you tell me that if…?'

'I can't tell you why I'm going to say something I haven't said yet,' smiled Onu Lek.

Estrel visibly bristled at being patronised like that.

'Something might happen,' Onu Lek continued, 'between now and then, to make me feel it is better to hide the truth from you. I cannot imagine what that would be. You know the truth now.'

'So you admit you lied?' Estrel was fighting to speak through the gritting and grinding of his jaw.

'It would appear that I will lie…'

This didn't do much to mollify Estrel. It wasn't doing much to reassure Haezle.

'…but I can't admit to something I haven't done yet,' he finished.

Estrel lost what little grip he had left on his temper.

'Why can't I ever get anything approaching a straight answer out of you?' he demanded. 'It's always vague suggestions and riddles. Nothing's ever clear cut, nothing's ever direct. Nothing's ever straightforward…'

Onu Lek remained silent in the face of this spittle-flecked outburst. Haezle wanted to jump in, things were getting out of hand. Her loyalties were to the old monk - she'd only just met this new guy. But they seemed to know each other well enough for Estrel's frustration, inelegantly as he was expressing it, to be justified.

She certainly couldn't find fault in his line of argument. Until, suddenly, she could.

'What if he didn't lie?'

Estrel stopped talking. Both men turned and stared at her. Haezle took a step back, the intensity of their stares too fierce, too hot for her to stand that close to.

She had to think fast. She wasn't sure where she was going with this yet.

'Except that he obviously did,' insisted Estrel.

It was Haezle's turn to bristle, now. There was something in his tone, something in the way he straightened up and leant forward, something in the way he was flexing his fingers, almost closing to a fist before he opened them out again. There was something she didn't like.

There was a threat in the air. Maybe not of actual violence, but it sparked and itched at Haezle. And she wasn't having any of it.

'Maybe something changed. Maybe he told you the truth at the time. But it's not true anymore.'

'This happened first,' spluttered Estrel. 'How can this have changed?'

'You came back. Aren't you planning to change things?'

'Unless he always came back,' Onu Lek cut in. 'Unless this always happened.'

'You're not helping,' scolded Haezle. 'This isn't a joke. Do you actually understand how all this works?'

Onu Lek was generally vague. He did usually speak in metaphor and allusion, if not actual riddle. Maybe he didn't really know. Maybe these were all theories. Maybe he was making it all up as he went along.

But she had theories too. She was a Reader. She'd seen with her own eyes, she'd interpreted with her own wit and logic. Her divinations were not any more concrete than Onu Lek's dissembling, if that's what it was. But she had a feeling that she was on at least as sure ground as he was.

Haezle realised Onu Lek hadn't answered her question.

'Do you? Do you understand how this works?'

Onu Lek said nothing, which told Haezle everything she needed to know.

'The pair of you…' She took a breath and allowed the half-thought she'd had and almost dismissed to form fully. 'So, if we're allowing that Estrel here can travel back from the future and have any kind of influence on what happens now…'

Estrel was screwing up his face, like he was trying to figure something out. Onu Lek remained impassive as ever. It was annoying Haezle now, too. It was a wonder she'd tolerated it so well up to this point.

Neither of them seemed about to say anything, though,

either in agreement or protest at what she was laying out.

'…then we have to allow that someone else might already have done that. That someone might have got ahead of you, gone back further, changed something else. Something that did this.'

Haezle waved her arm over the blank pages of the book. Estrel screwed up his eyes, looking like he was about to burst and had to hold it in.

'A paradox,' he spluttered.

'Maybe,' conceded Haezle. 'Although I don't know too much about that. Or any of it.'

She turned to Onu Lek.

'Could a paradox have caused this? Screwed up the timeline, undone what happened before. Anything like that?'

'No, no, no,' Estrel interrupted before Onu Lek could answer. 'I don't mean like that. There's something I remember now. Something might have happened.'

'Something?' asked Haezle. It seemed vague. 'That *might* have happened?'

'Something bad.'

CHAPTER 19

LAGRANGE

I wake in the early hours.

I'm in a bed, which is a good start. The way my tongue feels, as if it's three sizes too large and coated with a layer of sand, tells me I drank a significant amount. I also didn't stick to beer.

I roll onto my side, teeter on the edge of the bed, and roll back just before I fall. My heart is now pounding, causing a thumping noise in my head that is all the louder because I realise I can't hear properly. My ears are ringing. I must have been somewhere loud.

I recognised the layout of the room, though, just then, before I rolled back and shut my eyes again. I'm at home. This is my bed. That is a relief.

I'm not alone. I can feel warmth radiating from beside me, I can smell expensive scent that is almost smothering the tang of sweat and sex I can detect on the sheets.

I stretch my limbs. I feel worn and chafed and satisfyingly spent.

I roll the other way and wrap my arm around the naked man lying next to me, pulling myself up behind him, burying my face in the back of his neck. He grunts and pushes himself against me. The hairs on his body are coarse and the skin on his upper arms is rough, dry. My fingertips tingle with the memory of the rest of his body.

I take in a breath. I can taste him. We definitely fucked. I'm sorry I don't remember it better. I'm sorry I don't remember who he is.

Whoever he is, he's not responding to me and my half-hearted attempts to instigate another round and, when I exhale and get the full effect of my morning breath, I conclude it may be for the best. I roll back out of bed in the opposite direction and pad into the bathroom.

In the mirror, mouth foaming with toothpaste, I can see that I don't look good. There's a tint to my skin that's almost green. I'm not sure that I should be doing this to myself.

I've got no halfway, that's my problem. I'm reserved, and awkward, and careful, until I'm not. Then I'm… this.

I vaguely recall meeting him. It was in the same bar, the one where I met Kamla. I was about to give up, to go home, when he'd come out from the back room. He'd looked crestfallen. He'd lost the game already, told me he was terrible at cards.

I'd been pondering the whole money-power equation, and I thought that maybe this was an opportunity fallen into my lap. So I had started out trying to seduce him. Just not in the way that I eventually had.

I'd bought him a drink. His drinks were stronger than my drinks, and he refused to drink alone.

That might have been an excuse. He was certainly my type.

I hear the front door bang, and emerge back into the bedroom, still naked, toothbrush still in my mouth, to find my bed empty and his clothes taken from the messy pile at the foot of the bed.

That is a good thing. I need to go to work, and we avoided

any morning-after awkwardness. I still have the memories. Some of them.

Also, a gnawing sense of guilt and anxiety, and a sense that I said things I shouldn't have said. Did I tell him what I did, where I worked? Did he sense why I'd approached him in the first place?

I rush back to the sink, spit the toothpaste, drop the toothbrush, hurry back to the pile of clothes and retrieve my own trousers.

My Com and my Authority token are still in my pockets, where I left them. I can feel the weight of them and pull them out after removing the cushion of napkins that I'd stuffed into my pocket in the bar. It is a tactic I employ whenever I am trying to disguise who I am. The napkins stop me from accidentally taking out something that would give me away. Like an Authority token.

In this instance, they also provide a handy sign that my conquest hadn't been through my pockets, hadn't been suspicious.

He hadn't even been curious. I don't remember who he is. He didn't seem to care to find out who I am, either. That should suit me, but I feel a little sad.

As if in response to my need to be distracted, my Com beeps in my hand. I look down at the screen. It is a message from Mortimer.

I'M EARLY, it says. I'LL GET COFFEE. DOUGHNUT?

Shit, that was what the anxiety was. It wasn't something I said; it was something I am supposed to be doing. My shift starts at seven today. For once, Mortimer is on time - *early*, in fact - and potentially making me look bad.

I check the time on my Com. I have twenty minutes. I place an order for a TransPod and throw myself into the shower for just as long as it takes to wash enough of last night away that

I'm presentable. I don't have time to make coffee, but Mortimer's taking care of that. *I'm not sure I could keep down a doughnut.* I drain a glass of water that feels cold enough to freeze my brain and make sure I have some of those new lemon things with me.

By the time the Pod is pulling up at the kerb, I am just about locking up, running for the open door, barrelling inside. The Pod is brand new, smells of plastic and adhesives. It's part of Toun's new fleet. They're driverless, self-piloted.

I sink down on the supremely uncomfortable bench seat and try to control my breathing enough to calm the waves of nausea threatening to incur me a hefty fine from Administration, for cleaning the inside of their shiny new TransPod.

At least I don't have to put up with a driver trying to talk to me or, worse, silently judging me via snatched glances in the rear-view mirror. We start to move. I start to think.

The water has helped. I could do with a painkilling shot, but I don't have a MedPack on me. There's the solid partition in front of me - I guess that there's no need to see the inner workings of the robot that's piloting this thing - which has a screen set into it playing a feed from a camera on the front of the Pod. People still like to see where they're going.

I place my palm on the screen. I'm right to assume it's a touch interface. The feed cuts and I'm presented with a menu. The options in front of me include ADJUST DESTINATION, EMERGENCY STOP and BOOK RETURN TRIP, but there's also FIRST AID, which is what I'd been hoping for. I tap the button on the screen and a small panel slides open underneath it, presenting me with the MedPack I so dearly need.

I reach out to retrieve it, but it's stuck. I pull harder, but I can't get it free, and then I notice the payment demand flashing on the screen. I pull my Com out of my pocket and transfer the credits. I don't know what made me think the meds would be free of charge. Nothing else is.

It's worth it, though. The shot does the trick, clears my head, but also makes the hard plastic of the seat easier to bear and takes the away the chill I was feeling from the air-con. I settle back, get as comfortable as I can, and sigh.

What was the point of last night, then?

It's about time that I confront this, I suppose. I set out with the best intentions, to do some homework, get some information. I'd failed with Kamla. She'd told me nothing of use, nothing I didn't already know. She came, she flirted, she conquered. That was very Kamla.

I'd let it get to me, though, hadn't I? That's why I'd approached... whatever his name was. I was trying to get from him what I couldn't get from Kamla. First some information, then some attention. Finally, a one-night stand, apparently.

I'd succeeded on the second two counts. What about the first one? Did I get any information that was worth having? It's so hard to remember when I can't draw aside the curtain of alcoholic haze.

I close my eyes. It's then that I see it. An image, close up, close enough to touch it with my face. *Skin.* I see clothing peel away and skin revealed. *A tattoo.*

I'd asked what it meant, and he'd fobbed me off, kissed me again, pushed me back onto the bed. I thought I was on to something, but he distracted me. I hadn't minded being distracted, at the time.

It was a moon, half in light, half in shadow. Across the middle, where light turned to darkness, there was a sword cutting across its full diameter, simple and sturdy, with a red stone at its pommel. I'd asked what it meant, and he'd fobbed me off.

I open my eyes. We've arrived.

CHAPTER 20

ESTREL

It was a shock encountering Lek like this. And yet, at the same time, it was very familiar.

The déjà vu was uncanny. If challenged, I would swear blind that I'd been in this situation before, encountered Lek fallen on hard times like this, almost been shocked out of my skin by encountering him on the street.

This had definitely not happened before. This was definitely not what Lek was supposed to be doing now. I'd met him on my previous trip back, which was due to happen in about three years, and Lek had been installed in his rooms in the Citadel. He'd been exactly where he was meant to be.

Now he wasn't. And whilst it *was* a shock, it didn't feel as much of a shock as it should have been. I reached for the memory itching at the edge of my awareness, but it kept dancing away. I had a sense that I wasn't remembering a previous encounter as much as I was *being reminded* of it. Like it hadn't really happened to me, not directly. It wasn't a true memory, more like the echo of something else that looked like this memory.

I didn't think that made sense. That was what spending too much time listening to Lek would do to you.

Regardless, I'd been looking for Lek and I'd found him. Something odd was going on, but I'd achieved my goal. And if anyone could tell me what the hell was happening and why it didn't make any sense, it was Lek. Not that he would tell me. But he could.

'Lek!' I said again, this time trying to convey some enthusiasm with my tone.

Lek looked at me in puzzlement.

'What's a Lek?'

That wasn't good. Had he had some kind of accident? Was that why he was here on the streets? Had he lost his memory?

'You're a Lek,' I told him, before I realised what I'd said. 'You're Lek. Your name is Lek. Are you OK?'

Lek shook his head.

'No, that's not my name. My name is…'

He stopped, looking confused. He glanced around frantically, eyes darting everywhere, until they settled on something and he smiled, relieved.

'Drainpipe,' he said. 'My name is Drainpipe. Mr Drainpipe to you…'

'Right…'

This was obviously a serious situation. I needed to get him somewhere safe, where I could get him some help, although I did not know where from. I needed him, though. I needed him back to full strength.

I was going to need some help myself. Help to figure out what to do next. Help to figure out how to get back. The only place that help was going to come from was Lek. That wasn't about to happen. Which left me on my own.

I thought back to the gateperson at the Citadel. She'd denied all knowledge of Lek, denied that there was any record of him. Was it possible that everyone had lost their memory? Specifically, their memory of Lek? What could cause something like that?

I knew the answer, of course. I could have caused something like that, not being careful, not guarding against wrecking the correct order of events. I had been careful, but I also wasn't the only person I'd encountered travelling in time now, was I?

There were other versions of me, but I wasn't even thinking of them. Evie Chaguartay had travelled back to stop me. Who was to say that she hadn't done it again? Who was to say how many of her there were running through time, doing battle with all the other Estrels, and the Leks? Had she managed to take Lek out of the equation?

Now I really felt like I was on my own. I looked at the crumpled bundle of ragged blankets at my feet, the confused old man peering out of them. It made sense, of course it did. She didn't come back to stop me, not really. None of what I did was my idea. I was just a piece in the game. I was on board with what we were trying to achieve, I was an enthusiastic and dedicated pawn. But I wasn't driving anything. That wasn't what I did.

Lek, on the other hand... She must have realised. Maybe she knew all along. If she wanted to stop us in our tracks, if she wanted to win - and if I'd learned anything about her in the years I'd been in Trinity, she always wanted to win - then it was Lek she needed to stop.

She had the machine, too. She had Continuity. Whatever she did, however cavalier and however cruel, it didn't matter what the repercussions would be.

She could create paradoxes with abandon. The timeline would hold. Contradictory or not, the laws of time couldn't stop her. Not while she had that machine on her side.

I was scared now. I thought we were ahead of her, at least by a few steps. Now, here was the evidence that she was in control. She held the cards.

A chill ran down my spine. How far ahead was she? What did she know? What had she discovered? If she wanted to stop Lek, why didn't she just kill him? There was nothing to stop her.

If she'd kept him alive, there must be a reason. What if the reason was me?

I looked around the alleyway, but I saw nothing in the darkness. I couldn't stay here, it wasn't safe. But I couldn't leave Lek, either.

'I need to get you out of here.' I stooped to lift him to his feet.

A warm gust of foetid air wafted up from the blanket mound as I slipped my arm across the old man's back and tried to lift him. Lek let out a wail, a long, pained cry, as if my very touch was causing him agony. I pulled back, stepped away, holding my hands in front of me defensively.

'I'm sorry, I'm sorry! But we can't stay here. We need to…'

Before I'd finished my sentence, Lek was on his feet, leaping up in an explosion of energy that sent blankets and dirt and filth and *Dear Creator, that stench* flying out in all directions. I recoiled, so I was already leaning backwards when he caught me in the chest with his shoulder.

He looked slight, starved and skeletal, but the force of the blow was enough to knock me off balance. I fell backwards. Everything went black.

Except not everything. There was a light.

I was lying on my back in an alleyway, unconscious. I knew that. I couldn't feel anything, but I knew there was blood leaking from the back of my head, stagnant water soaking into my clothing.

All I could see was the pinprick of light. It pulsed, tiny and red against the darkness. I tried to see it better, and suddenly I managed to zoom in. The light became a beacon, its rhythm matching my heartbeat, thundering in my head. Maybe it was the other way around. Maybe I fell into sync with the light.

All I could see, all I could feel, was the light.

It changed again, exploding into thousands of sparks, each shooting out from the centre and landing, taking hold, each one starting a fire that soon burned brighter than the light which had carried them.

The fires shot out in all directions, at great speed, lines sweeping and crossing and filling the available space. They forked and branched and burned brighter and brighter, my whole field of vision filled with burning, bright light.

It hurt to look at, but I had nowhere else to look, and I couldn't close my eyes, because I knew they were already closed.

If I'm not looking with my eyes, what is it that is hurting?

As the last, tiny spot of darkness was expelled by the bright, searing light, I cried out in pain, although I couldn't hear my own moaning over the sound that I realised was coming from the light. It fizzed and buzzed and screamed, blocking out the chance for anything else to be heard.

All I could see was the light.

All I could hear was the light.

All I could taste or smell or feel was the light. It burned brighter and brighter, its intensity drawing me in. Everything was in the light and, despite the pain, everything was going to be OK as long as it burned.

The moment I had this thought, the darkness fell. Like a shadow over the sun, in a matter of moments, the light was gone. I couldn't see it anymore.

But nor could I hear, or taste, or smell it, and I knew it

wasn't just hidden. The light had gone out. It had burned so brightly and now it was exhausted. It wasn't coming back. All that was left was the dark and the cold.

I didn't know what I'd seen, but I knew it was important. I knew that, without the light, there was no hope. I knew that…

'Estrel,' said a voice.

Lek's voice.

CHAPTER 21

CANNON

Cannon waited in the darkness. The ship creaked all around him. This low down in the *Dukey Run*, he couldn't feel the pitch and sway like he could on deck, but he could hear every board in the hold protesting at the tension and torsion as they fought their way through the waves.

He had a torch with him, but he hadn't lit it. That felt like a poor decision, where he was cowering right now. He didn't know what he'd been thinking. He hadn't wanted to draw attention to himself. But he'd brought the damned thing with him. On some level, he'd recognised that he was going to need some illumination.

That feeling of being on autopilot was a familiar one for him these days. He was living his life as if in a trance, barely thinking about what he was doing or how he was acting. It was only in the quiet moments, in the breaks in between the noise, that he had a chance to contemplate, to breathe, to recognise the broken way in which he was behaving.

By "these days" he meant since Estrel had come on board. Cannon didn't understand why, but ever since the stranger had appeared it had seemed, increasingly, that he had been orchestrating events. Cannon had never been the life and soul, but he'd felt himself shrink, day by day diminishing into a bit player, a background extra in his own life. He felt manipulated, moved about a board he couldn't see by a hand he didn't feel. But he knew it was happening.

He thought he was beginning to understand why. Estrel was remembering. He didn't ask questions, but every interaction he had aboard the ship brought something new back for him. It was too coincidental to be happening by chance. Estrel Beck was playing them, moving them around the invisible board like pawns, piecing together his past, bringing back to mind what he had come there to do.

It was the only explanation. Cannon hadn't planned to come down to the hold. He knew why he was there now though, just as when he saw the flicker of candlelight at the far end of the passageway he knew who it was. He waited for Estrel to approach, before proffering his torch, which was lit by the flame.

'You came,' said Estrel.

Cannon nodded. Obviously, he had. Obviously, he hadn't had a choice.

'So what's in there?' asked Estrel, turning to the door to his left.

Surely he knew? Surely all of this had been leading up to the point where he knew.

'What do you mean?' asked Cannon, just to be sure.

'Inside the hold,' said Estrel. His hand was already on the door, pressing, ready to push.

'I thought you already knew everything about me,' sneered Cannon. It wasn't much, but he felt a last gasp of defiance course through him.

Estrel laughed his strange, blank laugh again.

'I can be wrong,' he said with a shrug.

Cannon deflated, the defiance dissipated.

'It's an elephant,' he said.

He didn't know. Cannon had been wrong. Maybe he had been wrong about other things, too. Maybe Estrel hadn't been manipulating events after all. Maybe Cannon was too suspicious.

Maybe Cannon was jealous.

Estrel had been washed into his life, befriended him, then befriended the rest of the ship. In a matter of weeks, he belonged more than Cannon ever had. Cannon didn't want to admit how much that hurt.

Maybe Cannon was protective.

He'd sworn that buying the elephant, despite not being entirely sure that was what he'd done, was the worst thing ever to happen to him. It had trapped him, bound him to this circus and its endless voyage across an eternal sea, to a destination that he was no longer certain existed.

At the same time, he wasn't ready to let it go. He thought that, if pushed, he might be inclined to guard it with his life, protect it at all costs. He might be ready to kill if threatened.

That was a strange thought. He didn't know where it had come from. It wasn't the kind of thought he usually had.

He realised Estrel had his ear to the door, listening for something. His fingertips pressed gently against the wood and he flexed them, as if trying to feel what was on the other side.

Estrel took his ear away and muttered to himself.

'What was that?' asked Cannon. He didn't know what the other man was doing, but he needed to know in case it was a threat to his continued possession of the elephant he'd never wanted.

'I said, I thought I'd be able to feel it out here...'

Feel what?

'You're sure it's an elephant?' asked Estrel. 'A real, live elephant?'

Cannon spluttered. He couldn't believe he'd been so silly. The whole thing was a massive misunderstanding.

He'd thought Estrel was after his elephant. The grand, bejewelled, jet black *statue* of an elephant that sat in the hold of the floating circus. *Not* a real, live elephant.

'That would be some kind of reckless folly,' he said, 'carrying a live elephant in the hold of a wooden ship.'

Estrel's face softened, a small smile creasing his cheek.

'I guess so,' he sighed. 'It was a lot to hope for. I thought that, maybe… I'd heard that… Well, never mind. You're right. It would be reckless. Foolhardy. Besides…'

'Besides…' grinned Cannon, very much relieved that his worst fears hadn't been realised. There was nothing to be suspicious of, nothing to be jealous of, nothing to protect. Estrel was just a poor unfortunate soul who'd been washed overboard from whatever vessel he'd been travelling on and was now trying to make the best of a bad situation. He'd thought they had something magical in the hold and he'd wanted to see it. Simple as that. Nothing to worry about.

Cannon turned to head back up the passageway. He wanted to get back to his cabin and have a lie down. He didn't like being down here and now that it turned out there was no need…

'Besides…?' asked Estrel.

Cannon turned back, puzzled. He thought it was obvious how that sentence ended. Apart from anything, it was Estrel who had started it.

'Besides, it's not as if there's any such thing as an elephant,' he finished anyway.

'I'm sorry?'

'There's…' Was he really about to say this? Did he really

need to? 'There are no such things as elephants. They're mythical. Fictional. Made up. They don't exist.'

'Ah,' said Estrel, nodding slowly. 'I see.'

'OK…'

This bit of the conversation was weirding Cannon out. Just when he'd been feeling better about things. He turned away again, this time determined to have that lie down. He could figure out what Estrel's intention might be when he was rested. He felt an incredible weight of fatigue pressing down on the back of his neck.

'Then tell me, Cannon,' said Estrel. 'What is that noise?'

Cannon stopped again, turned back to the door again. He was ready to dismiss whatever Estrel had heard. The bottom of the ship, the depths of the ocean, all the life within, it had its own soundscape, its own array of groans and moans and noises that no one could identify. It would be nothing.

Except that wasn't what this was. He knew it wasn't the moment he heard it, even though it was unlike any sound he'd heard before.

The sound rolled and rumbled and squeaked and it echoed around the hold on the other side of the door, vibrating through the walls and the floor. Cannon felt it inside his bones. It was a sound of anger and fear, and it was a warning and a cry for help.

Cannon's mouth hung open as Estrel pushed harder on the door and it swung inwards.

The hold seemed much smaller than it had before. It wasn't, but there was certainly less space. His elephant was gone, and in its place there was a much bigger, much greyer, much more alive creature.

It did look like an elephant, but it was wrinkled and calloused where before it had been smooth and shiny. It no longer wore its crown of jewels, but a ring of fire surrounded the top of its head in a way that seemed to defy science, as well as posing a significant safety risk.

It had nothing on its back, neither howdah nor tapestries, but thick ropes attempted to hold it down, to restrain it and contain it with the ship's hold.

Cannon suspected that, if it chose to, it would not take much for the creature to break its bonds.

The elephant's trunk snaked around in front of it, probing, searching the darkness for something that probably wasn't there because there wasn't room. Behind it, its tail flicked the back wall as it swung with an air of agitation, each of its three pointed ends swish-swish-swishing; less defiant, less proud.

Cannon was gripped with a sadness. This creature was majestic, in its own way, but it had been reduced by its circumstances. He had no concept of how it might have found its way into the ship's hold, but he couldn't help feeling, in part, responsible for this poor animal's plight.

Also, he was petrified and dearly wanted to run away.

'It can't be real…' he stammered, because he couldn't think of anything else. It clearly was real.

'I don't think you understand that word,' laughed Estrel. 'It's as real as this boat. Which is to say, given the nature of the reality we're currently inhabiting, as real as you want it to be. As real as you need it to be, as long as you really don't want to drown.'

Cannon stared at him. All the words made sense, but he did not know what the man meant by them.

'Is this why you're here?' he asked. It was interesting, because he didn't know what he meant by those words, either.

'Yes,' said Estrel, a big smile stretching from ear to ear. 'Yes. I rather think that it is.'

He swung the door shut and tugged it firmly to make sure it couldn't swing in again. Then he turned and retreated up the passageway the way he had come, in the opposite direction to Cannon's quarters.

Cannon contemplated leaving him to it, whatever he had to do. He wasn't convinced as to Estrel's intent. He wasn't sure that he wanted any part of it, but there was something that he couldn't let go of.

He felt that all of this, whatever this was, was his fault it some way. He couldn't rationalise it; he'd been tricked into owning an elephant, tricked into joining the circus. He'd been tricked into befriending Estrel and tricked into causing… whatever had happened inside the hold while he hadn't been looking.

But it was still him. At every step, he was involved. He was the common factor, therefore if anyone was at fault, didn't it have to be him?

Cannon sighed and followed Estrel down the passageway.

CHAPTER 22

LEK

'You don't seem very pleased,' said Keyes, putting down his quill and fixing Lek with a very firm stare. 'This is it. You've been chosen. Your quest will be successful; you too are on a path to join the venerable Order of the Brotherhood of the Citadel. You are about to be gifted the secrets to the universe... I thought you'd be happier about it.'

Lek wasn't happy. He thought he had a plan. He already looked forward to his newfound freedom. Now it had been snatched away from him by him getting the very thing he'd just decided he didn't want.

Sometimes the universe has a way of testing you. Sometimes you know yourself better than the universe does.

It seemed he wasn't doing a very good job of hiding his disappointment. He wasn't sure if that was important or not. He thought maybe he should be playing along. He didn't want to offend Keyes, of course, so masking his disappointment at the old man's appearance was a courtesy, at least. But he also wasn't sure whether that was only about avoiding social awkwardness, or whether the ramifications might be greater than that.

Who was this man? What power did he have if Lek displeased him? He hadn't expected to meet anyone on his quest. He'd decided that the pages he sought would be hidden, waiting for him to collect. He didn't expect to be handed them. He certainly didn't expect them to be written in front of him.

Which made the question of who wrote them rather more pressing. Everyone was vague about this in the Citadel. The books were "*from the universe*" and contained "*wisdom handed down from The Creator*". The Brotherhood were no more specific about things than that. Not publicly, at least.

That raised a question.

'Are you… are you a god?' asked Lek. He then realised what he had said, 'Are you *the* God? The Creator?'

Keyes crinkled his forehead in confusion.

'Are you…?' He trailed off, as if unsure how to complete the question. Lek got the distinct impression it had more to do with disbelief that the question needed to be asked than anything else. 'I just told you my name…'

'You did, but…' Lek felt a churning in his guts, reminding him he was really quite drunk. 'I'm sorry. I wasn't expecting you.'

That, at least, was true, and might go some way to explaining why he was acting so strangely. He also noted that Keyes hadn't denied being a god. He should probably tread carefully, so as not to antagonise him.

'Look,' said Keyes, picking up his quill to underline something on the page with a dramatic flourish, 'it's your first time. It's my first time. This is a weird situation. I don't think I'm any better prepared for this than you are.'

'Right.' Lek nodded enthusiastically. He stopped, but the world kept on wobbling up and down for a few moments, which was disconcerting. 'Didn't get off to the best start. Let's chalk that up to experience and move on?'

It was a hopeful suggestion, which conveniently ignored the fact that "moving on" might look very different depending on which side of the desk you were.

Keyes seemed to realise this.

'It might be helpful if you could confirm, though, that you are here for this. That you are committed to the Trial?'

'Oh yes,' lied Lek. 'Absolutely, completely.'

He didn't know why he said it. He'd been given an out.

But he still wasn't convinced this guy wasn't a god. Sometimes the universe has a way of testing you. Lek suspected that failing the universe would not give him the sort of freedom he had been looking forward to.

He had to appear to be all in, whilst looking for a way out.

'So how does this work?'

Lek took a step forward and peered at the marks on the page. They weren't letters that he recognised, they weren't words that he knew. They seemed abstract - characters rather than pictures - but he wasn't prepared to commit to an alphabet.

'I give you this text,' said Keyes with a slight weariness. 'You take it with you. You collect enough to make a book. Then your quest is complete. Did they not...?'

'And how many is that? To make a book?'

'That rather depends on how long the book is.'

'Right. Yes.' Lek paused. 'So how many is it to make *this* book? *Your* book?'

'Ah!' Keyes responded to this far more brightly. Something twinkled in his eye, and the first suggestion of a smile curled at his lip. 'That is a much better question. I was worried, if I'm completely honest, but I think you may just have the makings of an Acolyte after all...'

Lek smiled. He was proud of that. He'd asked a good

question. It was incredibly, stupidly basic, but he felt a warm glow.

He caught himself in the feeling. He needed to cut that out. Thinking like that was only going to get him sucked in, to commit him to something he wasn't equipped for. He should be looking for a way out.

'Ten,' said Keyes.

Ten didn't seem so bad, Lek thought. He found one by sitting still and getting very drunk. Although maybe they wouldn't all be as easy as that. He thought back to Pietro's map.

'So how will I know where the other nine are?'

The effort it took him to subtract one from ten was a reminder that he was still pretty drunk. Maybe he should ride this wave and collect the rest while he was on a roll?

'You won't.'

'Sorry?' Lek wasn't sorry and hadn't misheard. 'How am I supposed to find them, then?'

'How did you find this one?' Keyes answered the question with a question. Then he asked another. 'How did you find me?'

Lek let out a loud, belly shaking laugh.

'I didn't! At best, you found me. But I'm not sure that's what happened either. I didn't search for anything, haven't even left this room. I didn't move, just stayed in one spot, me and my patience. And my wine.'

He nudged an empty bottle by his foot with his toe. Keyes looked unimpressed with his speech. Lek wasn't surprised. He was sure this wasn't how you played the game, not how you quested the quest. But he'd done it anyway, and he'd come up smelling of roses. He'd beaten the system.

'Or…' countered Keyes, 'I waited until you were on the verge of giving up and then I brought you what you needed. I don't think you were listening to what I said earlier. You've been chosen. Your quest will be successful. This is going to happen. It doesn't actually matter what you do.'

He explained it quite patiently. The expression on his face betrayed the fact that he wasn't feeling it.

'I don't think that's… Is that really how this works? You said this was your first time, too. How do you know?'

'I know this because I do.' Keyes looked at Lek as if Lek was supposed to know what that meant, as if it wasn't a meaningless circular argument.

Lek shrugged back, petulantly. Keyes stood up and rolled the paper into a tube. He held it in his right hand whilst he opened a drawer in his side of the desk and took out a long red candle.

Lek snatched at the page, pulling it away from the other man's grip. He let it unroll a little, revealing some of the markings that Keyes had made.

'What does it say?'

Keyes shook his head.

'You aren't supposed to know that. You know that much of the Law of the Citadel, surely? I know you must be quite green, as an Applicant, but…'

'I know, I know,' snapped Lek. 'It's the Readers who read, the Readers who interpret, the Readers who divine. But wouldn't it just be simpler to write the secrets of the universe in Rove, or Ashuanan, or even Rosaanan? Something that somebody actually speaks, at least?'

'And how small do you think the universe is, that there is any language that could be recognised by everyone who receives its secrets? What do you know of the beings who have no knowledge of the tongues of your world, would not even recognise them as language at all? You presume a lot. We present the secrets to everyone, in the same way, equally accessible…'

'Which is to say, not accessible at all,' grumbled Lek.

Keyes pursed his lips. Lek rolled the paper back up, and slipped it into his bag, which wasn't smelling any better than it had earlier. He was amused to find that he seemed to have tucked an empty wine bottle into one of the compartments.

'So this is it?' he asked. 'This is where I start?'

'This is where you start,' confirmed Keyes, sitting down. The moment he did so, he seemed to fade. Lek was sure he could see the form of a very large wine rack appearing behind him. Only Lek was seeing it *through* him.

Marvellous, he thought. *It's a dream. Or a hallucination. I'm going to sober up and none of this is going to have happened…*

It struck him that this might not be a terrible thing. He could revert to the plan he'd made earlier, the one where he ended up free. If only he could remember what it was.

Lek let his legs crumple beneath him and he fell into a cross-legged position on the floor. It had been a mistake to get this drunk. Sleep was still required. He could sleep, and then he could figure out what came next in the morning.

Lek slipped onto his side and, making himself as comfortable as he could, which was to say not very comfortable, he closed his eyes and lost consciousness.

But the Book of Keyes was begun.

Sometimes the universe has a way of testing you. The universe is vast, and ancient, and everywhere. You are very small and you know very little. Of the two of you, it's the universe that probably knows what it's doing.

CHAPTER 23

HAEZLE

While Lek's story had been unclear, Estrel's was nonsensical. It sounded like the half remembered retelling of someone else's dream, which in some ways was what she thought it was. Estrel seemed certain that it had happened to him, but couldn't answer any of Haezle's follow-up questions to her satisfaction.

There was a machine.

'What kind of machine? What did it look like?'

'Like a huge metal cage, with an elephant inside…'

'An elephant? Was it a shrine of some kind?'

'No, not a shrine. It was in a laboratory.'

'What's a…? Never mind. It wasn't in a temple? Were you in Ashuana?'

'No, it was here, in Trinity. The elephant was real.'

'Real, what do you mean?'

'Real, not an idol. It was alive!'

'It… OK, OK, this isn't relevant. Or possible. What did the machine do?'

'I don't think I ever really understood that. It prevented

paradoxes, maybe? No, it allowed them and it protected them.'

'Protected them? Protected them how?'

'I don't know.'

'No, wrong question, sorry. It protected them. Why did it do that? What does protecting them mean?'

'It allowed them to exist. Alongside the things they would contradict, alongside the things they would break…'

Haezle watched as the colour drained from Lek's face at this part of the discussion. She was none the wiser, if she was completely honest, but that Lek looked scared was enough.

She realised that there was something else she didn't know.

'Who built it? The machine?'

'Evie Chaguartay.' Estrel almost spat the words.

'But she's…' Haezle started, before she remembered Estrel was apparently not of their time.

'She's…?' pressed Estrel.

'She's a just a little girl,' said Haezle. She'd seen Chaguartay's daughter on a channel broadcast. It was a standard Candidate profile piece, all puff and nonsense. The little girl had seemed sweet enough. 'But, obviously, she'll grow up.'

Estrel looked twitchy. She was afraid of what he might be thinking at that moment.

'We're not going to do anything,' she said sternly. 'To her. She's just a little girl. She hasn't done anything yet. We're not monsters.'

She wasn't a monster, is what she meant. She didn't know much about Estrel.

'No, that's not what I was thinking,' muttered Estrel, seeming as if that was very much what he was thinking.

'How bad is she, anyway?' asked Haezle. Not that she was going to adjust her position, but she wanted to check what kind of potential for evil she was giving the benefit of the doubt to.

'She destroys the city,' confirmed Estrel. 'She tortures people, kills people. She brings Trinity to its knees. We tried to stop her, we're still trying…'

'Who?'

'Me.'

Haezle didn't follow up on that answer. It seemed to belong with the chaotic nonsense she'd been getting when she'd been asking about the machine.

'Those are not the worst of her crimes,' said Lek.

Haezle took him in again. He was still pale, but he looked weaker, too. His eyes had sunk, his skin seemed to collapse under his cheekbones, giving him the aspect of a spectre. He was stooping as well, his neck bent and his head bowed.

'Are you OK?' she checked.

'No,' Lek intoned, sombrely. 'And if she had truly managed to do what Estrel says she has done, then none of us will ever be OK ever again. Reality cannot take the strain of that kind of power. We will all be wiped out, blown to oblivion…'

'What would be the point of that?' scoffed Haezle. 'Surely she has aims, has a reason for doing what she's doing? How's she going to achieve any of that by destroying the universe?'

'Maybe she doesn't understand,' said Lek. 'maybe she doesn't care. It doesn't matter which. She must be stopped.'

'Fine, good.' Haezle felt they were finally all on the same page. Different parts of the page, and trying to read in different directions, but on the same page at least. That would have to do for now. 'So how do we do that? Stop her?'

'The book.' Lek nodded. 'The book has the answers.'

'The Book of Keyes?' sighed Haezle. 'The book that we've just spent the last hour despairing over because, somehow, possibly because of the actions of a woman from the future in her insane quest for power, has had the contents of its pages wiped from existence?'

Lek was already halfway out the door at that point. He'd moved quickly for someone who had appeared so frail.

'Where are you going?'

'I wrote it once,' snapped Lek. 'I can write it again.'

Haezle was certain he'd said "write", which she knew couldn't be correct. She'd followed him out of the room and down the corridor, Estrel in tow. She had meant to ask him to clarify what he'd meant, thought she could do so as they walked, but she found herself too scared to do it and so she asked nothing and she learned nothing.

Something was wrong with the book. That was what they had to focus on now. Everything else could wait. She'd probably misheard him, anyway.

So they'd set off for the cellar. But then Onu Lek had got lost, and seemed unable to find the correct location. Even now that they were there, she wasn't convinced. Haezle had no reason to believe that this wasn't the cellar where Lek had first encountered Keyes and begun his trial. Given the way he was looking around vaguely at the walls and ceiling, she also had no particular certainty that it was.

There were dozens, maybe hundreds, of similar cellar rooms underneath the sprawling structure of the Citadel. There could be several more outside its perimeter, pushed out and closed off by the ever shifting ground which undermined Trinity.

Perhaps it hadn't been the best idea to build the city on top of a plague pit. They weren't quite in the Catacombs yet, but it was only ever a crumbling foundation away. Estrel pottered around the cellar, making thoughtful noises.

'Anything the matter?' Haezle asked him.

'No, no,' Estrel replied absentmindedly. 'I mean, maybe. This place, it seems familiar…'

'At least it seems familiar to someone.'

Haezle shot a glance at Lek, who was on his hands and knees, running a finger between the flagstones. She looked back at Estrel, who was facing the giant rack of wine bottles attached to the far wall.

'I think I've been here before,' he said with renewed certainty.

'OK,' said Haezle.

She didn't find this as surprising as it seemed she was meant to, judging by Estrel's tone of voice. He was from the future, *fine,* but he was also from Trinity. There was nothing to say that he hadn't been here before. Of course, he could have just been to one of the other many similar cellars instead.

'No, I mean, I think it's important. I think...'

Estrel stopped and turned, gazing around the dusty room, up to the uneven ceiling. He swept his eyes across the thick wooden props that were stopping it from falling on them, for now.

'I think this is the last place I was...' he said, and then he spun on his heel and went back to inspecting the wine bottles.

'What does that mean?'

'The place I reset,' explained Estrel, without explaining anything. 'When I looped, before someone else took over. Before Lek brought me back.'

'Before Lek...?'

'Not this one.'

'Ah.'

Haezle watched Estrel point at the bottle in the top left-hand corner of the rack, and then count his way across. One to the right, seven down, then another six diagonally towards the opposite corner.

He took a step forward and removed the bottle he'd settled on, twisting it around and inspecting the label.

'You need a drink?' asked Haezle with a note of sarcasm.

'No, I've found a message.' Estrel held the bottle out in front of him.

Haezle took it, bringing it close so she could read it. The original print on the label was a faint purple and borderline unreadable, but someone had scrawled a new message over the top in black marker.

THE ECLIPSE IS THE END.

Underneath that was a symbol of some sort. It looked like a moon, half in light and half in shadow. There was a sword across the middle of it.

'What does this mean?' she asked. 'Who's it a message from? The handwriting is terrible… Look, these are obviously Es but they look more like Fs…'

'It's from me,' said Estrel. 'It's a message from me.'

'Another you? A you from another dimension?' asked Haezle, handing the bottle back. *Another puzzle that needs figuring out*, she thought. She didn't have time for cross dimensional riddles.

'No,' said Estrel. 'It's from me. From actual me. This version of me. Different time, same place. I was here, and I wrote this so that I'd find it. It's an Echo.'

CHAPTER 24

LAGRANGE

I can see that he's got something, Stam Chaguartay. He's got this crowd in the palm of his hand. To be fair, if you come to Administration, stand in the foyer of their building and give a long and detailed speech about your plans to develop a whole new public transport system, they're going to give you their undivided attention.

He's got an idea to build an underground railroad. He reckons he can take ninety per cent of the traffic off the streets, close the TransWays and turn them into green spaces. He's pitching a pastoral paradise inside the city walls. It sounds lovely.

It's obviously bullshit. You can see it in the faces of some of the Exec. Ernold Toun is fuming, and I don't think it's because he's only just launched his shiny new fleet. Not only because of that, anyway.

You've got to be careful tunnelling under Trinity, surely? The very existence of the Catacombs, which were never built to be the subterranean labyrinth that they now are, demonstrates that, I would have thought. They just kind of collapsed into being, taking the lower cellars of the Citadel with them. It wouldn't be good if that happened to a tunnel carrying train passengers.

That doesn't seem to bother the assembled masses of Administration staffers. It's a big new project, with a massive budget. It's their job. I get it. The sound of their sighs of relief drowns out the dog whistles about putting the "hard-working people of Trinity" first and protecting their "birthright privilege".

I don't know what their "birthright privilege" is meant to be, and I'm not aware of anything of the sort being under threat. He's mentioned "illegal" immigration twice. I don't know what that's meant to mean, either.

I turn away. I've had enough of this. I can't imagine this working once anyone gives it more than a moment's thought. He's an outsider, Chaguartay. Ironically, he's a foreigner, an immigrant himself, albeit one with a strong case for having contributed significantly to his adopted home thanks to the massive investment he's made in the manufacturing sector.

I expect Borate and Drayen will expose this nonsense. It's unlikely that Chaguartay will get an opportunity to debate them in person, not publicly, anyway. It's rare to get a third-party Candidate and Chaguartay doesn't even have a party, not a recognisable one, certainly not one with a presence in the Dome. Chaguartay himself doesn't have a seat in the Dome. He's starting from so far back that it's inconceivable he'll get anywhere close to the mayoralty.

Still, he's hit a nerve. That's probably to be expected in this economy. We need a boost; we need some hope. I guess that's all these guys are doing; indulging in a little hope. I can't blame them for that.

I turn away from the crowd, and as I do so, I feel the vibration on my hip from my Com. Tapping my earpiece, I join the channel.

'Lagrange,' I mutter, confirming my presence without talking over the stream of chatter.

'Sim, where are you?'

The chatter stops abruptly. It was mostly Greaves giving a running commentary on the security situation. They have eyes on the entire crowd, watching out for the slightest sniff out of place. It's a big operation for a non Dome member.

It's not normal procedure, but then Chaguartay has kind of ripped up the rulebook here.

'Behind the Candidate,' I say, reporting my position, 'one o'clock, second-floor balcony…'

'Perfect,' says Greaves with an audible note of relief. 'I've got a blind spot. Can you see the back of the crowd?'

OK, Greaves is *supposed* to have eyes on the entire crowd. Seems like we've not fully pushed the boat out for Chaguartay after all.

'I can,' I confirm. 'What are you looking for?'

'Two men, black shirts? Probably not standing together. I think they're trying not to make it obvious.'

'Make what obvious?'

I can see one of them, standing back from the main crowd, arms folded. He's regarding the assembled staff, not looking at the podium. I can't see anything that suggests he might carry a weapon. He's not wearing a jacket, his sleeves are tight, the line of his trousers seems uninterrupted. I'm a long way off, though, and looking down on him.

'I see one,' I report. 'Do you need me to get closer?'

'Hold back until you see the other,' advises Greaves. 'I need to tell Mortimer where to go and he's stuck backstage, running through corridors, right at this moment.'

Figures that he'd be nowhere useful. Thank the Creator that I'm here.

'OK,' I say. 'What are we concerned about here? This one doesn't look like he's carrying a weapon.'

'We don't know,' confesses Greaves. 'Maybe nothing, but they're not meant to be here. They're not Administration personnel, they're not with Chaguartay's entourage. They're just kind of lurking, for want of a better description, and it's making me twitchy.'

Greaves usually only gets twitchy with good reason. That's enough for me. I scan the crowd again, looking for the second guy.

A door bangs to my right and I throw a glance to check who it is. I half expect to see Mortimer stumbling out, blinking into the light. It would be typical of him to have got so lost that he'd ascended two flights of stairs without noticing.

It's not Mortimer. It's a teen dressed in a black shirt who, on seeing me, turns abruptly and disappears back the way he came.

I'm already giving chase. I make it across the balcony and to the door before it's finished swinging shut. My hand is to my ear. I'm yelling at Greaves that I'm in pursuit. I hear him curse before he agrees with my snap judgement, and he barks orders at someone else to locate Mortimer and to get him on the tail of the other man.

I cut the comms. I don't need to be distracted like that. My quarry isn't as far ahead of me as he should be given the head start he had and he's having to actually open the doors I'm able to barrel through behind him. I catch up to him at the stairwell, shoving him in the small of the back and pushing hard, pinning him to the rail. I've got him trapped under my weight, so I know he won't fall, but he will have felt that he was about to as he was shoved forward and his torso bent over the two-storey drop.

I grab his arms and hold them behind him, pulling him

back from the edge and slamming him hard against the wall behind us. He lets out a groan.

'Got you,' I say, exhilarated by the chase and the opportunity for some mild violence. All in the name of apprehending a suspect, of course. Nothing gratuitous. It's cleared my head, though, got the blood pumping.

'I didn't do anything!' yelps the man.

That's a giveaway. If turning and running the moment you see an Authority agent isn't a strong sign that you have been doing something that you shouldn't, immediately denying having done that thing, before you're even accused of having done it, is.

I keep his arms twisted up his back with one arm, while I pat him down for weapons with the other. I'm using my weight to stop him from breaking free, leaning on him, pressing his face against the wall. It's less of a pat and more of a rummage.

He's not armed though. I pull some cuffs out of my pocket and clip them, with my free hand, around his wrists, which allows me to back off enough to spin him around.

He spits in my face. That's not friendly. I knee him in the bollocks.

'You're not supposed to be here,' I snarl, 'which you are evidently aware of because you tried to run away from me. You can tell me all about what you haven't been doing now, or I can take you down to Authority and you can tell someone else. Doesn't matter to me…'

I tap my ear again, rejoin the comms channel.

'Sim!' cries Greaves. 'You get him?'

'I got him, the disgusting little toerag,' I confirm. 'He's not armed, he tried to run…'

'Any idea what he was doing on second?'

'I don't think he had time to do anything on second. But

he's carrying nothing. Literally nothing. Not even a Citizen's License.'

'Right, so he'd come to take something?'

This is a good question. Maybe he had. Stupid time to come and steal from Administration, though, the very morning it's crawling with Authority.

The teen laughs. This is very irritating. He can't hear Greaves, so I assume that it's in response to my comment about him not carrying anything.

'What were you hoping to steal?' I ask him.

He shakes his head, grinning, despite the pressure I'm exerting on his upper ribcage with my forearm.

'You don't get it,' he gasps, as I push the air from his lungs. 'It's coming. You can't stop it. Everything is going to change. Fade to black…'

I don't know what he means by this, but it's fitting because that's the moment he does, indeed, black out. It's not the most constructive thing I could have done, I reflect, as I let him crumple to the floor at my feet. I'm going to have to wait for him to come to before I can take him anywhere now. But it was immensely satisfying.

I wipe a sleeve across my face. I suspect his spittle has dried by now, but it makes me feel marginally less disgusting.

I crouch to check his pulse, make sure that I didn't accidentally kill him. I didn't, but as I put my fingers to his neck, I see something that makes my blood run cold.

He has a tattoo on his neck, hidden by his collar. It's a moon, cut in half by a sword.

CHAPTER 25

ESTREL

'Are you real?' I asked the voice.

I didn't bother to ask where I was this time. This was the sort of thing that usually happened when you spent a lot of time with Lek. He had a tendency to create difficult, dangerous situations, and then haul you out of them when it got too complicated, depositing you nowhere while he figured out his next move.

I didn't let the sensation of the ground against my back, or the faint breeze across my brow fool me. Just because you feel it doesn't mean it's there.

It was different this time, though. This place was dark. Usually there were bright lights, maybe a bit of ethereal mist. But the light was all gone. This time, there was nothing.

I could feel it, the nothing. There was a pull, a nagging tug on my arms and my legs, on my skin and my breath. A void, sucking in everything, consuming everything. *Ending* everything?

I shivered, pushed the uncomfortable thought away, and called out again.

'Lek? Lek, are you there?'

The face of the old man floated into view. Not the shrivelled and starved creature from my encounter in the alleyway, but Lek. Actual Lek. My Lek. Still somewhat shrivelled, but wizened, not worn down.

'Estrel?' He was bathed in a faint luminescence. 'What are you doing here? How did you get here?'

This was concerning. I had assumed it was Lek's doing.

'I don't know,' I said. 'I fell. I might have hit my head. I assumed you brought me here.'

Lek looked serious.

'I don't think you should stay.'

'Do I have a choice? How do I get back?'

Lek looked around, although I wasn't sure what at. There was nothing to see. There was nothing there. Anywhere.

'I'm working on that,' he said, looking back at me.

The light was more intense when he looked straight at me. It was coming from him.

'Lek, you're glowing…'

'Of course I am. How else would you be able to see me? I'm an important figure. You need to pay attention…'

His face creased into a big smile. It should have been reassuring, but it wasn't. Lek had a tendency to use humour as a cover of last resort. If he was truly scared, he'd use a joke to hide the fact.

'…you're glowing too.'

I held up a hand in front of my face. It was inches from my eyes, but I struggled to make it out in the dark. Still, there was a faint reflection of a pale white light which must, indeed, have been coming from my own face.

'What does that mean?' I asked.

'I don't know,' sighed Lek. 'It kind of depends on what this place is.'

'I am glad you're here, at least. I was worried that something had happened to you. What was that in the alley? I thought it was you for a moment but…'

'That was me.' Lek locked eyes with me. 'That is who I am now, in that timeline. In any timeline, in all likelihood.'

'But that's not how I remember you? That's not how I know you.'

'You're remembering things that never happened now…'

I wasn't having that.

'No, I know what I remember, and you're a Cleric. You live in the Citadel. You're…'

'I was. I'm not anymore. I never was, anymore.'

'That doesn't make sense.'

Actually, it kind of did. I was getting the hang of things. I thought I could unpick the timelines and the paradoxes and the consequences that would explain where we'd found ourselves.

But Lek was frustratingly vague at the best of times and in these moments, all I wanted was some plain speaking. I needed to hear what had happened, at least what he thought had happened, in straightforward terms, as a matter of fact as he could make it. Then, with everything clear, we could make a plan.

I just felt that we were going around in circles. I sometimes wondered if Lek liked it that way. I sometimes wondered if he was capable of thinking any differently.

'Which Estrel are you?' he asked.

It was a perfectly understandable question, in the circumstances. Probably the only circumstances in which it would be.

'I'm the first one,' I said. 'The original. I arrived in Trinity on the day of the bombing, lived through the rise of Evie Chaguartay. I joined the resistance and lost Mouse. I travelled back in time to fix things, but things got worse. You sent me further back to give you a message, to fix things once and for all, but…'

'It wasn't enough,' said Lek. 'She went back further, faster. She found me, living another life, before I was even an Acolyte to the Brotherhood, before I found purpose and destiny…'

I understood.

'So that was you, in the alleyway. That was who you would have been if…'

'She trapped me,' he snarled. 'She trapped me and fixed my path in a way that undid everything I built, everything I learned. There is none of that left now, nothing to oppose her.'

'Except me?'

That was how these conversations tended to finish. But then I realised something else.

'And you?' I suggested. 'You're still here. She didn't eliminate you entirely. Tell me what to do to get you back! I'll go back and fix it!'

Lek shook his head.

'No. I'm not here. Not in any meaningful sense of things. That machine of hers…'

He almost spat as he said it, but I got a distinct sense that he couldn't spit. I didn't trust he was really there at all. I wasn't completely sure that I wasn't dreaming him, unconscious in a puddle, abandoned in an alleyway.

'…it doesn't destroy what should have been. It just pushes it to the margins, holds it there until it withers and dies.'

'You're dying?'

'I might be. I certainly don't feel as substantial as I used to. Can you see through me?'

It was hard to tell, with there being nothing but darkness all around us, but maybe…

'I think I can,' I said. 'I thought that your light was just a bit fainter, that my eyes had adjusted to the brightness, but come to think of it, you're looking a more grey than white.'

'Hold up your hand,' he said.

I did as he asked, at least I thought I did. I couldn't see anything. Where, before, the light emanating from my face had illuminated it, now there seemed to be nothing there.

In panic, I held it in front of Lek's face. It appeared to be no more than a wisp of smoke passing across his cheek.

'It's not there?' I choked. 'My hand isn't there?'

'It's there, just,' said Lek. That "just" was not very reassuring. 'There's not enough substance to reflect your light. Not enough to block mine.'

'So what, you can see through me too?'

'That's what made me think to ask. You've been getting fainter for the last few minutes. I think we're in the same boat.'

'Wait, but… I didn't get wiped from the timeline. Did I?'

Lek shrugged. He was not going out of his way to make me feel better about this.

'Maybe you did. You hit your head when I - that other me, from the street - pushed you away. Maybe you died.'

'Maybe I…' The words died on my tongue.

'I think this place is death,' said Lek.

Death? I panicked. I didn't know what to do. My mission had failed, Lek was gone, all was potentially lost. Now I was going to die.

'How do I get back?' I asked again, determined to fight the helplessness that threatened to overwhelm me.

'That's not really up to you or me.'

'What do you mean?' I was desperate now. 'It can't end here. I have to get back. I need to fight.'

'You don't. You can't fight this.'

'That can't be true! I, what, just have to give up? You can't be advocating that. Not after everything…'

Lek was shaking his head.

'You can't fight it. It's out of your hands. You can't get back, you have to be brought back. You need to be rescued.'

Those last words seemed fainter. I had to strain to hear over the sound of…

'I think you're going to be OK,' smiled Lek, warmly, and this time I did feel reassured.

He was right. I was going to be OK. As Lek faded away, his voice now only a whisper, I could hear another voice. A familiar voice.

A light rushed towards me, extinguishing the dark.

'…can you hear me?' asked the voice.

Mouse's voice.

Part Two

CHAPTER 26

CANNON

They weren't on the *Dukey Run* anymore. Cannon had been in his bunk, tossing and turning and trying to escape into sleep, when he had heard an explosion. Silence had fallen for a moment, just long enough for Cannon to wonder if he'd imagined it.

Then the screams began and the corners of his cabin inverted and the water gushed in. Cannon had time to snatch a breath before he was engulfed. He blacked out.

Cannon awoke on a rowing boat, headed for the shore. His throat and chest burned, and he had a tender spot on the back of his head, but he was alive and seemingly intact.

He scrambled into a sitting position, noting an additional collection of bruises and scrapes up his legs and back.

'You're awake,' said Estrel, without breaking stroke.

There was no one else in the boat. Cannon looked around. The sea was calm, barely a ripple on the water, just the steady, pulsing swell bearing them along. Behind them, in the distance, he could make out the blur of a shoreline, cliffs and coves. The sun was shining in an almost clear sky.

There was no sign of the *Dukey Run*.

'What happened?' he croaked.

'There was an explosion. The ship sank.'

He didn't seem about to add anything. That was fine, because Cannon had many questions.

'An explosion? How? What exploded? What about…?'

'The crew? The animals? Gone. They sank too.'

Estrel sighed. Cannon got the impression that this was a drag, having to explain to him. But maybe, he thought, he was being uncharitable. Estrel had rescued him, had got him into a boat to safety. Perhaps he was just tired. Perhaps he was still processing what had happened himself.

'It's OK,' he said. 'They didn't suffer. They can't have.'

'What do you mean?'

'They weren't real.' Estrel was deadpan and matter of fact. 'No more real than the ship.'

'Or the elephant?'

Cannon surprised himself with how easily he seemed to accept the information he was being given. On one level, he knew that he'd spent months aboard the ship, had interacted daily with his shipmates. He'd made friends, rivals, actual relationships with real people.

On another level, he felt that none of it had happened. He remembered how he'd told Estrel the story of how he joined the Floating Circus. Even as he told it, he would have, if questioned, denied that any of it was actually true.

Estrel hadn't questioned it. Cannon suspected he'd already known. Maybe he'd always known, ever since he'd arrived on the ship. Perhaps that was why he'd come. Perhaps he'd come to rescue Cannon.

From what, Cannon wasn't sure yet. He looked across the ocean that surrounded them. From here would be a start.

'I might have been wrong about the elephant,' admitted

Estrel.

'Wrong? Wrong in what way?'

'I said that it wasn't real either.' Estrel dipped his oars and adjusted their course. 'That wasn't right.'

'It was real?' Cannon had a pang of sadness, the thought of an animal drowning, even one that… *hang on…* 'You're saying that it *was* real? An *elephant?*'

'Impossible, sure. But it was definitely real. I should have said that it was unusual.'

Estrel lifted his leg and tapped the wooden box he was sitting on with his heel. Cannon hadn't noticed that he was sitting on a box. There was a rumbling from inside, the hint of a squeak.

'What's in the box?' asked Cannon, confused.

There had been a definite suggestion, from Estrel's actions, that the elephant was now in the box. That was impossible, obviously. Far more than "*unusual*".

'I don't know,' replied Estrel. 'Not any more.'

'You did know?' Cannon checked.

'Maybe.'

This wasn't proving to be a very satisfactory conversation. If Cannon were to pick up the hints he thought Estrel was dropping, then he would assume that, somehow, the elephant that couldn't exist but that Estrel was adamant had been real, was now in the box. That was obviously ridiculous unless the elephant had shrunk, or somehow there was more space inside the box than there was outside of it.

Had the animal imploded? Was that what had sunk the ship?

Estrel didn't seem prepared to say any more on the subject, however, so Cannon hadn't wanted to ask. They had reached the shore, pulled the boat up the beach and taken shelter in a cave. They made a fire from dried-out driftwood and some kind of kelp that gave off occasional puffs of foul smelling smoke, and they waited.

As far as Cannon could tell, Estrel had a plan. He hadn't divulged it, but every time Cannon had asked what they should do, Estrel had just murmured reassuringly and muttered something about waiting, and a long journey ahead.

'What are we going to do for food?' Cannon asked.

Estrel didn't have a great track record for answering direct questions, but Cannon wasn't sure how long he was supposed to wait and he was hungry and the pangs pulled at his stomach, wearing down his already thin patience.

'Can you fish?' asked Estrel.

Cannon couldn't, and he said so.

'I guess, then, that we just have to wait. We might be here a while, though. *Let me tell you a story…*'

Cannon wasn't sure why he said that again. He thought Estrel had already said it. Sometime earlier, sometime before. He'd said it and he'd pulled the same dramatic expression. His intonation was identical, the way he'd hung onto the end of the word story, as if enunciating the ellipsis.

It was odd. Maybe it was just in Cannon's mind, some kind of spookily vivid déjà vu. He shook it off. Estrel was starting his story.

'There was a Tree,' he began. 'This was a long time ago, mind you, and already the Tree was ancient. Some people say that it was the first ever tree, but most people accepted that this was ridiculous and that there were almost certainly other trees.'

Cannon agreed that this was probably the case, although surely one tree had to be the first tree?

'The Tree stood strong and tall, enduring while those other trees, especially the ones that had come before it, withered and died and rotted to nothing. Everyone who passed, because the people hadn't yet decided that staying in one place was better than keeping moving, saw the Tree, and remembered the Tree and, over time, it became part of their stories. That is why people believed the Tree had always been there. It was a comfort to them to know that, whatever happened, the Tree would be a constant.'

Cannon wondered what the relevance of this ancient tree was. Was that where they were going? Right at that moment they were huddled, sheltering in a cave, of course, but Estrel had mentioned a journey. He seemed to be a man with purpose and Cannon wasn't keen on getting left behind on a beach, so he hoped he would be going too.

'One day things went as they tend to in these sorts of circumstances, and someone who was in very great need and didn't have anywhere else to turn, couldn't think of any other way, came to the Tree and asked it for help. Probably, people thought that a strange thing to do - to ask a tree for help. But that was not as strange as what happened next...'

Cannon realised where the story was going.

'Is the Tree some kind of god?' he asked. 'Did they ask it to heal them, and it did?'

'They did ask it to heal them,' agreed Estrel with a smile. 'And then they got better. Their wounds healed, their fever broke, they made a full recovery. Whether the Tree was a god is not for me to say or, indeed, particularly relevant...'

'I'd say it was pretty relevant to the person who was healed?' argued Cannon.

'Maybe so,' conceded Estrel. 'Although I'd say that the most relevant thing was that they healed. The rest of it is just a story. I find, in general, that the gods are nothing special, they just have the best stories. Usually, they are more than happy to tell those stories themselves. At least in that, the Tree is an exception.'

'So what happened to the Tree? I assume that *is* relevant?'

'Indeed…'

Estrel smiled again. Cannon saw no warmth in Estrel's smiles any more. They weren't remotely comforting. They held secrets. Cannon wasn't sure that those secrets were things he wanted.

'They built a city in the shadow of the Tree,' he continued. 'A vast city that became the centre of the world, at least for a while. The Tree was, indeed, special, but not in the way everyone thought it was. It brought balance to what had been a harsh terrain. It took root where nothing had previously grown and it survived on what moisture it could pull from the earth. The more it pulled, the more it brought forth, until the land was green and alive. It bore fruit, and because of its size, that fruit was enough to feed a small settlement, then a village. Before long, the town of Trinity was established and…'

'Hold on. So this is a story about greed. About how Trinity grew too fast and took too much? They killed the tree, didn't they?'

'They did,' sighed Estrel. 'But not the way you're thinking. The Tree was a marvel, and could have gone on providing, gone on growing, until its bounty supported even the modern city-state.'

'But it didn't, did it?'

It wasn't a question. Cannon knew that the modern city-state of Trinity was not supported by a giant tree. Nor, indeed, was it the centre of the world.

'The people of Trinity, or should I say, the wise men of Trinity, because that's who it was, continued to tell their stories of the Tree. It was, indeed, raised to godhood, whatever that might mean to you. It means little to me. But it was the end of the Tree. They built too close, they dug underneath it to tap the energy its roots provided. The Tree was suffocated. It couldn't reach the earth and the earth couldn't nourish the tree. And just like all the trees before it, the Tree withered. Then it died. Then it rotted. And Trinity rotted with it.'

He was silent for a moment. Cannon listened to the crackle of the flames, and the moan of the wind, and the sigh of the waves on the shore. The white noise of the world held him.

Cannon wasn't ready for a quest or a mission. But, unfortunately, that felt like the kind of story that usually preceded that kind of thing.

'So was that a metaphor, or whatever?' he asked wearily. 'Or did it actually happen like that?'

'That is the question...'

Estrel stood and stooped to look outside of that cave. He seemed to strain to hear something and now Cannon did the same. He thought he could sense the beating of hooves, far in the distance, up on the opposing cliff.

'...but we're going to see if we can answer it. Soon.'

He turned back from the mouth of the cave and kicked sand into their fire. It spat and fizzled as it went out, leaving Cannon sat in darkness, staring at the silhouette of Estrel, framed by moonlight.

'We?' Cannon asked. He knew the answer, but he thought he should check.

'Oh yes,' laughed Estrel. 'You may not realise it yet, my friend, but you're an important part of this story. It couldn't be told without you. Bring the box.'

Again, the laughter was cold and without humour. Cannon had gone way beyond not feeling reassured. The sound terrified him.

He pushed himself up from the floor and bent to lift the small crate. It was surprisingly light, considering what it was meant to hold. Carrying the box and reluctantly accepting his fate, Cannon followed Estrel out of the cave.

CHAPTER 27

LEK

It has come to my attention that someone else has been telling my story. I don't know who it is yet, or why they have been doing it. People tell stories for different reasons. Sometimes stories are for enlightenment. Sometimes stories are for manipulation.

Every story you hear, you need to ask yourself why it's being told. This is my story, and I intend to be the one to decide that from this point onwards.

Sometimes stories are true, and sometimes they are fictional. Sometimes they are both and sometimes, *sometimes* they start out being one and end up being the other.

I am worried that this might be one of those stories. From now on I intend to tell it to the best of my recollection. It's my story, after all. It happened to me.

I thought the Trial would be easy from that point onwards, much as I hate to admit it. When I woke up from my brief nap, I decided that, as it was going well so far, I might as well continue after all.

I had, of course, got lucky with the first pages, getting

drunk and having them fall into my lap, so to speak. That was a large part of the problem. I'd got drunk. I was still drunk at that point and, having swiped a last bottle for the road, was still getting drunker.

I have little memory of the next few hours, for obvious reasons, but I do recall that when I recovered my awareness of my situation, I carried significantly more bruises and cuts than I had before.

I don't know where I went. I've been to the Catacombs subsequently, of course. Sometimes I have wondered, as I wandered, whether I'd been down this particular tunnel, or encountered that particular dead end, before. On a few occasions, I tried to seek my route, find evidence of my presence, to retrace my steps.

There was nothing to find. The Catacombs are hard and rocky and leave a far more permanent mark on you than you ever will on them. They are a maze of passageways, constantly intersecting and passing over and under each other, with sinkholes and rockfalls to further complicate the picture, the structure and layout shifting at random intervals, in unpredictable ways. They form a three-dimensional maze that has so many permutations that they may as well be infinite. I will never know where I went.

When I regained the senses that I'd dulled with wine, once the wine had run out, and then done its job, then faded away leaving me with what seemed, at the time, to be an unreasonable amount of pain, I found myself stood in front of a door.

The door was wooden and solid, attached to the wall with large strap hinges. There were many doors like it all over the Citadel. But none of them were painted blue. That marked it out as being something out of the ordinary, and therefore something I should investigate.

There was no handle, so I pushed at it, although the hinges were obviously attached the wrong way round for it to swing inwards like that. It didn't budge.

I pocketed my torch and, with both hands, tried to get my fingernails between it and the wall, to prise it open, despite that fact that it looked far too heavy for me to do so without breaking my nails and grazing my knuckles on the rough stone of the wall.

That was exactly what I got for my effort, and the door still didn't move. I sat down for a while, inspecting the fresh damage to my hands, as well as the pre-existing injuries that my sandalled feet and bare shins had sustained while I'd been too drunk to know where I was stumbling, or to feel the consequences. I think there was grit between my toes. It might have been sand.

It took a long while, far too long, for me to realise that there might be someone on the other side of the door, and that they might be supposed to open it from their side.

Slowly, I noticed a scratching, scrabbling sound. Something *was* there, something was trying to get out. I probably should have thought harder about what it was, probably should have considered that something trying to get out from the other side of a door that had no way of being opened was better off remaining there.

I just wanted to find out what was through the door, though, so I leapt to my feet and hammered on it. I don't know what I expected. Maybe I thought that whatever animal - I was certain now that it was an animal - was behind the door had an owner, and that owner would hear my knocking and let me through.

That isn't what happened, though. All my banging and shouting did was to rile up the creature until its scratches became more frantic. The wood shifted and creaked, even before I heard the twin thuds of what I assumed were the front paws of a gigantic animal rearing up and supporting itself as it stood on its hind legs.

'Hello?' I shouted. 'Is there anyone there?'

The response I got was in the form of a low growl, followed by a series of vicious yaps. I took a step back from the door in shock.

Now I could see it better. From a few paces away, the door seemed to be bowing outwards. I could see hairline cracks appear in the paintwork, the grain of the wood acting as fault-lines, weak points where the wood could flex and break.

There was a further bang, then a creak and a groan from the door, which bulged alarmingly. There was a silence. I drew back, closed my eyes.

The door exploded in a shower of splinters. I heard it; I felt the rush of air. But I wasn't pricked by a thousand shards. I didn't feel so much as a dull thud against my head.

I opened my eyes. There was now a gaping hole, framed by the ragged edges of torn wood. What was left of the door hung at an angle, because two of the three hinges had somehow been ripped from the stone wall where they had been attached.

But that was it. There was no debris, no sign of the parts of the door that were no longer where the rest of the door remained, hanging. No chunks of wood, no splinters, no sawdust. I hadn't felt myself being hit by any of that stuff because I hadn't been hit by any of that stuff. Nothing remained.

I lie. That wasn't it. There was something else, something on the other side of the door, which I could now see clearly through the hole I presume it had made.

It wasn't exactly a dog. There was a general resemblance to something dog-like, something that may once have been a dog. It could have been a distant relation, or a much cross-bred descendent. Its hide was thick, like leather, tight over the tensed muscles underneath. It had fangs curling out of its mouth and down below its jaw-line. Its claws looked so sharp they almost glinted.

Even thinking about it now gives me cause to shudder. I didn't have time to do so then. It reared up, those lethal claws pawing at the air as its hind legs tensed. It sank back, ready to leap, and then launched itself through the air, before taking off with a snarl and a roar as it flew towards me.

That's as far as it got. Frozen to the spot in fear as I was, I wouldn't have stood a chance if it had reached me, and reach me I was certain that it would.

But it never got past the threshold. The moment the creature passed the destroyed door, ripping what was left of it away as it squeezed its hulking form through, it faded away. I watched the animal in cross-section as it vanished, from nose to tail, a writhing mass of flesh and bone and viscera until...

Nothing. There was nothing, no creature, even less door than there had been before, just an empty space before me and the lingering smell of musk and sweat and earth and spoor.

I stood up from my crouched position and cautiously approached the doorway. The smell intensified, but there was still no sign of the animal that had lurked there.

I reached out and touched the jagged edge of the remaining door. My finger pricked with a splinter and I instinctively stuck it in my mouth, tasting the blood it had drawn.

It was real, then. The door, at least, had been real. The destruction, at least, had been real. Did that mean that the beast had been real? Where did it go?

I put my foot through the doorway. I hadn't focused on the room beyond when faced with an apparently rabid beast that commanded my full attention, but now it was gone, I had no better idea of what was through the door. The light was dim, and any shapes I could discern in the murk were vague and unclear, almost like they were out of focus.

My foot, now it was across the threshold, also seemed to have lost some definition. I could feel a numbness tingling at the ends of my toes, as if there were a physical aspect to this indistinguishability.

I chose to take another step.

CHAPTER 28

HAEZLE

Haezle was no longer confused, but she was annoyed, and exasperated, and ready to give up and go home.

'Who do you think you are?'

Estrel just stared at her. He didn't say a word. It did nothing to enhance her opinion of him.

She stared down at the wine bottle in his hand and, more particularly, the symbol that had been drawn onto the label in black marker. He'd seemed so pleased when he'd found it. It seemed idiotic.

'What do you mean, it's an Echo?' she'd asked.

His response had been a very broad grin.

'I should probably tell you a little more about myself.'

He seemed ridiculously pleased with himself. Haezle found that off-putting. She said so. He looked crestfallen.

'No, it's important,' Estrel insisted. 'This… this is a message.'

He waved the bottle around in front of him.

Haezle shrugged.

'Sure, a cryptic message. I specialise in those. "*The eclipse is the end*". You said you left it. Who's it for?'

'Me,' said Estrel, his grin sneaking back in. 'It's a message for me.'

'Why are you leaving messages for yourself?'

'Because I wasn't sure that this was something I needed to know. I don't understand what it means.'

'But you just said it was a message for you.'

'It is. But not "*me*" me. Another me.'

'There's more than one of you?'

'There's more than… I told you about this.'

He had. Haezle hadn't really believed him.

'I thought it was a metaphor. I thought it was a hallucination. I thought he…'

She jabbed an accusing finger in Onu Lek's direction.

'…had put weird notions in your head and… I don't know. I didn't think you meant actual, real life versions of you, walking around leaving and finding messages.'

'Well, I did. I also told you I'm a time traveller…'

'Tell me again.' Haezle softened her tone, tried to soothe the bruised ego of the man in front of her. 'Why are there multiple versions of you? And why are you leaving each other coded messages, rather than just telling it straight? Come to that, why leave messages at all? Can't you guys meet? Does the universe explode if you do?'

'I… don't know,' admitted Estrel, weakly. 'But we don't tend to meet. Most of us are from parallel realities…'

'There are parallel realities? So there are more of me out… somewhere?'

'No, I don't think it works like that. It's just one day. There's one day where a time loop was created and… I…'

Estrel trailed off, looked at Lek for help. Lek shrugged. He didn't look like he was following things any better than Haezle was. He also didn't really look like he cared all that much.

'I don't think I'm explaining it very well. It's not been that long for me. I've not been travelling very long.'

'Travelling? Through time?'

'Yes. I think that, for most people, if there's more than one of you, then that's why. Evie White. Chaguartay-White…'

'Right. That's the same person as the little girl running about out there? Or someone new I don't know?'

'OK, I'll pick a name. Evie Chaguartay. That's who she is now. That's what he called her when he laid this all out for me…'

Estrel pointed at Onu Lek, who shrugged again.

'I have no idea what you're talking about,' he said.

'That's another thing.' Estrel was becoming visibly distressed. 'You should. You should know all about this! Why don't you know about this? You always know. You're the only one who understands! I thought you had special powers! I thought you could see all of time? That's what you told me. Was that a lie, to get me to go through with all of this?'

Haezle stepped between the two men to diffuse the situation.

'Let's just try to stay on topic. Can you do that for me? You mentioned a time loop. That's what created so many copies of you. Someone put you in a time loop. That was Evie Chaguartay? All grown up?'

'No.' Estrel looked surprised. 'No, Evie Chaguartay didn't put me in a time loop. Why would she…?'

Haezle was finding this increasingly exasperating. She couldn't find the right questions to get a straight story, but she couldn't just let Estrel talk, as he seemed incapable of saying anything that made sense.

'Who did then?'

'I did! Well, one of me did…'

'You put yourself in a time loop?' Haezle paused, waiting

to be told that she was wrong again, but it didn't seem like that was going to happen. 'How?'

'I don't know the details. It was a different me. Me from the future. On a different timeline.'

'You from the future, but on a different timeline, put a past version of yourself into a time loop. That sounds incredibly dangerous, reality-wise. I thought you were being careful of things like that?'

'I didn't know anything about it at the time. The me who went into the loop. That was how we protected ourselves.'

'You put yourself into a time loop without your own consent? Didn't you…? No, but you know about it now? Is that because you got out of the loop?'

'I didn't get out. I was supposed to kill Evie Chaguartay, apparently. I didn't manage it.'

'But you're here now. Am I in the time loop?'

'No, I am out now. After it failed, I kind of carried on. I don't really understand that, either. But he pulled me out…'

Estrel pointed at Onu Lek, who continued to look baffled by everything that was being said.

'That was when I realised. It all kind of came to me, in a rush - the loop, the future, everything that had brought me to that point. It all came crashing into my brain as the timelines collapsed and…'

Haezle felt a jolt of sympathy. It must have been overwhelming. Haezle could see the strain on his face. That didn't sound like something she'd want to experience.

'He said that it hadn't worked. The time loop,' Estrel continued. 'He said that she'd changed the game, and he needed all of us to fix things. He said we could stop her from ever coming to power and that everything would be better. He said that…'

Estrel trailed off. There were tears in his eyes.

Haezle was sympathetic, but she wasn't satisfied.

'I think I can guess why he thinks he should do that. I know the Order. I know what monks are like. I even get where the book comes into it. I suspect that if I ever get my hands on a complete copy again, I'll have a head start on interpreting it. But I don't understand you. Why you?'

'Yes, I don't understand that either,' said Onu Lek suddenly. 'I've been trying to follow all of this. I agree with you, Haezle, that this sounds absolutely like the sort of thing I would do, given the opportunity. It also sounds like, in the future, that opportunity is exactly what I'm going to get. But I'm confused by you, young man. You seem to talk so much and understand so little. You're not a scientist, or a soldier, or a monk, even. Why did I pick you, and, more to the point, why did you go along with it?'

Estrel screwed his hands up into fists and lurched around to face Onu Lek. For one awful moment, Haezle was worried that he was going to hit the monk, but she realised that he'd made the fists to bring his hands under control, to avoid doing just that.

'Yes, Lek, why did you pick me? You should know. You usually know. You usually know everything. What's going on? Why has your time travelling omniscience deserted you?'

Onu Lek shrugged.

'You seem furious with me,' he observed. 'I can't give you any answers. It doesn't matter how loudly you shout.'

'I'm suggesting,' snarled Estrel, through gritted teeth, 'that you're putting it on. That you're not as clueless as you're making out and that, right now, this is all an act, presumably for her benefit.'

He punctuated the "her" with a finger pointed at Haezle, rudely, forcefully and without looking around.

'You're angry, Estrel, I get it,' she said, hoping that calling him out on his behaviour might prick something, release the head of steam that he'd built up. 'Why would Onu Lek lie to you? Why would he lie to me?'

'Why would he do anything? Why would he send me back here? He knew something was wrong, he knew that there was something up. With the book, with this version of himself. Whatever's going on, this one…' - and at this point he swung his pointing finger back around to point at Onu Lek - '…is no use to me. I'm stuck here. I can't do anything. I've been sacrificed, for some reason. I want someone to tell me why.'

'I don't think that's true,' said Onu Lek with a small, irritating smile.

'Don't think what's true? I haven't been sacrificed? I might as well have been.'

'No, I mean, it's not true that you can't do anything. You can help me.'

'Help you do what?'

This question came from both Estrel and Haezle. For her part, Haezle was astounded. Onu Lek had spent hours acting as if everything was completely baffling to him, and being no help whatsoever. Now, suddenly, he seemed to have a plan.

She shouldn't have been astounded. This was typical behaviour. This. This was what monks were like.

'Help me compile the book,' smiled Lek. 'Again.'

'Help you…?' Haezle began and then stopped talking.

She looked at Estrel pleadingly. This couldn't be right. She looked up to Onu Lek. She respected him, respected his judgement, his wisdom. Was he really just planning to repeat what he'd done before, all over again?

'Maybe he's right,' Estrel said. 'The book was lost in my time. Maybe he sent me back to find it and maybe this is how it has to be done.'

'Lost, not erased,' said Haezle.

'Perhaps something got lost in translation. Forgotten over the years.'

'Perhaps somebody just needs to say what he means and stop talking in riddles all the time.'

Haezle was a little surprised that had come out of her mouth. Onu Lek looked affronted.

'I thought you were here to help me?' he said to both of them.

Haezle said nothing.

'I'm here to help me,' said Estrel, simply. 'I know that now. I'm here to save the woman I love....'

And there it was. This wasn't what Haezle had expected to hear, but that was the answer to her earlier question. It made her angry.

'You're here for what? I thought you... Aren't you risking the whole of existence, everybody's lives with all this messing with time? And you're telling me you're doing this for what? A woman?'

'Yes, a woman,' replied Estrel. 'Mouse. The woman I love. That was why the original me created the loop. That was why this splinter of me was created. I loved her too, in my reality. I can't let it be in vain.'

'You're here to help yourself by saving the woman you love? Saving yourself? You're not even doing it for her?'

'I...' Estrel looked thrown. 'Of course I'm doing it for her. I just... I misspoke.'

'How did she die?'

She asked the question more forcefully than she had meant to. She wasn't trying to hurt Estrel. But she had to know. Because she had been about to agree that, given circumstances, finding the book, compiling it again was the best course of action.

Now she wasn't sure what she was doing it for. But it

needed to be something more important that some guy's heartache.

'How did she die?' she asked again.

'She… there was a meeting. Evie Chaguartay gassed the place. Everyone died.'

'And that destroyed you? That left you desperate enough to come back to do this? That…?'

'No!' It was Estrel's turn to look affronted. 'I fought. I led the resistance. We tried everything to turn the tide, to bring Evie down. But it wasn't enough, and then Lek told me I could have both. I could have Mouse back and we could stop Evie Chaguartay in her tracks before she ever hurt the people of Trinity.'

'But if she hadn't died, you wouldn't have fought?'

'I… well, not the way I did, no. But it's not like I was pro-Evie. I just thought that democratic means…'

'If she hadn't died, you wouldn't have fought,' Haezle concluded for him. 'But I bet she would have. I bet that's why she died. Don't you think that needs to mean something? How do you think she'd feel about all of this? What gives you the right to erase her sacrifice?'

She could see that Estrel was seething. Haezle hadn't meant to push things that far. She couldn't take them back now.

'Come on, Lek,' snarled Estrel. 'We've got a book to compile.'

CHAPTER 29

LAGRANGE

It's a mess at Administration, a big mess. Fortunately for me, way too big of a mess for Cadets to be left to clear things up, calm people down, or make sure everything's locked down so that nothing else happens. They've not even sent us chasing after anyone who got away. They've sent us back to base.

This sounds like a bad thing. It sounds like they're cutting us out, putting us down, but I don't care. Because clearing things up after something like that is an enormous hassle and, back at Authority, I've got use of the Mainframe.

I've got use of it, but it isn't a lot of use to me, because me and computers don't get on. I can barely operate my Com. Fortunately, Mortimer is a different story.

Not an entirely different story. He can barely operate his Com, either. But he knows his way around the Mainframe.

I don't have an actual image of the tattoo. I didn't take pictures and, well, it's a tattoo. I could hardly take it with me. Not without taking a body along too, and that would have been obvious.

Mortimer tells me we can't do an image search off a

description, not in the time we have, which isn't a lot. So I've drawn it on a piece of paper. I'm not great at drawing, and it turns out I'm not great at remembering what this tattoo looks like. To be fair, both times I've seen it, there's been a fair amount of adrenaline pumping through my system, albeit for very different reasons.

The resulting sketch is, well, sketchy. There are rough lines and smudges and bits that are overdrawn several times because I can't quite get them right. It's not good enough. We have found nothing.

'How long, exactly, would the text search take?'

Mortimer sighs and runs his hand through his hair.

'I don't know. If we're lucky, a few hours…'

Fuck him, we probably had a few hours. We wasted forty minutes on this nonsense of a sketch, which is delivering zero results so far.

'Well, we'd better hope clean-up takes even longer than expected, because we're getting fuck all from this approach. How do we run the text search?'

'You tell me what it looked like and I type it in.'

Mortimer's tone is unhelpfully sarcastic. For once, I manage to ignore that.

'OK…' My mind has gone blank. I'm not certain that my lack of artistic skills was necessarily the most significant issue before. 'It was round. Like a circle. Like, properly, a circle. Not actually the same shape as the moon.'

'Right, a circle.'

I ignore him.

'There's a sword down the middle, straight down the middle. The blade is pointing downwards and, on the left of that, it's skin, no ink. On the other side is black. There's no texture or anything, no craters, no patterns to show…'

'That it's a moon?' Mortimer cuts in. 'So how do you know

it's a moon?'

It's a good question. Damn him. He doesn't really do good questions, which makes it harder to ignore him. Harder, but not impossible.

I manage it without breaking a sweat.

'I know it's a moon. You need to put moon…'

He's put "circle". I watch while he deletes it and types "moon".

'The hilt of the sword is fairly simple, I don't know, bog standard sword…'

'Bog standard sword? I can't put that. It's not a description.'

'It's plain, all right? Don't mention the hilt. The hilt isn't important. It's plain. There's a stone in the middle, though. A red one. Like a jewel.'

'A ruby?'

'Maybe a ruby, maybe some other red stone. I'm not an expert on stones, either. Those are the important…'

I don't need to finish the sentence. Because far from taking hours to run the text description search, we have a result already. Mortimer hadn't even typed the bit about the stone yet.

There's one entry. One. And it's classified. All that comes up is the image, the same symbol that I've seen tattooed on two different men.

'Is that it?' asks Mortimer.

I just nod. I'm staring at it. This version isn't a tattoo. It's graffiti. There isn't enough wall to know exactly where it is, but the brickwork, the alternating rows of two different lengths of stone, the grey of the rock - that's so quintessentially Trinity that I would not even imagine that it was anywhere else.

It might be the city wall itself. There are words painted underneath. They are redacted with big, black rectangles, only the edges of the letters poking out. There isn't enough for me to guess what they say.

'Why's it classified?' I wonder.

Although what I really mean is *"who got it classified*?" Because that's a top level intervention, hiding it from the rest of Authority. Even at a pretty junior level, which Mortimer and I are, there isn't a lot we don't know about the citizens of Trinity and what they get up to in their spare time. Sometimes at work, too.

There's a short list of people who could have done it. Borate, obviously, and his Senior Oficiers, which includes his son, Gerstley, plus Canto, Ranieri, Pestril and the new guy whose name I can never remember until about five minutes after I should have used it. So far, I have failed to make a good impression on that guy.

Anyway, it has to have been one of them. I have nothing to narrow it down with, other than that Borate senior has been conspicuous by his absence ever since he decided to run for the mayoralty. But I would imagine it takes a matter of moments to classify information in the Mainframe. Plus, his position and ambition mean he's got a lot to lose.

Where does that leave me? I basically have two questions which, in fact, are the same question: why is it classified versus who classified it. One will lead me to the other, but I have no way of narrowing down either.

'What does it mean?' asks Mortimer.

Now that, surprisingly, is an excellent question. A question that might lead us to why it was classified. A good question that might lead us to who got it classified.

So a better question, at this stage, than either of mine. I give Mortimer a look, make sure he can see the surprise on my face. It's genuine. I'm impressed, but he doesn't take it that way.

'OK, OK, that was the obvious question to ask…'

It was, but I didn't ask it and now I'm the idiot.

'…but do you know? What does it mean? What's it a symbol of?' he asks.

'I don't know. I've only seen it twice before this and both times it was tattooed on. That's a pretty major commitment to a symbol, so it must be something important.'

'Is it like an initiation of some sort? Swearing allegiance to a cause, or a philosophy…'

'I don't know. The two guys who had it didn't have a lot in common.'

'Right. The guy you choked out and…'

I realise I haven't told Mortimer exactly where I saw the tattoo the first time. For good reason, because it's none of his fucking business, but it's understandable that he'd ask. However shit I think he's going to be at it, he is also in training to be an Oficier. He's collecting information, trying to fit the pieces together, looking for patterns.

Men I've wrestled - that's the pattern.

'The first one was a rich kid. Financial markets, that kind of thing…'

My kind of thing… Deep breath, I didn't think this was how I was going to come out to Mortimer.

'It was on his back. Pretty prominent, but kind of hidden, like it was a secret, only for trusted people to find. Whereas the guy at Administration had it on his neck…'

'More proudly,' ponders Mortimer, breezing past the revelation about my sex life. 'Or at least less ashamed.'

I guess it didn't have to be a revelation about my sex life. I could have met him at the gym.

'He didn't seem like the kind of guy who believed in shame.'

I think he's right, though. A footsoldier displaying it proudly, a money man hiding his true allegiance, the same symbol daubed on a wall. It feels like a cause.

Damn, Mortimer is coming up with the goods today.

'So the symbol belongs to a cause,' I solve aloud. 'A new one, at least to Trinity, because it's barely been seen. And the one place it has popped up, all information has been withheld.'

'Have you heard anything? You spend more time in the Docklands than I do…'

I do, mostly because Mortimer spends all the time he *is* down there jumping at his own shadow. Docklands isn't so dangerous if you know the right people to name drop at the right moment. I do.

It's helpful to me, though, that Mortimer is keeping his distance from the more unsavoury end of the city. I've got some leads, some ideas that could land me a collar that would make my name, bump me up to Oficier without the need to take the exams.

I don't need competition in that. Heaven help us all if Mortimer got promoted above me.

'No, I've heard nothing. It's strange. How did this appear from nowhere? Only one entry on the Mainframe… there's some kind of organisational structure to this thing. It can't be just two guys. So how has hardly anyone heard about it?'

'I guess we need to know what's in that redacted file. We could break into Borate's office. We might find something that will point us in the right direction…'

And just like that, Mortimer returns to form.

'That is a shit idea. Probably the worst plan you've ever proposed.'

'You've got a better one?'

Mortimer is sulking. But I do.

'I'm going to talk to Antonio.'

CHAPTER 30

ESTREL

I was home.

This had never really been my house. It was Mouse's before I arrived in Trinity and it remained her property the whole time we were together. But we shared this space for years. Happy years. It became my home.

After Mouse died, I carried on living there. No one seemed to care. I didn't really know if she owned it, which seemed unlikely given the general state of her finances, or if she rented, in which case her landlord would have to be very understanding about the chaotic and unpredictable nature of her income. Also, I never saw a landlord.

I was just wondering if Mouse had been squatting there all along, when Mouse banged a mug of tea on the table in front of me.

'Milk?' she asked, her tone snappy, like she'd stopped worrying about me and was growing tired of my presence.

It had only been an hour. But the stranger she'd found battered and bewildered on the street seemed to be fine now, because I was, and whatever charitable urge she'd had probably dissipated. It was normal. I would not take it personally. She didn't know who I was.

It would make sense if she was squatting. No one would trouble her, given the protection afforded to her by her association with Eamer - Docklands Kingpin and quasi-General of the Black Knights. I wondered why it had never occurred to me before.

I wondered why I had never thought to ask. I was sure I'd offered to pay her rent, but she'd dismissed the idea. It hadn't come up again.

A lot of things hadn't come up again. We'd had ten years, more or less, which you would have thought was plenty of time to learn everything. It wasn't any time at all.

'No, no milk,' I said with a smile.

I knew the fridge didn't work at this point. I had no idea where Mouse was keeping the milk, but it wasn't anywhere cold.

'Good,' shrugged Mouse. 'I don't have any milk, anyway.'

She sat opposite me, on a high stool like the one I was sitting on, and rested her elbows on the table, cradling her mug between her hands.

'I'll just drink this and then I'll get out of here,' I said.

I meant it, even if I was desperate to stay. I hadn't planned this. I knew it wasn't a good idea. But I didn't have a lot of choice. I was fine now, but I'd needed someone to rescue me from that alleyway. I'd needed someone to rescue me from that other place, too. Mouse to the rescue.

This wasn't what I wanted, anyway. I wanted my Mouse back. This wasn't my Mouse. This was who she was before we met, and that was an era that we definitely hadn't talked much about.

This wasn't my home. It was Mouse's home. Mouse's house and Mouse's home. The kitchen with its broken fridge and unidentifiable slime coating the floor was Mouse's. The migraine inducing flickering of the overhead light was Mouse's. The living room with its disgusting, lopsided couch and the screen, where the right half took five minutes longer than the left to warm up, was Mouse's. The empty cartons and bottles and, upstairs in her bed, condoms and pill pots, those were all Mouse's life before me.

But she was still Mouse. I'd missed her. So I sipped my tea slowly and watched her fidget and mumble to herself. Several times she appeared to think of something she needed to do in another room so she'd get up and leave, only to return a minute to two later, looking distracted and nervous.

It was so familiar, so beautifully, awkwardly familiar. My heart ached with love. And I couldn't help myself.

'Something making you nervous?' I asked casually.

Mouse's gaze shot upwards, and she stared straight at me. Her eyes narrowed with suspicion.

'What? No! Nothing that… I've just got stuff to do, that's all. I'm busy, very busy, and you seem OK now, so you probably should go? Right? You've probably got places you need to be as well?'

She knew I hadn't. We'd already had that conversation, after she'd brought me inside and given me a clean cloth and a bottle of liquid to clean myself up. It didn't have a label, but it stung like damnation and I assumed, from that, it was the right sort of stuff.

I hadn't needed showing to the bathroom, but I had to let her do it, anyway. It was the cleanest room in the house, if you ignored three weeks' worth of neglected laundry spilling out of a plastic box in the corner.

Afterwards, I'd found her in the kitchen, messing with the kettle, as if she was locked in an internal battle whether to offer me tea or not.

I sat down. She leant against the counter, arms folded, staring. It might have appeared confrontational, but I knew it was defensive.

'So… Estrel, is it?'

It was weird, her not knowing my name. I'd had to pretend I hadn't known hers. I didn't ask whether it was her given name. I didn't do that the first time we'd met, either. I mean, the first time we'd met for me.

The list of people who knew that she was really called Miriam was incredibly short. She wouldn't be impressed to find out that list was longer than she knew.

To be fair, Mouse was a given name, too. It wasn't like she'd picked it for herself. It's not that it didn't fit. It absolutely did, in the sense of her being quick-witted, adaptable and observant, but no one would describe her as being timid, or particularly gentle, or playful. Not to her face, anyway. Not unless you were me, anyway. But not this version of me, and not this version of her. It hurt that I'd lost that. It hurt even more that she'd never known it.

I realised Mouse was waiting for me to confirm my name.

'Oh, yes. That's right.'

'So what were you doing in the alleyway behind my house, Estrel? This isn't a great part of the city.'

I needed to be careful, keep things vague.

'I was trying to find someone. I needed some help. He wasn't who I thought he was, though, and…'

Mouse was nodding, seriously.

'You know that there are safer places you can go to get that kind of trade?' she asked.

It took me a moment to realise what she was talking about.

'Oh no,' I protested, 'I don't mean that kind of… help. I've only just arrived in town and…'

She didn't seem to be listening to what I was saying.

'...well,' she continued, 'maybe not all that much safer. But unsafe in different ways, and certainly a lot cleaner. Well, somewhat cleaner. You should go down to the Docklands. Anything that might take your fancy is on offer down there. Quite a lot that might not, too…'

This was the sort of tangential monologue that I'd got used to. It was comforting to be caught in the headlights of another one.

I was getting sentimental. This was not usually a comforting experience, it was a relentless one, like being run over by an rampaging mob, where what you meant and what you actually said were trampled underfoot, squashed together until even you had forgotten that they were ever separate things.

I was fighting myself, resisting every urge to be honest and open up to the woman I loved. I wanted to tell her what had happened, between us, to us… I wanted her to know what the future held and, most of all, I wanted her to believe me and to do something different, to save herself.

The logical flaw here was the expectation that she might believe me, that she might believe "Hey, you don't know me but in the future we're going to meet and fall in love and then you're going to die and I'm going to come back in time to save you. And also the city."

That didn't sound like Mouse, and I wouldn't have respected her if she had believed me. It was ridiculous. That was before we got to the part about it being dangerous and threatening the fabric of reality.

Much as it hurt, it was safer if she thought I was looking for sex on the streets.

So I let her believe that, and now, with me feeling substantially better, and with my earlier mission unfulfilled, she assumed that my need remained.

I put down my mug.

'I don't really have anywhere to go,' I admitted. 'I'm very new in town. But Docklands, you said? Is that somewhere I might find a place to stay?'

I knew it was. I was proud of myself for thinking to ask this question.

'Kind of depends on your standards, but, like I said, it's clean…ish and safe…ish. If it's that or an alley, then Docklands is definitely a better bet.'

A small smile twitched at the corner of her mouth. I recognised this too. I hadn't actually missed it, but…

'Especially if the alley is in The Alleys.'

I was a joke, and a joke that I understood. But, as someone who had supposedly only just arrived in Trinity and with no prior knowledge of the place, which in some senses was true but in others definitely wasn't, it was a joke I had to pretend not to get.

That it wasn't funny really helped me keep a straight face.

'OK,' I deadpanned.

Mouse shrugged. She was used to her jokes not landing.

'Well, I'm due at work in half an hour. I can take you down there, if you like.'

This was unexpected. Five sentences ago she was trying to get rid of me. Now she was offering to take me where I was pretending I needed to go. It was time for another question that I already knew the answer to.

'Do you work in The Docklands?'

I was pleased with the superfluous definite article. It made me sound extra green.

'I have a thing in a bar,' she said.

This was a succinct way of putting her odd combination of the roles of bar manager and underworld fixer.

'Cool, are there rooms to rent in the bar?'

'Not rooms you'd want to spend more than an hour in, no… Look, give me ten and we'll head out. I need to find something to take with me. My boss gave me something to hold for him. Go make yourself comfortable in the front room. The screen should sync to your Com…'

I drained my mug, the remaining contents of which were cold and grainy. They made me grimace, but I avoided the urge to spit them back into the mug.

Mouse disappeared out of the kitchen and up the tiny staircase. The third and seventh steps already had their trademark creak, but the top one didn't yet bang with that annoying, stride-breaking flip that it had done once Jo Jo had "borrowed" the nails to repair his door ram. That came much later. We all had a lot to suffer first.

I slipped out and round the corner into the living room. Making myself comfortable would be a tall order, but I pushed the empty, grease-stained plastic containers and cardboard boxes back up the mini-mountain they'd been part of on the far side of the sofa. Having created enough cushion space to sit down and pointed my Com at the screen on the wall.

Jack White appeared in front of me, on the steps of the Dome. I recognised this. It was his speech, the "End of the Black Night" one. It was clever, equating Chaguartay's term of office with a bad dream, while implicitly connecting him with the criminal fraternity that had his patronage.

I'd seen it a dozen times before, maybe more. This was the moment that he declared his intention to take the fight to the Mayor. The words turned out to be hollow; the man was a charlatan. In his defence, he was being used. We were all deceived. By his wife, who was plotting with her father all along to prolong Trinity's nightmare.

I knew all this. But I watched it again. It was a moment of history being made. But the right-hand side of the screen took five minutes longer to warm up than the left, so I didn't see what was wrong. Evie White wasn't standing by her husband's side, as she was in every other version of this scene that I had ever seen.

Something had changed. If I'd noticed, I might acted sooner, and I might have avoided what happened next. Somehow. Maybe.

As it was, from that moment, it was doomed to happen.

CHAPTER 31

CANNON

They were headed for Trinity, it seemed. *Still* headed for Trinity, but this time, overland. That was what Estrel had told the coach driver before he bundled Cannon into the carriage and pulled the shuttered door closed.

Cannon didn't get a good look at the driver. He could see them now, the back of them, anyway, through the small window in front of him, just behind Estrel's left shoulder.

They sat hunched over, a large hood pulled down over their head. The way it hung in loose folds around their shoulders, Cannon would have been surprised if it didn't entirely cover their face. It must have been impossible to see the horses or the road ahead.

It didn't seem to matter. Both horses were determined and surefooted, which was no mean feat on the pitted roads they were taking through the countryside. They crossed steep hills, if not actual mountains, with sheer drops that dwarfed the cliffs from the shore they'd washed up on, but the horses didn't break stride, didn't flinch from their task. They kept on galloping, perfectly in synch, with a metronomic rhythm that would have lulled Cannon to sleep were it not for the crunching lurch of the carriage with every pothole they clattered through.

They didn't seem to need the coach driver, who sat with the crop held loose in their grip. Cannon hadn't seen them apply it once.

'It's almost self-driving, this carriage,' he observed.

Estrel glanced over his shoulder and nodded at the hunched form of the coach driver.

'Yes, I suppose so,' he mused. 'It's funny how some things come back around. There are no new ideas.'

Cannon wasn't sure what he meant by this, but he did sense a lighter note in Estrel's tone. It was a relief. They'd sat in heavy silence since the start of the journey. He didn't know where that had been, so didn't know how far Trinity was, or how long it would take them to get there. Impressive as they were, he thought that the horses would tire at some point, and they'd have to stop for a while.

Where, he had no idea; he hadn't had a glimpse of civilisation the whole time. But that made him all the more pleased that he was in the carriage. Estrel hadn't given him a lot of choice but, if he'd been left behind, it was evident that he couldn't have a walked far enough to find refuge before he'd starved, or fallen off an escarpment, or got stuck in a bog.

He could hear wind and rain against the shutters now. The carriage rocked as it was buffeted by the gusts. This was no weather to be out in, and no terrain to be out on. He was better off inside. With Estrel. Who at least seemed to be in a better mood.

'You seem different,' he said, hoping it would be taken for the compliment he'd intended.

Estrel furrowed his brow.

'It's tricky,' he mumbled. 'Hard to say. But I think I am.

Different.'

Cannon wasn't sure what to say to that.

'Right, good,' was all he did say.

'I'm experiencing some things that I was once told are called "temporal ripples",' he said, by way of a non-explanation. 'It's disorientating, but I'm kind of learning as I go...'

'Aren't we all!' grinned Cannon nervously, although he was relieved to be having something close to a normal conversation.

'No, I don't mean that,' said Estrel. 'Maybe it's time I was straighter with you, Cannon. I don't know. You've been through a lot, too, haven't you?'

Cannon nodded. He had. He also wasn't completely sure that was what Estrel was talking about.

'I've been travelling a long time,' Estrel continued. 'Like, a long time.'

He smiled, as if he'd made a joke. Cannon didn't get it.

'Do you remember how you came to be in the ocean?' he asked.

It was the one thing that had never seemed to come back to Estrel. Cannon wondered about the event that triggered an amnesia that deep-seated.

'No. I don't, but I don't think that's important. I think I'd been there for a long time. I think it's how I got back to your ship.'

'Back to our ship? You mean you were on the ship before? You fell into the...'

'No.' Estrel cut him off sharply. 'You're not listening well enough, Cannon. I don't mean "got back" as in returned. I mean, I travelled back to your ship.'

'Travelled back?'

Backwards? Back... what else could he mean?

'Through time. I'm not… I thought you'd realised this. I'm from the future.'

Wait. What?

'I'm not…' began Cannon.

What? Wait…

'Cannon,' Estrel looked concerned. 'You do know that… I thought you knew that…?'

'Thought I knew what?'

He was feeling sick to his stomach. What Estrel appeared to be saying made very little sense. He understood, at a basic level, what the future was, but that was another of those troubling time-related concepts that made his head spin. It wasn't for him to understand. It wasn't for him to worry about. So he'd thought. He had a horrible, growing suspicion that it was.

'I come from the future and you come from…' Estrel stopped. 'No, that's not fair. You need to find it for yourself. Tell me about yourself, Cannon.'

'I… I…' Cannon cast around for a story, an anecdote that he could share and put this whole nonsense to bed. 'My name is Cannon. I'm a performer. I joined the Floating Circus to see the world. You know this…'

'It's not true though, is it?'

'It *is* true! It's as true as…'

Tears pricked at Cannon's eyes. He could feel his face turn red, feel the vein pulsing in his temple. The pressure in his head seemed to build until he was certain that he was going to explode.

'Tell me a story about yourself.'

Estrel's voice was soothing, and brought him back into the carriage. He felt the hard, wooden bench under him, planted his feet firmly on the carriage floor, at least until another pothole in the road threw them both into the air, crashing back down with a bruising thud.

'Tell me a story about *before*,' said Estrel, again.

Cannon screwed up his face in concentration. He tried to think about "*before*". He tried to remember what "*before*" was supposed to mean.

'I lived… in a village,' he said, eventually.

That seemed normal. That seemed plausible. He was fascinated to see that it felt real.

'Good,' said Estrel. 'Tell me about the village, tell me about something that happened, anything that happened.'

'The festival!' cried Cannon. 'Every year there was a festival. I remember it from being small, all the food and the dancing. There were animals… shows, like…'

'That's good,' Estrel encouraged him. 'What's the last festival you remember? Before you left, before you joined the circus?

'It was… there were…' Cannon got a warm flood as the feelings associated with memories he couldn't quite grasp came flowing back. More tears welled in his eyes but, instead of frustration and anger, he felt warmth and belonging.

'Don't force it,' warned Estrel. 'Just let it come.'

'There was cider,' grinned Cannon, suddenly.

'It sounds fun.'

Estrel seemed engaged, encouraging. Cannon hadn't seen this since the early days on the ship. He'd missed having a friend.

He tried to remember more, desperately wanting to preserve this moment, to please his friend. There was nothing there.

'I… I…'

Cannon stammered to a halt. He started blankly at the shuttered window. His memory was as limited as the view.

'It's OK,' said Estrel, gently. 'This is often what happens.

This kind of travel isn't normal, it's not natural. We aren't built for it. Our *brains* certainly aren't. So they put up defences. That's all this is, a defence mechanism. You can't remember your life from before because your brain can't handle it…'

'You remember,' Cannon pointed out. 'You couldn't to start with, but you remember now. You keep remembering things. The temporary ripples…'

'Temporal ripples,' Estrel corrected him. 'And yes, you're right, I do. But I've been doing this longer than you. I've done it a bit more often than you have. I'm learning. Adapting. Someone once told me that, once you're practised enough, you can see all of time. All at the same time. You can see everything that ever happened to you, will happen to you, might have happened to you, but for the roll of the dice, or the flap of the butterfly's wings.'

Cannon thought about that for a moment, and it terrified him with its vast possibilities and infinite contradictions.

'I don't think I'd want that,' he said quietly.

'Nor should you. Don't push it. If you're ready, it will come. I've spent a lot of time getting better at this. I have work to do.'

'What kind of work?'

'The sort of work that is more important than whether I want to stay sane.'

'You're going mad?' asked Cannon.

Estrel seemed very relaxed about this. It seemed to be a sacrifice that he was willing to make, and Cannon wondered what the cause was that was so important that he'd give his own mind for it.

'I am going mad,' said Estrel. 'But I've met wise men. And believe me, there's nothing about their situation that would make me want that, either.'

CHAPTER 32

LEK

The room I stepped into was not dark, or murky, or ill-defined. It was white. The brightest of white. The walls were white; the ceiling and floor were also white. The fluorescent light from the square panel lights in the ceiling bounced off every surface, reflecting a painful glare.

There was little in the way of furniture. In one corner there was a pile of sacking that looked like it might have been used as a bed, a half-empty water bowl and some large bones, picked clean of any trace of meat and with huge dents and grooves ground into them, presumably by the teeth of the creature I'd seen before.

As my eyes adjusted, I saw scratch marks on the wall and a patch of darkness where the floor had been dug at until it wore away. There was a powerful smell that brought tears to my eyes.

This was certainly where the animal had come from, then, but the environment looked very different from this side of the door. I turned to look again at where I'd come from.

This didn't seem to be any normal doorway. There was no

way this room was part of the Catacombs. In different circumstances, I might have found this stranger than I did at the time, but I was taking on an Acolyte's Trial. I had been given no indication of what I should expect. Perhaps this kind of thing happened all the time. I wouldn't have known.

This is, or at least was, not my normal way of thinking. I guess that since this time I have become rather more used to the unexpected and inexplicable happening. Although, of course, since this time I have also got significantly better at expecting and explaining these occurrences. Regardless, I'm impressed at how well my younger self took this turn of events in his stride.

The door looked very different from that angle. It wasn't made of wood for a start. A hole, of about the same size as the one I'd stepped through, had been torn through the metal. The twisted barbs at the edges of the hole were burned black. It must have taken a considerable amount of power to break through.

I walked back towards the hole and touched the sharp edge, the same curiosity that had burned at me only moments earlier demonstrating conclusively that, sometimes, I never learn. I pulled my hand back, again sticking my finger in my mouth to soothe the wound, tasting blood.

This door didn't look like it worked the same way, either. There weren't any hinges or handles, and it seemed like it would just disappear inside the wall to open. I didn't know what would trigger it. I didn't think it would open anymore, either. There was no need to open it anymore, to be fair.

Now that I was closer, I could see through the hole and was only a little surprised to see that it wasn't the dark stone passageway I'd come from. It was hazy, as if shrouded in a thin mist, but it was unmistakeably a corridor. It looked to be part of the same building - the walls were white, although the floor was a grey concrete. Immediately outside the door there was a small section with black and white tiles laid out in a chequered pattern.

I stuck my head out, which was bold in comparison to how tentatively I had come through the other way. I heard a quiet popping and felt my teeth twinge, but was otherwise unaffected.

Physically unaffected, anyway. I couldn't believe my eyes. Suddenly I was back in the Catacombs. The same stone walls and half-collapsed ceiling, the same smell of damp and dust, with a distant drip-drip-drip the only sound, all present and correct.

No snarling mutant dogs. No long white corridor, no chequerboard flooring. I swung my torch up and down the passage as a last check and then straightened up and pulled my head back into the room.

Fizz.

Buzz.

I was back. The view through the hole reverted to being the unreachable corridor.

This was odd. I could only conclude that this door was some kind of portal through space. I'd crossed through into somewhere else. It seemed to be two-way, but only for me as far as I knew. There was no sign that the dog was currently running through the Catacombs. It seemed to have stayed wherever it was meant to be and disappeared down that corridor, the one I didn't seem to be able to get to. If that's where the creature was, then I wasn't concerned about not being able to get there. I thought it made me rather safer.

These were all perfectly logical, if not especially sensible, conclusions to come to. At least, they were with the knowledge I had at the time. Of course, now I know. The door wasn't a portal through space. I didn't travel any further than the distance my legs took me - a few paces into the room, at that point. But I did travel in time. The stone passage in the Catacombs, the long corridor in what I now know to be Research, they were are the same thing.

The building of the giant, underground Research complex didn't begin until many years later, after Chaguartay took power. It had started small, but grown quickly, and soon ran into the same problems that anything built underground in Trinity encountered. It was part of what had put a stop to the building of the Chaguartay Line almost as soon as it had started. Half of the city of Trinity had, over the years, sunk under the surface. Its compacted form made up the Catacombs and, since it had been there first, it wasn't getting out of the way for anyone or anything.

Not even Chaguartay, who, if the stories are to be believed, tried to detonate large amounts of explosives in the Citadel's foundation in order to clear the blockage. That, they say, is why its towers lean so dramatically.

Research was a sprawling, unplanned structure. However, an underground railway, to be of any use, needs to go from point A to point B in a reasonably straight line. Research could go around and under what was there before it. It stood to reason that, sometimes, when there was already a passageway running where a corridor needed to be, they just repurposed what was already there. That's where I'd come from. And this was where I'd ended up. In pretty much the same spot, but about sixty years in the future.

I didn't know that then, and I don't know whether I would have done anything differently if I had known. I was curious, and I wanted to explore this strange new place I'd found myself in. I think I would have done the same thing if I'd known it was, in fact, a strange new time.

I marched across the room, towards a similar door that -

now I knew what I was looking for - I spotted opposite the one that had been broken out of. There was still no obvious handle, or access panel, or any other method of opening the door that I wouldn't have known to look for because I had never needed to conceive of such a thing.

So, instead, I beat on it with my fists and shouted at the top of my voice.

'Help! Can anyone hear me?'

I paused, put my ear to the panel to hear what was on the other side of it. I could hear nothing except for a low, electrical hum. I resumed my banging.

'Hello? Help! Help! I'm trapped!'

I hoped that someone on the other side knew what this room was used for, and that they would come to my rescue, confused how someone had become trapped in what was, essentially, a cage for a rabid animal.

There was still no response, though. Either there was no one there, or they didn't care. I stopped banging, looked around for something else to attract attention with.

'What are you doing in there?' came a voice, tinny and buzzing with static.

I looked up, above the intact door, because that was where the voice appeared to be coming from, but I could see nothing.

'Yes, up here,' said the voice. 'I know you can hear me. What are you doing?'

'I'm trapped!' I shouted at nothing.

'No, you're not,' said the voice. 'There's an enormous hole in the door behind you. You can go out that way. Maybe you can retrieve my Hybrids for me…'

Hybrids? Plural?

I wanted to say that I couldn't go back out that way because *that way* wasn't the way he thought it was. I was keen to explore this new place. I felt certain that the next stage of my

Trial, the next set of pages I needed to collect, were somewhere here. I didn't think I was going to explain that properly, though. I didn't really understand it myself.

'I was trying to avoid running into him again,' I said instead.

Him? Them?

There was a pause, radio silence. Then a crackle and a hum.

'You'd better come this way, then,' said the voice.

The door in front of me slid open.

CHAPTER 33

It was early morning, and the roads throughout the centre of Trinity were jammed. Haezle pulled her scarf around her face, trying to filter the thick air through the dense knit and reduce the volume of particulates she was inhaling. The wool tasted of metal and oil. She suspected it wasn't doing anything.

Estrel and Onu Lek had disappeared down a staircase into a lower level, taking several bottles of wine with them. Onu Lek had insisted it was an important part of the process. Haezle had found her own way out of the Catacombs, stuffed her robe into a cubby and marched out of the Citadel.

She was done with them. Their motivations were wrong-headed, their actions nonsensical. They seemed to have appointed themselves as some kind of guardians of time.

She'd be worried about it if she thought they were even vaguely capable of achieving any of their objectives. Then, the entire fabric of reality would be at risk. As it was, they were just going to get drunk and lost in some tunnels. She hoped they made it out in one piece, but that was all the luck she wished them.

Haezle crossed the road between the cars. They weren't moving, so there was no need to wait to find a crossing. The texture of the surface changed with every lane, each one added separately as the TransWay had grown. Haphazard. Unplanned.

That was Trinity. Constantly expanding except, as a walled city, there was nowhere to expand. So everything just got crammed into the same spaces, buildings on top of buildings, roads on top of roads.

She picked up her feet a bit to avoid tripping over the join between the last two lanes, then turned sideways to squeeze between two vehicles that were bumper to bumper. Trinity was a mess. She looked up at the leaning towers of the Citadel. It helped when the buildings that were already there sank down into the ground. It made room for the new stuff.

Onu Lek and Estrel were under there, down in the Catacombs. Maybe it wasn't so bad if they blew the whole place up. Maybe they could travel back to the start, to the beginnings of Trinity. They could have a quiet word with the Founders, get them to do things differently.

Maybe they could get them to skip building the walls. Maybe they could get them to look after the Tree. *See,* she thought, as she tripped up on the pavement. *I have good ideas. I wouldn't waste the opportunity to fix things. I'd make a difference.*

Haezle paused to let a knot of youths pass, then nipped across the wide walkway ahead of the wave of factory workers that were headed the other way, chattering and bouncing on their way home from a night shift. They seemed energised by each other's company.

It wasn't like that in the Citadel. She couldn't imagine laughing with her fellow Readers. She didn't even have that kind of relationship with Isaak, who she considered a friend. If she thought about it, she wasn't sure what he would find funny. She'd never seen evidence of a sense of humour.

When she thought about it like that, it didn't seem like somewhere she belonged. Given what had happened in the last twenty-four hours, maybe she didn't anymore. Maybe she needed a new career.

Haezle ducked down a narrow alley, cutting through between the shops on the strip to the yard beyond. Her foot splashed in what she hoped was a puddle, but might have been something altogether more unpleasant. She didn't look down. It was usually best not to.

About halfway down the alleyway, the overpowering smell of urine began to be overpowered itself, eclipsed by burning herbs, pungent and tacky. Haezle stopped breathing through her mouth, and welcomed the scents of home, spice and vinegar floating in before she stepped into a wave of hot fat, sizzling meat that she could almost taste on the breeze.

The courtyard beyond the alleyway was filled with lean-tos and shelters made from iron and canvas and the occasional brick or concrete block, although those were scarce. Even with the amount of building happening in any part of Trinity at any one time, Administration had every site locked down, and it was hard to salvage anything.

This was a messy, chaotic settlement. To Haezle, it was home. To a significant proportion of the politicians in the Dome, it was an eyesore that needed eradicating. They described their homes as shacks, the courtyard as a shanty town. The residents of the courtyard called them tents, and the courtyard was the Commons. It was a way of life, one that they had no choice about, but one that they embraced, anyway.

Haezle tiptoed across the central Commons. It was early, and she didn't want to wake anyone who didn't want to be woken. The carefully stacked pots and pans, and the benches and fire pits that filled the centre, were a trip hazard. One that, if triggered, would make a noise that would raise the dead.

On the far side of the Commons, there was a door set into the wall. Negotiating her way across without incident, Haezle approached it and tapped lightly at the small window in the middle of it.

A face appeared in the glass, indistinct through the grime and grease on one side and the grey pollution coating the other. She didn't need to recognise it, though. She knew who it was, and it seemed the face knew her too, because the door opened and she slipped inside.

Konoroz was dressed in singed whites, a blue apron around his waist, the long ties of which were wrapped multiple times around his ample waist, tied too tight so that they looked like they were going to cut him in half. He turned back to the grill, inspecting some patties, tipping them up with his slice, letting them fall back with a slap and a sizzle. The last one he flipped, satisfied that it was sufficiently well done on the underside.

Haezle breathed in the aroma of Konoroz's grill. The foul odours of the street were gone. In here was only warmth and nourishment.

'You're up early?' asked Konoroz.

'Up late.' Haezle stifled a giveaway yawn and took a seat on top of a box.

Konoroz nodded, giving her a sideways smile.

'Not like that! I was at work.'

'They're working you too hard, those monks.'

'Maybe. I'm not sure if I have a job anymore.'

'Something went wrong?'

Konoroz reached into a box underneath the grill, which wasn't much more than a metal sheet attached to a gas burner, and produced a flatbread, which he dropped onto the hot plate, moving it around to pick up fat and flavour before leaving it to crisp.

'I don't know if there's anything left for me to do, if I'm honest. There's a problem with my book.'

'So? Read another book. I know you're fond of your old monk but…'

Konoroz waved the tongs in his other hand in the air to signify something that Haezle couldn't necessarily identify, but completely understood.

'I don't know. It doesn't usually work that way,' she sighed. 'And I haven't exactly parted with Onu Lek on the best terms.'

'Hmm?'

Haezle took a deep breath.

'I might have told him he was a selfish idiot with a god complex, who was more interesting in puzzles to solve than the people whose lives represented said puzzles. Not in so many words, but I think he got the hint.'

'Is that true?' asked Konoroz, turning his attention away from the grill and raising an eyebrow. 'It sounds like it might be true?'

'Oh, definitely true. I effectively accused him of being a man.'

Silence hung in the air for a moment. Haezle felt suddenly awkward.

'I mean… not you, of course. I mean, you're a man, but not…'

She realised that Konoroz's shoulders were shaking with the effort of not laughing.

'Whatever.'

Haezle folded her arms. She could hear the shouts of children from outside the galley, running footsteps hammering past the door. The Commons were coming to life.

'People are waking up, they'll be wanting their breakfast soon,' said Konoroz. 'Pass me that cooler.'

Haezle looked around, but couldn't see the cooler he was referring to.

'You're sitting on it.' Konoroz gestured to her seat with his tongs.

Haezle flushed with stupid embarrassment.

'Sorry,' she muttered, standing up and heaving the cooler up by its plastic handle. It was much heavier than she was expecting. 'What's in here?'

'Heavy fish,' said Konoroz.

Haezle wasn't certain if that was just an adjective, or actually the name of the fish. She would have asked, but the effort of carrying the chunky box all of three feet left her gasping and breathless.

'You're not kidding,' she spluttered as she straightened up.

Konoroz bent and pulled the lid off the cooler, tossing it into the far corner. A cloud of air escaped, surrounding Haezle with a gust of wet fish, rotten eggs and cheese left out in the sun. She gagged, then choked a little, bringing her hand to cover her mouth and nose. It was rather too late.

'Is that stuff OK?' she croaked from behind her hand. 'It smells rank.'

Konoroz grinned, removing whole fish from the box with his tongs and slapping them onto the grill.

'Old fish is the best fish. Tastes like experience.'

To be fair to Konoroz, the moment they hit the grill the evil stench was burned away, and Haezle got a tantalising hint of crispy skin and succulent flesh underneath. To be fair to Haezle, no one was supposed to experience this particular Ashuanan delicacy in its raw form.

'I have something more suited to your delicate constitution,' said Konoroz, sliding one of the meat patties onto the golden flatbread. He grabbed a squeezy bottle from beside the grill and liberally squirted its contents on top, before wrapping the bread around the meat and using that to pick it up and hand it to her.

Haezle sank her teeth in eagerly. She hadn't eaten since the previous evening, and she hadn't stopped moving since then. She hadn't realised quite how hungry she was, although, to be fair, the questionable fish had suppressed her appetite for a moment. Now it was back with a vengeance and she devoured the food, barely pausing for breath, not even noticing the burn from either the hot meat or the hot sauce.

'Thank you,' she said, muffled.

The door burst open and a small child, four or five years old, burst in, running and waving something in his hand. He skidded to a halt inches from the grill.

Heart in her mouth, Haezle recognised him as Ani, Konoroz's grandson.

'Boy!' shouted Konoroz, trying to scold whilst hiding his obvious delight at the surprise visit.

'Sorry, Poppa.' Ani's reply came in the form of a stage whisper.

'You came to learn how to cook? You're a good boy, thinking about your Poppa. Where's your father?'

'I don't know,' said the boy. 'Do you like my aeroplane?'

He waved the paper aeroplane in his hand, flying it around his head, looking at Haezle for approval. She nodded appreciatively.

Konoroz flipped a fish, which leaked onto the hotplate, causing a sizzle and cloud of new, peculiar odours.

'Urgh! Fish!' cried Ani, dropping his plane and running back out the way he had come.

Konoroz chuckled, turning to watch him go.

'He's a good boy,' he said again. 'If he doesn't spend too much time with his father, he will do fine...'

Haezle was familiar with Konoroz's disappointment in his

own son, so it didn't matter too much that she wasn't really listening anymore. She bent down to pick up the aeroplane from where it had dropped on the floor.

Something about the piece of paper it was made from had caught her eye, seemed familiar somehow. As she unfolded it, she could see exactly what it was.

The paper was a poster or a flyer of some sort. There was writing on it, but it wasn't any kind of script she was familiar with. It looked like the abstract symbols you might find in a library book at the Citadel.

That wasn't what had grabbed her attention, though. On the poster there was a hand drawn symbol. A familiar one - a moon cut in half by a sword. The same symbol that she'd seen on Estrel's Echo.

'Fuck,' she whispered.

CHAPTER 34

LAGRANGE

It's a stroke of luck. I don't really believe in luck, as a matter of course, but I'll take this. We've got a very limited amount of time to find anything out, and I need to talk to a lowlife. Normally, that would require me to head down to Docklands, hang around a bar - typically the Bosun's Locker, because then I can use Kamla's influence to help me grease some wheels.

It would be a long, drawn-out process, involving a lot of drink, potentially some drugs, and probably a fight or two. More importantly, that would be a nighttime activity, but it's ten in the morning and we don't have time to mess around. Fortunately, we have a member of Eamer's crew in the cells. To make things better, it's Antonio, and I think I can work with Antonio. I just need to persuade him he can work with me.

Getting access isn't as hard as it should be. I know L, who's manning the desk this morning, well enough that she won't ask me too many questions about why I want to interview a detainee - something that would normally fall to a Junior Oficier, at least. It helps that said Junior Oficiers, and their Senior superiors, are mostly out at Administration trying to wrap up the mess from the Chaguartay rally, so that even if she was inclined to follow up there isn't anyone to follow up with.

Every cell has an attached interview room, and that's where Antonio is waiting for me. As Cadets, we're not supposed to enter a room with a detainee on our own, it's against protocol, but I don't think that I have anything to worry about with Antonio and, besides, Mortimer isn't going to be a lot of use to me. If anything, it's less of a risk leaving him outside. He stays in the lobby with L, watching us on the screens.

Antonio doesn't seem that pleased to see me. I suppose he's not enjoyed our hospitality all that much.

'What do you want?' he demands, as I slide myself onto the bench opposite him.

'I've just come to talk,' I say, which is true. 'I hear you've not been doing a lot of that.'

'You sent that cunt down. I'm not talking to him.'

"That cunt" is Pestril. He's not, incidentally, he's a decent guy and a Senior Oficier with a strong reputation for fairness and actually solving cases and preventing crimes. That's a unique combination. I admire the guy. I wouldn't go as far as saying I would want to be like him. Admirable as he is, people call him a cunt behind his back.

'I told you, I can't be the one to interview you. There is a pre-existing relationship that could compromise my impartiality.'

'Fuck that. You're just scared to talk to me because you know what she did.'

"She" in this context is Kamla. Kamla played a big part in Antonio screwing up enough to find himself detained. Kamla didn't entirely follow protocol. I did explain what protocol was, and she definitely paid no attention to anything I said.

Frankly, it's a mess. If it gets out, Antonio is certainly going to get out scot free and I need to hope to The Creator that no one realises my part in the whole affair. That would be the point where we move from Antonio being a criminal caught in the act of criminal behaviour, albeit with a somewhat nonsensical plan, to Antonio being the victim of entrapment.

That wouldn't look good for me. As far as I know, Antonio is the only person who could actually put two and two together and rat me out. It sounds like he might be getting close. Fortunately, I now have a new plan which has fallen into my lap entirely by chance. I am a lucky bastard.

'I'm sure I have no idea what you're talking about, but none of that matters anymore, Antonio. I think I can get you out of here. I just need some information. I think that the higher-ups are going to be so grateful that any previous misdemeanours might be considered by the by.'

'What about our "pre-existing" relationship?'

'Don't worry about that. Things have changed.'

'I don't trust you.'

That was what I was worried about. He knew who I was before he was arrested, knew what I did for a living. Many Authority agents hang out in Docklands. Many Authority agents will turn a blind eye to the activities of their companions, and not always because they're being paid off.

That's not me. I do feel at home where the morality is more optional, but I take my job seriously. I believe in this city and there's a line which I won't cross. Nor should anyone else.

Antonio isn't so bad. He doesn't really deserve to be in here. Kamla stitched him up, and I'm still not sure why. She is deadly when she's scorned, though, and that might be part of it.

All of this is irrelevant if I can't convince him I can get him out if he tells me what I need to know. Then the pressure's on to actually get him out of here before he realises it was all bullshit and tells someone about Kamla and me. One problem at a time, though.

'Look, Antonio, I know this hasn't gone to plan. Any of it. But I really need your help. And you know I'm straight up. If you tell me what I need to know, then I won't let you down. You know I won't. I suspect that this information is no skin off your nose, anyway…'

I stop talking. There's an art to persuading people to do what you want, and it involves far less talking than most people would imagine. The silence hangs between us. Antonio sneers. I absorb every bad vibe he's bombarding me with. None of it matters, not if I can get him to cooperate.

I'm sure he knows. He must know. What am I going to do if he doesn't know?

'What?' he asks.

I'm in. I take my Com out of my pocket and flick the screen on. I don't need to find the image, I've already loaded it. It's not the best quality; it's a photo of a screen, with all the glare and reflection you'd expect. But it's the real thing, not my poor quality half-recollection, and I can see the spark of recognition in Antonio's eye the moment he clocks it.

'You know what this is, don't you?'

He nods slowly, looking carefully at me through hooded eyes.

'Do you?'

I admit I don't. He picks up my Com and tilts its screen towards himself.

'I guess the cat's out of the bag, then,' he says. The way he says it is curious. It's like a sigh, but it's not weary. If anything, he seems excited. He's almost breathless with it.

I'm excited. Those words, the idea that there was a cat to be let out of anything. I lean forward.

'What does it mean?'

Antonio laughs.

'That's what you want to know? That's the information you're going to get me out of here in exchange for?'

It seems a fair exchange to me. The air between us is almost fizzing with the promise of whatever this is. Antonio laughs again and I think I've made a mistake.

'I'll tell you everything. Don't worry,' he says. 'But I'd better tell you quick, because in about an hour you're going to know all about it and then I've got no currency. Our deal still stands, though. Even when everything I've got to say becomes common knowledge…'

In some senses, he's talking himself out of a deal right now. But I think he knows I'm desperate. I think he knows I want to know fast.

I'm not certain why I want to know so badly. There's no case here, nothing to solve. Nothing that will get me ahead, nothing to feed my ambition.

But I found it first. I saw the connection. I uncovered the conspiracy. And something is about to happen, something big. If I know what it is, then I might have a chance to stop it. That could mean something.

'It's the Clippers,' says Antonio. He jabs a finger at the Com, leaving a large, greasy fingerprint on my screen. 'This is the symbol of the Clippers of the Black Night.'

'Who are the Clippers? What's the Black Night?'

I've never heard of either of them, but the way he says it imbues it with meaning that he seems to expect me to understand.

'Well, that's the question.' Antonio leans back and folds his hands behind his head. 'It might be a movement, it might be a cult. It might be an actual, literal Black Night. It might be an eclipse. What everyone agrees is that it's going to change everything.'

'Change everything? Change everything how?'

'We're going to tear this city down. Whatever the Black Night is, most of us don't care. It's a moment of transition. A moment of chaos. We're taking over…'

"Most of us don't care…" are the only words I hear.

'Who does care?' I ask.

'You should care. You should all fucking care. I like you, Sim, but you're one of them. You're part of the problem. You and all your Authority chums are going to find yourself strung up from the city walls…'

'No, no… you said "most of us don't care". So somebody cares. Who cares?'

'Who do you think? Eamer's obsessed with this shit. He's like you. He won't let anything rest unless he understands every detail. He's been seeing some psychic…'

This does not sound like Eamer.

'Eamer's been seeing a psychic?'

'Well, maybe not a psychic. But he's got a new best friend. Weird woman. Wears funny clothes. Talks all sorts of nonsense. Got some really strange ideas about the way the world works. Like she believes in magic or something… she's got him believing he's got some kind of destiny to lord it over the rest of us. I don't know. I reckon there's every chance someone shivs him the chaos we're about to unleash. I'm sorry that I'm going to miss it. Stuck in here. But at least that means no one is going to shiv me…'

Eamer. Eamer's the key. I don't listen to anything else Antonio's saying. I'm on my feet.

CHAPTER 35

ESTREL

We took the miniTram to Docklands. We didn't talk en route. Mouse liked to sit on her own and stare out of the window, so we did that. I was in the seat behind her. I spent the entire rickety journey staring at the back of her head.

It seemed a bit creepy on my part, but I couldn't help myself and she didn't seem to notice. To be fair, it wasn't as creepy as it could have been. I ached to touch her. I didn't know how much longer I could be in her company without giving myself away.

I needed to be somewhere else. I couldn't bring myself to do that, either, though. Which is why, once we arrived at Eamer's, I accepted her offer of help to find me somewhere to stay.

She was being very nice to me, a complete stranger from her perspective. I did ask about that.

'I don't know,' she'd said. 'It's funny isn't it? I don't usually help people for free. There's something about you, Estrel…'

Talk about making my heart sing and my stomach drop simultaneously.

'Blame the universe?' she suggested. 'I feel like I need to make sure you're OK. I can't explain it.'

'Well, thank you,' I said.

'I don't like it,' she laughed. 'So don't get used to it. I seem to owe the universe a debt, although I can't imagine why. This ends the moment I discharge myself from that obligation.'

So Mouse's debt to the universe meant she was sorting out my accommodation. I did need somewhere to stay. I couldn't exactly sleep on Lek's floor now that Lek wasn't who he was meant to be. I didn't know who had his quarters in the Citadel, but it was fairly certain that they wouldn't see it as their job to put me up.

It was, of course, something I could have done myself. I had never been in Trinity in exactly this time period before, but it was close enough to when I had that I knew where I could crash, where wouldn't ask questions, where I wouldn't have to sleep with a knife in my boxers in case I got robbed while I slept.

But I couldn't admit to that, either. I had to continue to play dumb. It was just as well I had Mouse on my side. Even if she was taking her sweet time to sort anything out.

For the time being, I was sitting in a booth in the corner, nursing a pint. My intention had been to bide my time, quietly drink my beer, watch Mouse at work, talk to no one, do nothing, leave the timeline as alone as humanly possible. Then Fricker had slid into my booth.

I knew Fricker. I'd done business with him in the past. My past, his future. He was a technological genius. He could hack anything, convert anything, rig up whatever you wanted to do whatever you needed, given a little time and appropriate payment.

But that wouldn't be for a few years, and it wasn't like we were close. Which was why it was weird that his first words to me were *"Hello Estrel"*.

I stared at him over the rim of my glass.

'Who?'

Fricker grinned.

'It's OK Estrel, it's me. You don't have to worry. No one else can hear us.'

'Why would I worry about anyone else being able to hear us? And my name's not…'

'OK, OK, OK… Have it your way. But you can trust me, you know you can. It's me, it's Fricker. We did that whole…'

I put my glass down. Fricker shouldn't have known who I was. We hadn't met yet, not from his perspective. Except…

There were a lot of me. In the place outside time where Lek and I had escaped to, after the thing with the two Evies, after I'd shot and killed Oficier Lagrange, there had been a lot of me.

Lek had sent me back here. I didn't know exactly what happened to the others. It stood to reason that he'd sent them somewhere, too. Maybe someone had turned up not that long before me. It would be possible that Fricker and I had already met.

Was it possible that Mouse and I had, too? If we had, she wouldn't be pretending not to know me now, would she? Whoever this other Estrel was, it didn't seem that he'd been completely reckless. Fricker knew who I was, but Fricker wasn't exactly important to me. Not like Mouse was.

It struck me that maybe he hadn't known. Perhaps he was a version of me who had never met Fricker, who had never had need of Fricker's specialist services and had been plucked from his timeline without ever having met the man. Maybe he'd been careful about Mouse, but hadn't known to be careful of Fricker.

Was that possible? I needed to ask Lek. Lek had the answers. Lek always had the answers.

Except he didn't. Not here. Not now. Because of that, I didn't have them either. Was that my fault? Had another of my parallel selves caused whatever had happened to Lek?

There had been a lengthy silence between us now. Fricker was looking twitchy.

'Thanks for the Com, man,' he said, eventually. 'It's a neat bit of tech, the ComN. It was good to get the chance to take it apart.'

'I don't know what you're talking about.'

'Good, good.' Fricker grinned, more confidently. 'I've got the right guy, then.'

'I don't understand. Why would you think I brought you a Com to take apart?'

'Oh, because you did. You did. But not "you" you. Not this you.'

'I don't understand,' I said, again.

'You warned me about this.' He grabbed my pint glass and took a swig. 'Thanks, needed that. Right. So. Once upon a time, not that long ago, I met you for the first time. You told me you were a time traveller, and we did some business. The thing with the Com. It will come in handy next year when it finally comes out…'

That was messy. Why would I give Fricker a new model Com device a good year before it came out? What was I up to?

'So you've met me before?'

'Yeah, yeah and, like I said, you told me you were a time traveller and that things could get complicated if you weren't very, very careful. So you said that every time I met you I should pretend like I didn't already know you, right…'

This, I realised would actually explain a lot about my relationship with Fricker in the future. I always assumed he struggled to remember things like faces, or names, or entire past conversations with people. I'd put it down to some nasty solvent fumes he was inadvertently inhaling in the course of his work.

'You're not pretending not to know me now.'

'No. No, I'm not. Because that was the other thing you told me. You told me that one time I'd meet you, right here in Eamer's, on the eve of the eclipse.'

He spread out his hands and raised his eyebrows. He looked very pleased with himself. I was less impressed. This was obviously a future version of me, who therefore had knowledge of what the current version of me had done before him. Basic time travel logic, but…

There had been tens, maybe a hundred, versions of me with Lek, before I'd come back here. I'd assumed that they were all a result of aborted time loops. That they were failed Estrels who had lived out their lives on doomed timelines the moment they'd got to the end of their day and failed to kill Evie White, until Lek had rescued them and given them purpose.

Maybe it was more complicated than that. Maybe my footprints across time were messier and more significant than I'd thought. This didn't sound like a good thing. I needed to talk to Lek. But Lek was gone. Turned out I could only talk to Fricker.

'So what's different now? Why aren't you pretending not to know me now?'

'You said this was a crossroads, a turning point. He said you have choices now, choices that you'll lose if you don't take this opportunity.'

'What choices? What are you talking about?'

His words had a ring of truth to them, though. I'd had a mission to complete, without any choices available to me. There was a plan, and I had to execute it. Things had changed now. Without Lek, I had choices.

'I can't tell you that, but I think I can help. Well, maybe it's help. I don't understand it, but you said I should give you a message…'

A message from my future self? If anything, this was better than taking Lek at his word. My future self had knowledge about what was about to happen. He had to have my best interests at heart. I wasn't sure if I could say either of those things about Lek.

'…well, it's not so much a message as a question. Like I said, I don't understand it but…'

'What is it?' I demanded.

A question seemed less helpful than a message, or an instruction, but I wasn't in a position to be choosy, I supposed.

'OK, OK, calm down. What I'm supposed to ask you is this: *"What is the elephant for?"'*

CHAPTER 36

CANNON

'Two pints of Reader's, and whatever you're having, Effie...'

Effie nodded her thanks and gave Cannon a look up and down, apparently checking his angle of presentation and to what extent he was being supported by the bar. Satisfied that he was in a fit state to continue drinking, she turned to the pump to draw the cider.

It was late in the afternoon, and not yet evening, but on a day like this, you had to be on your guard early. The entire village was out and the entire village was thirsty.

'No, dont get mehat,' slurred a voice from over his shoulder. 'Wouldn't drink that man's piss...'

Effie paused as she finished filling the first glass.

'That's not actually what we're serving here, Manda,' she called to the unseen girl, 'but how about I get you a glass of water to be going on with? Mr Reader's cider is generally appreciated around here, but I understand your tastes may be a little more refined...'

Cannon grinned into his armpit. He'd offered to buy Manda a drink due to a sudden surge of magnanimous affability. He'd just finished his fourth pint and was gently soaking in a happy place where he was content to sit and watch Effie work, where chat came easy and he realised the benefits of a wide circle of friends because it suddenly seemed that he had a wide circle of friends.

Manda Charlotte was not someone Cannon would usually consider a friend. She wasn't someone who would normally look twice at him. He didn't think that was something that made his social life any the poorer but, for now, he was enjoying her company.

'Is there anyone's piss you would drink, Manda?' he asked. 'Out of interest?'

Manda swung around, elbowing another patron in the spine, but ignoring his grunted expression of pain. Her wild eyes gave away the afternoon she'd had, the sheen of sweat across her shoulders and décolletage speaking to undue exertion in the afternoon sun or an excretory system keen to expel toxins in whatever way it could. Probably both. She fixed Cannon with a steely stare and slowly licked her lips.

'I'd drink yours, Cannon,' she purred, and then cackled, swiping his fresh pint from the bar top and running off, leaving him with a large glass of lukewarm water.

Cannon once again saw the benefits of keeping his circle of friends small and turned back to the Alderman.

'Sorry, you were saying...' he said, as a sign that he'd finished being distracted by drunk women at the bar.

The Alderman pouted and shook his head.

'Don't 'emember,' he slurred. He was more drunk than Cannon had realised.

'A permit,' he prompted, 'for the market. It shouldn't be a problem?'

'Don't see why not.' The Alderman quaffed more of his ale. 'It'd be good to have someone selling pickles again...'

'They're ferments,' Cannon corrected him, but the Alderman didn't seem to notice.

'That chap that used to sell the pickles, you know, erm...'

Cannon didn't know who was being referred to, so he stayed quiet.

The Alderman didn't seem to notice that either, and appeared to fill in the blanks in the conversation himself. He nodded vigorously in agreement with something Cannon hadn't said.

'Exactly! Exactly! Onions that would make your bum tweak.'

Cannon wasn't sure what it meant to have one's bum tweak. He thought it must be quite a pickle to cause that reaction.

'So my application would be welcome?'

The Alderman held his hand up high.

'It would be a welcome change!' he declared, sweeping his hand down in a demonstrative gesture, the meaning of which was lost on Cannon. 'A pleasant distraction from all the elephant licensing…'

Cannon's mind reeled with the questions that presented themselves. He took a moment to consider which he was going to ask first.

'Who's applying for an elephant license?' Cannon asked, then immediately regretted not asking something else.

'Circus,' replied the Alderman.

'The circus has elephants?' asked Cannon.

The circus had rolled into town the previous day and, to date, had appeared to be quite small scale. Cannon hadn't paid much attention, but if they were going to do an elephant show, that usually meant a few fireworks. That would be what the license was for.

'Nope,' the Alderman shook his head and leaned in conspiratorially. 'Between you and me, there isn't even any such thing as an elephant license. We've had no cause to invent one. No-one brings elephants through Bramshall…'

Cannon was confused. It seemed that the Alderman was talking about real elephants.

'On account of them not being real?' checked Cannon.

'On account of them not being real. Although perhaps they didn't mean a real one. But they applied, so we made one.'

Cannon nodded. He was learning a lot about local politics.

'…put all kinds of conditions on it,' continued the Alderman in a

husky, hushed voice. 'Dung disposal, maximum load for the green, water consumption levies… all sorts. Make it seem more official. Not just like something we made up on the spot. Cost a pretty penny too.'

Cannon nodded. He could imagine that it would.

'…then they turn up yesterday and it's seven people and a dog. Possibly a mangy-looking monkey, although that could have been another dog. One caravan which they all seem to live in and a trailer in which they keep their big top. Which should, more accurately, be called a "top" because I don't know if you've seen what they're erecting on the village green, but it's not very big.'

Cannon hadn't and was far less interested than he had been a few minutes ago to do so. Perhaps his first instinct had been the right one.

'No elephant, then? Why did they want the license?' he asked.

It seemed like the obvious question.

'That,' said the Alderman, stabbing a finger at Cannon with one hand while he used the other to tip up his pint mug. It was already empty and so he stared into the bottom with a combination of disappointment and confusion. '…is the question.'

'That's interesting,' said Estrel.

'What's interesting?'

Cannon was confused. Confused by Estrel's comment, confused by the story he'd told, confused how he could remember something so clearly, so vividly, when it was so obviously impossible and definitely hadn't happened. To him, or to anyone else.

'How it all comes back around,' clarified Estrel. 'To the elephant. It's all about you and the elephant.'

'It's not about me. That never happened,' insisted Cannon. 'And it's not about an elephant. Elephants don't exist.'

Estrel held his hands up.

'I'm just saying,' he said. 'Why don't you try again?'

'Manda?'

Cannon's voice was hushed and guarded. He wasn't even sure that this was the way she had turned as she left the beer tent. He didn't want anyone to hear him lurching about in the dark, shouting for Manda Charlotte, because a man lurching around in the dark, shouting for Manda Charlotte, was usually on the lookout for something very specific.

'And I'm not,' he said under his breath. 'I just want my pint back.'

On one level, he did want his pint back. He was running low on funds and couldn't afford to be losing drinks or he'd have to go home. On another level, one that he wasn't completely ready to acknowledge yet, he was looking for something.

Not something from Manda. He would have been at pains to point out, but she was a helpful excuse to leave the tent and have a look around. To check out the circus.

It was chillier in the autumn air than he'd expected, though, and he was developing second thoughts. Maybe he should just retrieve his drink and head back through the glowing portal back into the beer tent.

No, the drink was just an excuse. She'd probably drunk it by now, anyway.

'Manda?' he rasped again.

'In here,' came a voice from the bushes.

Cannon headed toward the call.

'No, wait!' called Manda again. 'a'ma pissing. Give me a…'

There was a rustling and a commotion from a bush several to the right of where Cannon had thought the voice was coming from, and suddenly Manda rose from the foliage, pint glass still in hand.

She lurched forward, lunging at Cannon in a way that might have been meant to be an affectionate nuzzle, but ended up being more of a headlong dive into his chest. She seemed to have started too early, and too far away, and ended up with her forehead pressed into Cannon's sternum in a way that wasn't entirely comfortable for either of them.

'Are you OK?' asked Cannon, who was by no means sober but felt and appeared, in contrast to his companion, like he was in possession of all his faculties, and some of hers as well.

Manda just sighed and handed him her glass. Which was his glass. Which felt worryingly warm. Cannon tipped the contents on the grass.

'Come on,' he said, steering Manda back towards the light.

They were friends now. Friends kept an eye out for each other. He could check out the circus in the morning.

'I'll see if I can stretch to another drink.'

'Lef' t-my knickers in the bush,' giggled Manda, lurching back towards the undergrowth. 'I should get them 'cos I'm not that easy…'

There was a great disturbance in the bushes and what appeared to be a snake curled down from a treetop. To Cannon's great surprise, it was followed by an elephant's head. Not a snake, then, he thought, whilst still trying to figure out which branch it would have to be coiled around in order to descend at that angle…

Estrel kicked the box, which was tucked under his seat. A small, muffled, squeaking trumpet sound emerged.

'Elephant,' he said.

'But that never happened! It's not possible that…'

'We've talked about this. Just because it's impossible doesn't mean it doesn't exist.'

Cannon gritted his teeth.

'I don't know what that was. That wasn't my memory. It was just a story. I must have heard it somewhere or… You heard the story. Even in the story, I didn't believe that it was a real elephant. There wasn't even any elephant.'

'It's OK, Cannon,' said Estrel. 'It's OK. You're fighting it, and it's upsetting you. That's understandable. I thought this might be the case, and it's not your fault. You're right, it isn't your memory. You don't have any memories. Not before the ship, anyway. All you have is stories.'

'What do you mean, I don't have any memories?' asked Cannon, scared. 'What happened to me? Why was I on the ship?'

'Nothing happened, Cannon. For you, there was no "before the ship". You're no more real than any of the rest of them. The Ringmaster or the Squirrel Sisters, or Bonzo or any of the others. You're slightly less real than the elephant in this box.'

Estrel tapped the box with his heel, again, for good measure.

'You ran away and joined the circus because your name is Cannon,' he said. 'It's a great story. But it's not real. And I don't think that's really even your name.'

CHAPTER 37

LEK

There was a man on the other side of the door. He was short and scruffy, with a bushy black moustache. There were what looked like pieces of straw stuck in the thick curls on the top of his head. It was very hard to tell how old he was, but if I had to guess, he was only just out of his teens.

'I thought I was the only one here.'

He shoved his hands into the deep pockets of the beige canvas jumpsuit he wore. I'd expected someone who would shout at me, demand to know who I was, maybe even point a weapon at me.

I definitely expected someone suspicious of me. I didn't expect someone who, on seeing me, would weaken their own defences by tucking their hands out of action. I glanced down at my own robes and sandalled feet. Perhaps I didn't present as a threat.

'I… um… Where am I?' I asked.

Given the non-confrontational nature of our introduction, I decided I had nothing to hide and that honesty was going to be the best policy. I didn't think he was ready for my description of stepping through a portal from another place just yet, though.

'Research, of course.' He looked puzzled. 'Are you OK? Why are you dressed like an *olde worlde* Cleric?'

I knew the word cleric, of course, from a linguistic point of view, but at the time the use of this term, with the all important capital "C", meant little to me. It wouldn't, pre-Dissolution. I also didn't know what he meant by "olde worlde" - he even pronounced the "e"s. But then, I thought I was still in my time.

'Maybe not,' I said, deciding that maybe honesty wasn't the best policy after all and that I should dissemble until I knew what exactly was going on.

I put my hand to my head, feigned unsteadiness. The man immediately stepped forward and took hold of my elbow.

'Come with me, Mr Citadel. Can't have you passing out in the corridor. Not with a pack of Hybrids rampaging about.'

I followed where he guided me, which wasn't far. We shuffled through the next doorway, where he rolled a chair across and pushed me down into it.

I looked around. The room was filled with screens. Most of them had an image of a room, almost identical to the one I'd found myself in. The view was from above the entrance - the one I'd exited from - across the room with a full view of the other door opposite.

Each one had a similar hole torn through it.

'You've lost a lot of animals today?' I asked.

The man cast his eyes across all the screens, shaking his head.

'The Hybrids? Don't know what got into them,' he said. 'Something spooked them. I'll be honest, I didn't think that the doors would just give in like that. It's not like they don't make a habit of hurling themselves against the walls when they're a bit riled up. I would have thought it was an explosion or something, but…'

'An explosion?'

I didn't know where I was. I didn't know *when* I was. You must remember that.

'Yeah, there was a bomb went off in Central about twenty minutes ago. Near the White Room. I thought they were overreacting when they insisted on evacuating everyone, but it turns out that I'm the idiot. Now I'm stuck down here with no chance of getting out. Not with bits of the complex exploding and the rest filled with Hybrids.'

'I'm sorry,' I said. 'I'm confused. Assume I know nothing. What's going on?'

He looked me up and down and seemed to come to a conclusion.

'Must have been one hell of a bender. I assume that's why the fancy dress? You lose your Com? Because you can't so much as unlock the screen without seeing all about how Trinity is blowing up left, right and centre.'

Trinity. I was still in Trinity. I wondered why I didn't recognise this place. I couldn't imagine what building it was part of - it certainly wasn't within the Citadel. I didn't imagine that it wasn't part of a building. I hadn't yet realised what the lack of windows, of natural light, really meant.

There was so much information coming in I didn't even stop to wonder what kind of workplace culture meant that someone wandering around, hungover and in fancy dress, was an unremarkable thing to come across.

"*Your world is Research*", they say in the induction. I have to come to learn that is a life sentence.

'Someone is bombing Trinity?'

'Closer to home than that. Someone is planting bombs. On the streets, in the buildings. It's either an attack from within, or someone has infiltrated us. It seems to be everywhere, and they got worried that there were going to be explosions down here and so they got everyone out. And I said "no" because I thought I should stay here and monitor the Hybrids… that's kind of my job… but also I didn't want them to get abandoned. They need feeding pretty regularly, you see, and I didn't know what would happen if I left, when they'd let me back in, how long they'd be on their own for. They're only babies really…'

He trailed off. I wondered if he knew that I'd seen one, if I knew that - however young they were - something less vulnerable and babylike was very hard to imagine.

'So there's no one else here. Just you and me?'

'Not sure,' he murmured, walking over to a console and flicking some switches so that the images on some screens changed. 'There's a few people wandering around. Not entirely sure who any of them are…'

I looked at the new images. There was a younger man in some kind of white overall, who looked bewildered and lost. There were several people in military style fatigues slumped at various locations, all apparently dead from some pretty gruesome firearms wounds.

No… wait… that guy is still alive.

He had little left below the waist, though. I couldn't imagine he'd live much longer.

'Hold on, I think we may have a straggler,' he said.

He pointed at one screen, where I could see another corridor, much like the one I'd looked down from inside the Hybrid's cell. A short figure in a lab coat was shuffling along it.

I assumed some kind of scientist. My companion had referred to the place that we were as "Research". Saying nothing, he activated the door and slipped out. It slid shut behind him and I was left alone.

I took stock. I didn't know where I was. I seemed to be in some kind of bunker, but one with a futuristic feel and levels of technology that were not commonplace in Trinity, and certainly not in the Citadel.

I was being told I was still in Trinity. That seemed impossible. This place was too strange, too foreign to be part of my home. The chaos that was being described above ground also seemed alien to me. It sounded like some kind of civil war was raging, and that wasn't something I could imagine happening. Trinity was, if not a happy place, certainly a satisfied place.

I concluded this had to be a different Trinity, somewhere with the same name but in a different part of the world altogether. That made sense of everything. Everything except the fact that the man had correctly identified my robes as being from the Citadel, even if he thought they were a costume.

I don't know if I would have got to the truth on my own, but that didn't matter. At that point, the door behind me slid back open, and the man reappeared, accompanied by a woman in a lab coat.

'I found Venn here wandering around,' he said. 'Looks like you're not the only one to have missed the evacuation call.'

'Vido told me he'd rescued some casualty from the party last night,' she said. 'You've missed a lot of…'

The woman stepped out from behind him. She wore thick, black-rimmed glasses, which she immediately pushed back up her nose. In the same movement, she tucked her shoulder-length brown hair behind both ears in what would become a familiar routine when Venn was preparing to inspect something.

She inspected me. For several seconds, there was silence. It felt a lot longer than that.

'Hello,' I rose from my chair. 'My name is…'

I hadn't introduced myself to the other guy. I didn't know what his name was, although I now assumed it was Vido.

'…Lek,' she finished for me.

I stopped, halfway through leaning forward and offering my hand. She knew who I was. I couldn't comprehend that. I lost my balance and thumped back down into the chair.

'You…'

I trailed off. My mind was whirring, thinking a million half-thoughts in a matter of seconds. None of them crystallised into anything coherent. I didn't know what to say.

'I didn't think you were supposed to be here, not now,' she said, furrowing her brow, which caused her glasses to drop down the bridge of her nose. She pushed them back with the middle finger of her right hand. 'But now that you're…'

She trailed off again, squinted at me. Still, I said nothing. I didn't know what she was trying to figure out. I do now, of course.

Eventually, she spoke again.

'You're so *young*.'

CHAPTER 38

HAEZLE

Sleep was for the weak. Sleep was for people without purpose. Sleep was for people without curiosity because, given how complex and mysterious the world was, when you truly looked at it, how could you bear to miss a single moment to explore?

Haezle was on her last legs, and she needed a mantra to keep her going as she trudged back down the streets and alleyways to the Citadel. She settled on the steady, driving rhythm of *"...sleep is for losers..."*. It helped.

Even if she hadn't already seen them, the symbols on the flyer would have sent her running back to the Citadel. The Library was the natural place for her to research the picture of the moon and the sword.

She couldn't leave it alone. To see it twice in such a short period felt like too much of a coincidence to ignore. She at least needed to understand what it meant.

It had appeared on the bottle that Estrel had pulled out of the rack - his Echo - which he had said was a message from inside his time loop. Did that mean that this piece of paper, too, was an Echo? Was this left by another Estrel? Had she found something that he was meant to find?

Was it important to him on his current mission? The words on the bottle's label - *"The eclipse is the end"* - they seemed more important now. He'd brushed them off, more interested in the Book of Keyes than the message he'd left himself.

Haezle couldn't help but feel that was a mistake. She hoped it wasn't a fatal one. For any of them.

Haezle passed through at the Citadel North Gate, ahead of a queue of kitchen staff who were getting their credentials checked. She wasn't sure why they'd be double checking the pot wash had the proper authority to work, but maybe there had been an incident she wasn't aware of.

The gateperson looked up from the paperwork they were studying and waved Haezle through with a familiar smile. Haezle waved back and hurried through, under severe stares from the back of the queue.

Maybe she shouldn't eat at the refectory today. Not that she would be hungry for a while. The breakfast she'd got from Konoroz sat comfortably in her stomach.

Haezle turned under the covered walkway and cut across the quadrangle. If you knew what you were doing, and approached it from just the right angle, you could find a path of narrow stepping stones that were invisible to the casual observer. This allowed Citadel staff to take a shortcut without spoiling the illusion of an impeccably laid lawn. Haezle hop, skipped and jumped her way across, and climbed the steps to the Library.

One thing she didn't need to research was the subject of eclipses. Eclipses we important to the history and mythology of Trinity.

There was an eclipse, so the story went, at the start. It was an eclipse that stopped the Founders on their journey, the sudden darkness preventing them from moving on. When the light returned, their journey had ended. Trinity was founded there and then.

There had been others. Every time they coincided with something significant. Usually something of significance to the Brotherhood. The death of the Founders, who collapsed simultaneously and died on the spot, coincided with an eclipse. The Brotherhood was established, and the Citadel built in their memory.

The sinking of the Citadel, creating the Catacombs, had been accompanied by an eclipse, at least in its initial stages. Arguably that was still happening, so she wasn't sure how much that had been a coincidence rather than an omen.

The confirmation of the current Superious, whenever that had been - and no one was still alive who remembered, improbable as that may seem - was announced in total darkness, despite taking place in the middle of the day. They must have had to look really hard to see the smoke.

All of those, in some way, seemed to be beginnings. Estrel's message had said, "The eclipse is the *end*". So this had to be a different eclipse. A new eclipse. The next eclipse? She didn't pay attention to the forecasts. She didn't know when that would be.

It was dark in the Library. It was always dark in the Library. Haezle walked through the central aisle, past all the high bookshelves, ignoring the muttering from colleagues about the lateness of her arrival. She cared little about that, although she should have let Guardian Whiteley know before deciding to take the day off. That didn't matter now. She was here anyway.

The door to Elara Whiteley's office was small and wooden and somewhat hidden behind a large bookcase. Haezle knocked quietly. It didn't do to interrupt Miss Whiteley's meditations too forcefully. Every Reader had a story about when they'd done that. They weren't pretty.

'Come!'

Haezle pushed the door open. It was heavy, and it dragged on the remarkably deep pile carpet. Some had noted that nothing in the - usually quite spartan - Citadel was as luxurious as Miss Whiteley's carpet.

It was dark inside, the only light coming from a flickering candle. Haezle slipped through as soon as the gap was large enough for her to fit, then leant back on the door and used her body weight to heave it closed.

She paused to give her eyes a chance to adjust. It took a few moments for her to realise that there was someone else in the office besides Miss Whiteley.

The man turned to face her. He was young, and he was dressed in clothes that were unfamiliar in style . Although they were recognisably a shirt and trousers, they looked to be made of fabric that Haezle had never seen before, cut with lines that seemed angular and uncomfortable to her eye.

She wondered if he was from Rosaan, maybe, or Øp. Somewhere more exotic than Ashuana. Or Trinity. She realised he looked surprised to see her, but in a way that suggested he had been expecting her, just not now.

'Haezle,' said Miss Whiteley from behind her desk. 'This is Juni…'

'James,' the man cut in. 'Sergey James.'

He stood and offered her his hand. Haezle, bemused, took a step forward and clasped it, pumping it up and down once before letting go. Sergey James had very warm hands, she noticed.

'Haezle Muñoz,' she said.

'It's so nice to meet you,' grinned James. 'I was going to say "finally" but… we'll come to that later. It's not really been that long. I… I'm jabbering. I'm just a bit surprised. You're early.'

She really wasn't. Haezle peered around James to check the expression on Miss Whiteley's face, which was best described as "stern". That didn't mean a lot. It was kind of default for her.

'I'm sorry, Miss Whiteley,' she said hurriedly. 'I should have let you know before now, but I need to take the day off. I had something of a long night and…'

'I know, dear. You're not wearing your robe.'

Haezle almost thought she saw the flicker of a smile. Even without this, the warmth behind the word "dear", which she'd never heard Miss Whiteley utter before, was disconcerting. So disconcerting, she didn't even object to its use.

She *knew*? How did she know? *What* did she know? She couldn't have inferred all of that from the fact that Haezle wasn't wearing her robe. Not wearing her robe would usually incur a punishment, not draw sympathy.

'I don't understand,' she said. Which was true. She was very confused by this conversation, by this man's presence, by the fact that he appeared to know who she was, not to mention his assertion that she was early.

Early for what?

'It's fine, dear.' *There, she said it again.* 'Mr James here has explained everything.'

Explained everything? What has he explained? What does he know?

Haezle looked back at Sergey James, who was still looking very pleased with himself.

'Well, then,' she said, coughing a little to clear her throat. She straightened herself up and tugged at the hem of her tunic, hiding some creases. She needed to look like she meant business. She wanted answers. 'Maybe he could explain it to me. Because I haven't got a clue what he's talking about, and I'm pretty sure he's talking about me.'

Sergey James's grin froze, uncertainty flashed behind his eyes.

'I… I just meant that you'd been quick. I don't think you're early *for* anything. But that's good, right? You being back early? You've got the book?'

Haezle's heart sank. She couldn't help but let out a significant sigh.

'The fucking book,' she muttered.

Miss Whiteley looked horrified at the outburst.

'Haezle…' she scolded.

'No, it's OK.' James put both his hands out, trying to calm things down, slow the avalanche of irritation headed his way.

'No!' shouted Haezle. 'It's not fucking OK. I've had it up to here…' She raised her hand up to her forehead. '…with you *men* thinking you know how things are supposed to be and trying to tell me what I should do and…'

She ran out of steam, chest heaving, gasping for air that she'd lost in the outburst.

'Where's Lek? Where's Estrel?'

James's concern was now carved into his expression. Haezle took a step back.

'I left them in the Catacombs. They went to find the book. Again. I didn't want any part of that nonsense. I left them to it.'

'You left them to it?'

'I left them to it. I don't care what's going on.'

'You're Onu Lek's Reader!' exclaimed Miss Whiteley. 'You don't care what has happened to the Book of Keyes?'

'I don't!' said Haezle. 'I'm done.'

'Then why are you back?' asked James, still confused.

'I…' Haezle didn't know where to start, didn't want to get into it. 'Who *are* you? Why do you care so much about the Book of Keyes?'

'Because!' He sighed, if anything more significantly than Haezle had, and collected himself. 'Because without it, we're doomed. And they will not find it without you.'

CHAPTER 39

LAGRANGE

Eamer's the key. Of course, Eamer's the key. I should have known that all along. I saw him in the Citadel. He doesn't belong there. I knew something was up then, but I got distracted, didn't follow it up properly. I didn't listen to my gut. That's the last time that happens.

I could have gone straight to Docklands before. I could have gone there last night, instead of kidding myself it was safer to meet Kamla uptown. I did get laid and getting laid put me onto the Clipper tattoo, but I might have found the same thing if I'd actually followed up on my instinct.

I should have gone straight to Docklands after the Chaguartay rally. I knew something was up then, something that I needed to find out more about, but again I'd copped out and come back to search the Mainframe instead of doing some proper police work.

I definitely should have gone as soon as I realised what the symbol probably was. I kidded myself that I didn't have time, that talking to Antonio would be easier. But I'd wasted time. He would never have given me what I'd get going to the source.

Well, I'm remedying that now. It's a short walk to Docklands if you take the direct route, but the direct route is along the TransWay and that's gridlocked at this time of day. It's gridlocked at almost any other time of day, let's be honest, and I value my lungs rather too much to walk through the clouds of fumes that envelop the walkways.

So I'm taking a scenic route, through the old town, down twisting side streets, up and down small flights of stone steps and across courtyards. If I wasn't in a hurry, this would be a pleasant stroll.

I'm taking a shortcut through people's lives. I see rugs being beaten; I see kids playing games; I see mid morning assignations that seem clandestine to the casual observer, even if they're actually entirely innocent; I see old men being helped across the street; I see tables on cobbles outside pop up cafés that amount to not much more than someone's kitchenette; I see musicians rehearsing in the park; I see stray dogs, and stray cats; I see dogs on leashes, and more cats; I see love and life and toil and mundanity and wonder. Or I would if I wasn't speed walking to the extent that my shins prick and burn with the effort.

I see the graffiti, too. I see the usual stuff: names and tags and cartoon images. I see grotesque tableaux and surreal vistas. I see moons, cut in half by swords. So many moons. Either they've materialised over night or I've really not been paying attention.

I see the words, too. Not redacted this time. Repeatedly. *THE ECLIPSE IS THE BEGINNING. THE ECLIPSE IS THE BEGINNING. THE ECLIPSE IS…* Then I see the mob.

To be fair, it's not really a mob yet. I dash up some steps around the side of a small chapel, two at a time despite the burning in my legs, and turn the corner into a grassy scrap of space. It's small enough that I have to stop in my tracks to avoid running into the group of young men who are gathered around a broken bench on the far side.

They're all facing away from me. They don't seem to realise I'm there. I see it, though. The symbol of the Clippers of the Black Night. It's tattooed on their forearms and on their biceps. It's sewn onto their jackets on patches. All of them - I count seven - proudly displaying an underground symbol that I've only just discovered existed.

Has this been hiding in plain sight the whole time? Did I just miss it? Did everyone else?

They're talking in low voices, in hushed tones. I can't make out what they're saying, but that instinct, the one I kept ignoring before, tells me that this is something I need to hear.

I can't infiltrate them, though. I'm wearing an Authority uniform. I stand out like a sore thumb as it is, caught frozen in the middle of a patch of wasteland.

I need to get to some cover, but there isn't anywhere. There are trees dotted around the perimeter of the grassed area, but they're small and sparse and wouldn't hide a squirrel.

I back away, slowly putting distance between me and the group. My sense of self preservation outweighs my desire to hear what they're discussing. My gut is torn between the two, but my head knows what's what. And it wants to stay on the top of my neck.

I don't look behind me. That's unfortunate. If I'd looked behind me, then I would have seen the others coming. I don't think I'd have been able to avoid them, but I would have had more time to make the decision I am forced into making on the spur of the moment.

Fighting isn't an option. The glance I give the group coming up behind me tells me there's more than two of them, which is the maximum number of strangers I'm willing to risk taking on. There's a growing group of others around the bench, too. People are drifting out of the shadowy alleyways that radiate off this area to join them.

I look around for something to brandish, to buy myself time by fending them off. There's nothing. I had to check my weapon in when I returned from the rally at Administration, but even with a firearm, I don't think I would stand a chance. They would realise I couldn't shoot them all at once and, through sheer numbers, they hold the advantage. I have to run.

But more figures are emerging from the shadows into the light and I don't want to bolt down some narrow escape only to find myself face to face with more gang members.

I make a snap decision. There are houses that face onto this green. My attention has been focused on the gathering crowd, but I've been taking in the peripheral details. There's a door on my right. It's battered, paint peeling off, at least one pane of glass missing. Someone has punched a hole where the lock is supposed to be, and it's hanging ajar. The front step is littered with paraphernalia that confirms its status as a tweak palace, if confirmation was needed.

I run. I hold an advantage because I know which way I'm going to go, so my weight is already shifted. The gang behind me, and the one moving from around the bench in front, don't have that information so they need to change course, shift their momentum. This costs them seconds and I'm crashing through the door before they really have time to give chase.

I career down a hallway where the wallpaper is black and spotted, and the carpet squelches. There's a body crumpled at the bottom of the stairs on my left. Their legs are tucked into a tatty sleeping bag. There's a needle falling out of their limp hand.

I hurdle their legs and carry on. To be honest, I'm getting numb to the desperate sadness I now regularly encounter in places like this. That's part of the job, the encountering and the numbness. You can't think about it.

Right now, I don't care. I need to get away. I've ventured into a part of town that it is not really advisable for me to be in, encountered a group of people who are conspiring to do something I am paid not to approve of, all while wearing a uniform that marks me out as someone they actively want to do harm to.

That all said, their pursuit seems more intense and furious than I would have expected. Of course they hate Authority. That's kind of what we're here for. But there are incoherent shouts and snarls that I find chilling and, as I barge through a door into the kitchen at the back, I'm hearing things smashing and breaking in the hallway behind me that suggest they've quickly armed themselves.

They must have been carrying those weapons because I couldn't find anything on the ground. That sends a jolt of panic through me. If they came tooled up, then they are looking for trouble. They are now a mob. One that is after my blood.

I drop my shoulder and charge at the back door. A figure slumped over the table raises their head from a pool of something I don't dwell on. The thundering of footsteps in the hallway spurs me on.

There's a backyard filled with rubble. I don't have time to consider whether it's safe, I just take a run up the most substantial looking pile of stuff. It crumbles away under foot but it doesn't actually cave in and my foot doesn't plunge to be trapped between concrete blocks. I only realise that's what could have been what was in store for me once I'm already halfway up.

Like I said, I don't have time. Windows smash behind me, and I know my pursuers are about ready to burst out into the yard. I make it to the top of the pile without incident and I'm within leaping distance of the wall. There's an alley on the other side which looks clear enough up ahead, but I can hear shouts and the sound of glass breaking from that direction as well, and I realise that the other half of the gathering mob have gone around the outside of the house to intercept me.

I could leap over the wall, and I might get away, but the initial fight-or-flight rush has faded and now I'm feeling the effort it's taking to get away. My legs are burning, my chest is tight. I'm struggling to pull in enough air to provide the oxygen my muscles need.

This might matter less if I was being chased by one guy. I'd be able to gauge how he was doing, chances are he'd tire too, chances are I could get away. But there's so many people chasing me. It would only take one of them to be fitter than me and I'd be hunted down.

I need to do something unexpected, before they catch up with me enough to see it and follow.

I glance to my right. There's a roof. It's some kind of shed, or outhouse. Said roof is little more than corrugated metal and chances are it's rusted and I'll fall straight through it…

But beyond that are more roofs, slate ones, tightly squashed together with narrow ginnels in between. And beyond those I can see what might just be my best chance at sanctuary. The Citadel.

I jump onto the metal roof, which holds. I make my getaway.

CHAPTER 40

ESTREL

Those words echoed through my head after Fricker had slunk back to his workshop.

"What is the elephant for?"

It sounded like a rhetorical question, but I didn't think it was. If I took it literally, then the answer was that the elephant was the heart of a device that allowed paradoxes to exist. It overrode the normal logic of the universe. It made the impossible possible.

This was a message from my future self. He wanted me to know, to think about the purpose of the elephant. I thought Lek had sent me back here to prevent the creation of the device. Now I seemed to be telling myself that I should use it. This was an instruction. I was certain of it.

I didn't know if this version of me knew about what had happened to Lek or not. I wasn't certain of the order of events, or whether normal cause and effect cared about that sort of thing. But that was kind of the point. Evie Chaguartay's Continuity machine broke that.

So maybe he knew, maybe he didn't know. Maybe he didn't

know, and then suddenly he did, because something had changed and that something had become something that had already happened. Maybe…

I was turning in mental circles. It didn't matter. What mattered was that I was here, feeling lost without Lek's guidance, trapped in uncertainty about what I could and couldn't do in Mouse's presence. And, if I was right, a future version of myself was telling me not to worry about it. It didn't matter.

Ultimately, I'd travelled back in time to save Mouse. That hadn't gone to plan, so I'd come back again to fix what we'd messed up the first time. Namely, the Continuity machine. But what if I didn't? What if I took advantage of it?

What if I used the fact that any paradox I created would hold to rescue Mouse now, get her out of Trinity? What was to stop me? Apart from the fact that Mouse didn't know who I was. At all, but in particular what we meant to each other. I didn't mean to her what she meant to me.

I could tell her. That would not, apparently, blow up reality in the way I had assumed. But how would she react to that?

That wasn't what I wanted. Even if she reacted well, I wanted her to fall in love with me, just like she had before. How could that happen if I told her she was supposed to? Mouse didn't react well to being told what she was supposed to do, but in these circumstances I didn't think anyone would.

I'd been through this before. I'd considered it before but it was too dangerous, not fair. Yet I kept coming back to it. Apparently I would continue to do so, in my future.

It still felt like the wrong thing to do, though. My heart hurt. My *heart* hurt. If I loved her. If I really loved her, and I did… Did I have to let her go?

Tears pricked my eyes, my breath caught. I gulped in a spluttered lungful of air. It caught again. Did I have to let her go? Was that the way to save her?

I managed a full breath in without spluttering. I exhaled through rounded lips, blowing out a jet of feelings to rid myself of them. I wiped my eyes with the heel of my hand.

Not a moment too soon. Mouse slid into the booth opposite me, where Fricker had been half an hour earlier. If she noticed I was emotional, she didn't say so. That meant nothing. She wouldn't have said a word either way, but it was reassuring nonetheless. I didn't have to protest that everything was fine.

'Got you a place to say,' she grinned, sliding a full pint glass across the table to me, and swigging from the beer bottle she clutched in her other hand. She held it just below the level of the table, so that you wouldn't have known she was drinking unless you caught her mid swig. It was very hard to catch Mouse in the act of anything.

'Right,' I said.

It was a good thing, I supposed. I needed somewhere to stay. And that place not being Mouse's house was potentially safer, certainly less difficult for me, at least until I figured out what to do.

But it wasn't with Mouse, and I'd waited so long. Regardless of the weird situation I'd created by being here at the wrong time, I didn't want to be apart from her.

'It's with Clar. They're... well, you don't need to know the circumstances, suffice to say their love-life is a whole drama of its own. But Jo Jo has moved back out to his mum's place, so Clar says their flat has space, and is usually empty, so you can have their sofa. Now that Jo Jo's not using it. Which I know, for a fact, is not where he was fucking sleeping. If you get my drift...'

I'm not sure I would have got Mouse's drift, but I knew the back story. Jo Jo moved in and out as the state of his relationship with his parents fluctuated. Clar and Jo Jo would be fine.

But that wasn't why my blood had run cold. Everything that Mouse had just said was true. I knew it had happened. But Mouse shouldn't have known about it. Mouse shouldn't have known Clar. They wouldn't meet for another eighteen months.

Suddenly, I was terrified, and I couldn't say a thing. I fought to keep a natural expression on my face, knitted my fingers together under the table to stop myself fidgeting.

'…they're going to drop by later and leave a key. I can take you there later tonight. Make sure you've got everything you need. They said to help yourself to…'

'No,' I said. I panicked.

'No?' Mouse's tone turned. She went from breezy, for Mouse, and helpful to something more stern. 'What do you mean, no?'

'I mean, it's OK, really. I can sort myself out. I don't… I mean, I don't really know this Clar. I mean, who is…'

I trailed off. Was I really about to misgender a close friend in order to maintain my clueless newcomer persona? I couldn't do it.

'…who are they?'

'They're a good friend of mine. You can trust them. If you can trust me, and you seem to, although all I did was haul you out of an alleyway, then you can definitely trust Clar.'

'You did a bit more than that,' I said.

'I made you tea,' she conceded. 'It was disgusting. I see now why you might have reservations about my judgement. Whatever, the offer's there. Take it or leave it.'

I didn't know what to do. After the drama with Lek, I thought I'd found myself in a situation I understood. I thought I understood it better than the people who were in it with me, certainly better than Mouse.

It turned out I understood nothing. The extent of the

changes wreaked across the timeline were revealing themselves at every turn. Lek, Fricker, now Mouse and Clar. I had no idea how far this went.

I had no idea what any of this meant for me. It didn't feel like it was going to be good. I didn't feel very safe.

Which was, ironically, why staying with Clar might be the best thing to do right now. Clar had always been an oasis of calm and safety, in every emergency that Trinity had ever thrown at me. I needed that right now.

Continuity should protect any paradoxical faux pas I might make with Clar, and I would be careful. Maybe some time away from Mouse would clear my thinking, allow me to come up with a better plan.

A better plan than declaring my undying love and seeing it thrown back in my face, ending in Mouse refusing to have anything to do with me, much less leave Trinity - the only home she'd ever known - on my say so, should not be hard to find. My emotional state was clouding my judgement.

I needed to be quick about it, though. Fricker had made a point that the instructions I'd given him, to pass on the question to me, had to apply if we met "on the eve of the eclipse". I didn't know why the eclipse would be important to any of this, but I felt like I had a deadline.

Nothing had happened, as far as I knew, last time around. I hadn't been in Trinity, but no news of unrest had reached Ashuana City, either from inside Trinity itself or from the refugee camps outside. There had been no reports of Trinity closing its borders, no issues with flooding or landslips to disrupt travel.

There was nothing that would prevent our escape that I was aware of. Nothing could have happened to Mouse. She was fine when I met her. Nothing could have happened to me. I wasn't here.

But things were more complicated now. I couldn't rely on what had happened before. I needed to make my mind up to a plan fast. Some space to do that might be helpful.

'You're right, it's a good idea,' I conceded.

I picked up the pint glass for the first time and drank the drink she had brought me. It tasted fresh, unlike anything that usually came from the barrels festering in Eamer's cellar. I lifted my eyebrows.

'You're welcome,' smiled Mouse, some lightness returning to her face.

She slid to her left to exit the booth.

'Let me know when Clar gets here…'

I looked across to the bar and recognised a familiar tall, slim figure, with long hair cascading from beneath the short brim of a black boater. I forced myself to stare a little longer, trying hard to feign searching for someone who I had spotted straight away.

'I won't need to,' confirmed Mouse. 'They're already here.'

CHAPTER 41

CANNON

'There is a battle raging across all of time,' said Estrel. 'It has been fought forever, but it has also only just begun. It is reaching the point where forces are massing and it risks spilling out of control, becoming an all-out war, with everything and everyone at risk.'

'At risk?' asked Cannon.

He was struggling to make sense of the concept of something that had only just begun also having been happening for all time. He was struggling with the idea of a battle across time. He thought that things being "at risk" was a relatively mild assessment.

Also, he didn't know what any of this had to do with his name.

He felt a shift in the pull of gravity as the coach climbed a steep slope. Estrel checked out of the window, through the blind, once more. Apparently satisfied, he returned to his monologue.

'Everything, everyone, everytime. Nothing could survive something like that. Whatever happens, whatever anyone -

you or I, but especially you and I - does, it must be prevented at all costs. There is only one way to prevent it.'

Cannon waited for Estrel to tell him what it was. Instead, Estrel seemed to change tack.

'There is a man. A *wise* man...'

This wasn't the first time that Estrel had mentioned wise men. It was the first time it had carried this specific, sneering emphasis, but Cannon had already understood that the epithet "wise" didn't mean to Estrel what it meant in general usage.

'...I used to follow him. At one time, as far as that phrase has any meaning for me anymore, I was something of a disciple of his. I took risks - with my life, with the lives of people I loved - in service of his plans because I believed in him, and believed what he told me.'

'He's on one side in this battle you spoke of?'

'He is. Together, we plotted and planned and fought. We won minor victories and lost enormous battles and took reality to the edge of a temporal war. Our foe was too clever for us. Or we weren't clever enough. Nothing we did was enough.'

'This isn't a war, though, yet? You said it wasn't... How did you stop them?'

'Oh, we didn't stop her. We couldn't,' sighed Estrel. 'I came face to face with her frequently, and every time I walked away alive but frustrated. There was no way to beat her. Maybe there was, at the start. She was smart, she learned fast. It didn't take her long to catch on, then catch up. Then she was ahead of us every step we took...'

Cannon was struggling. This all seemed so vast and abstract. He couldn't relate any of it to the cross-country coach journey they were in the middle of. He couldn't relate it to his time on the *Dukey Run*, or his confused memories about his home. He still didn't know what any of this had to do with his name.

'It sounds like you were trapped,' he observed. 'Going round in circles…'

'Quite literally looping around,' said Estrel, with a wry smile. 'I've trodden the same path, made the same mistakes, so many times. Over and over and over again. Do you know how exhausting that is?'

'Yes,' said Cannon. He didn't, but it seemed to be enough for Estrel.

'Just when I thought I couldn't go on, just when I felt as thin and worn through as I could possibly be, just at when I thought I was ready to give up because…'

Estrel broke off and stared at Cannon.

'You know how this has to end, right? If we're to avoid a war to end everything, you know what has to happen?'

Cannon raised his eyebrows, wobbled his head vaguely. He didn't know. He thought that was what Estrel was trying to explain to him.

'What?'

'Someone has to win. I was going to let her kill me. That's how desperate I got.' He shook his head and looked down, a wry smile spreading across his lips. 'It would have worked. That would have been the end of it. But so much would have been lost. That's when I learned what she'd done, and it was so… brilliant. Everything I thought I was going to lose… I…'

Estrel's voice caught in his throat, and Cannon realised he could see tears in his eyes.

'Are you OK?' he asked.

There was a burden that Estrel seemed to carry, and Cannon could see the toll it was taking. Estrel sucked in air through his teeth, raised up his shoulders and, with a small shake of his head, pulled himself back together.

'There was a woman,' he said. 'Another woman. I loved her, and she was gone. That's why I got involved, that's why I thought I had to fight.'

'What happened?' asked Cannon.

He could see the pain on Estrel's face. It was the first time since he'd woken up after he was pulled from the water that Cannon had seen him with his guard down. Estrel was vulnerable, and that touched Cannon.

'It's complicated, but… this woman, the one we were fighting. Her name was Evie Chaguartay. Her father had been Mayor of Trinity and he'd been a piece of work, but she was on a different level. The day I arrived in Trinity, she bombed half of it in order to gaslight the population into sweeping her to power. Once she was there, every decision she took was in her own interest, and no one else's. We signed up to fight, me and Mouse. First politically, but Evie developed a habit of killing her political opponents…'

His voice cracked again, and he stopped. Cannon realised he didn't want to finish the sentence.

'Mouse was your partner, right? And this Chaguartay woman killed her?'

'She killed many people, but yes, she killed Mouse. After that, I was fully signed up for the fight. I resisted, I resisted hard. I fought in the streets, shot guns, planted bombs. We were losing badly… she had an army of criminal thugs at her disposal. We weren't prepared for what that fight turned into. Maybe we weren't ready to become the people we'd need to be to win it.'

This didn't sound like a battle across time. This sounded like a conventional insurgency. But Estrel wasn't finished.

'That's when he came to me. Lek. Wise old Lek, guardian of time. Compiler of the legendary Book of Keyes. He had a plan. He said that we couldn't win from the point we'd got to. We were too far down a path that could only lead to our inevitable demise. The only path to victory was to go back in time and take a completely fresh direction. To fork the timeline at a point when it wasn't too late, to stack the deck in our favour.'

'And that's when you started to travel in time.'

Estrel nodded, a faraway look in his eye.

'I don't even know how long I've been doing it now. Back and forth, round in loops, my memories have been wiped and recovered so many times I think I'd go mad if I could remember it all. I kind of worry that's what's happening to me right now.'

He grinned. Cannon noted a certain manic energy with the grin which unnerved him.

'What was the plan?' he asked.

'Doesn't matter now,' scoffed Estrel. 'She was still, always, a step ahead. I don't know how she did it, but we still couldn't steal an advantage. We were still losing at every turn. Like I said, eventually I had nothing left to give. Just when I thought all was lost…'

Cannon realised what Estrel had been saying earlier.

'You switched sides?'

'It was more complicated than that.'

Cannon thought that he'd hit a sensitive topic. He didn't follow up. But Estrel seemed to need to get something off his chest.

'She built a machine,' he explained. 'She built a machine that let her manipulate time without all the usual complications. It should have won her the battle, stopped us in our tracks, there and then. But Lek did something. I still don't understand what he did, but he took away the thing she needed to make it work…'

Cannon couldn't help himself, but the next question asked itself before he realised it had formed in his mind. He knew it was important. Somehow, he knew this bit was about him.

'What did it need to make it work?'

There was silence. Cannon could hear nothing, not even the rush of the wind or the thundering of the horse's hooves. Perhaps time stood still for a moment, but just for a beat, nothing happened.

Then the world came rushing back in.

'Something impossible.'

That was all that Estrel said, but Cannon knew he meant the elephant.

'He hid it from her, and now you've found it for her?' he asked. 'Why?'

'Because then she wins and all of this ends,' said Estrel. 'It was going to end anyway, but this way there's a chance. I can save Mouse. It doesn't matter what else happens, I can make it so that she survives. I can break all the rules, I can destroy whole worlds if I need to. But I can save her. All I need is the elephant.'

'Why did he hide it…?'

Estrel cut him off before he could finish.

'Because he was wrong,' he sneered. 'He thought he knew everything, but he doesn't have a clue. The man is a fraud. I would love to see the look on his face when he realises what I've done. That I beat him. That he has nothing left, nowhere else to go…'

'No,' said Cannon, pushing to get a word in. 'Why did he hide it *on the ship*?'

Estrel stared at Cannon. Cannon stared back. The feeling of dread creeping up the back of his neck was horrible.

'He didn't,' said Estrel, sounding like he didn't think that this was something he should have to explain. 'You did. You're how he hid it, Cannon. Did you not realise that? He took the elephant, and he hid it in a story. Your story…'

'*I* made all of it up? Why would I? I don't know anything

about your battle or a machine or…'

'No, Cannon.' Estrel dropped back to a gentle tone. 'No, no, no… this isn't... I thought you got it. You didn't make it up. You're in the story, Cannon. You're the most important part of the story. You're the witness. None of it happened, none of it was real. But it *became* real because you were there. I misspoke earlier. I said Cannon wasn't your name. That's not quite right, but you're spelling it wrong. You didn't write the story. You *are* the story. Canon. That's who you are. You're the canon. That's why I didn't just take the elephant and run. I need you, Canon. Because you make the stories, and we're going to write a whole new one.'

CHAPTER 42

LEK

There was another prolonged, baffled silence.

'I need to get to my lab,' said Venn abruptly.

She walked up to the console that the man I now knew as Vido had operated before, and switched the feed that went to the screens on the nearest wall.

Rather than the cells, they now showed a collection of corridors. They looked near identical, but each had plans on the walls that were new to me then but very familiar now. These indicated locations that tallied with the labels in the bottom corner of each image, terms that, again, would become far more familiar from this point onward: R&D, Temporal, Consolidated, Genomics…

Venn scowled as she focused in on the Consolidated Research feed.

'Looks clear enough for now,' she muttered. 'What's the route to there from here?'

Vido moved alongside her and tapped some keys until a version of the Research plan appeared on another screen, larger and more readable. He stabbed a finger at the Zoological zone, then dragged it with a squeak across the glass, tracing a path from there to where Venn's lab was located.

'The most direct route is via the Hub,' he said, 'but that's just blown up, so I don't know you want to go that way. There seem to be Resistance Agents swarming all over it, or at least there were. They're mostly dead now, but I'd steer clear of the White Room. That was what they seemed to be interested in…'

Venn's head snapped around to stare at Vido.

'Is there someone in there?'

Vido shrugged.

'How would I know? There are no feeds in that section, and that's information way above my pay grade.'

'Hmmm,' Venn adjusted her glasses and rubbed her chin. 'So I need to find a route through Cybernetics?'

She flicked a few switches, and the screens changed. Still corridors, still almost identical to all the other corridors, but these had snarling, drooling Hybrids galloping down them. One by one, the screens filled. There was a pack of them, seven or eight altogether.

I checked the corner of the screens. These corridors were in Cybernetics.

'Not that way, then,' I said.

'Nope,' agreed Venn. 'That was my last option. I don't think I'm getting to the lab.'

She turned around and leaned on the console. She chewed on her lip, pushed her glasses back up from where they'd slipped yet again.

'You really are so young,' she murmured.

'You keep saying that,' I said. 'I don't know what you mean. For an Acolyte, I'm practically geriatric.'

That's when she laughed, and that's when she told me.

She told me of how we met, from her perspective, brought together by a man called Estrel Beck who was a time traveller from the future. She told me how he had travelled back from a point where Trinity was nearing collapse, ruled by a tyrant intent on taking everything she could for herself, even if it meant the destruction of the ancient city.

She told me that one day, some sixty-plus years in my future, I would see the solution, would figure out which was the pivotal day. I would calculate that if it was possible to kill this malevolent ruler, then a better world would emerge.

She asked me how I'd found myself there that day, and we pieced together that the portal I'd stepped through was a gateway to another time. She explained that I had travelled to that day in the future, the day it all changed. The day that the future depended on.

'I helped Estrel to put himself into a time loop,' she said. 'He will live today repeatedly until he figures out that he's supposed to kill her…'

'What do you mean until he figures out?' I asked. 'He went into the loop. Why doesn't he know what it's for?'

'It's an earlier version of himself. This, coincidentally, is also the day he first came to Trinity. We've intercepted that version of him. He's in the loop. He doesn't have a clue what's going on and every time he loops, he forgets. That's how it has to be. He can't know.'

'Why not?'

'Because any knowledge, any assistance from any of us with knowledge of the future, that could have serious implications for the success of his mission. He has to kill her, but he has to do it of his own volition, from his own motivations. If it happens any other way, we risk a paradox that would rip reality apart.'

'What if he never does it?'

It seemed like an obvious question. Venn rejected it with a quick shake of her head, which dislodged her glasses again.

She pushed them back up.

'He's got forever, and he only has to do it once. Eventually, events will conspire to give him both the motive and the opportunity. She does some pretty horrendous things today, and Estrel's on our side. Or he will be once he knows what's going on.'

'On our side? If I understand correctly, nothing's happened yet for you to take sides of?'

Venn ground her teeth. Now, I recognise this as a sign of frustration. It had taken a long time for Venn to be convinced of the merits of our cause. Even at this point, it was scientific discovery that was driving her. It's unusual to have someone from the future arrive to tell you that your ideas have merit.

That was enough for her to help us. She remained sceptical about why we felt we had to do what we were doing, but she was Research through and through. All that really motivated her was the "what". The "why" didn't need to be relevant.

'It doesn't matter,' she said, eventually. 'If she succeeds, no one benefits. Everyone loses. That's what he told me, that's what you told me. You wouldn't be attempting something like this if it wasn't of the utmost importance.'

That was important. This was my plan. I couldn't understand why, but I hadn't lived through the events she'd described yet. I also couldn't understand how, though. This felt very much outside my sphere of expertise.

'How did I…?' I couldn't quite find the right question. The tenses, for a start, were complicated. 'What makes me decide that this is the plan, though? It's really complicated, potentially reality ending and…'

'…there must be an easier way?' Venn cut in. 'That's what I said. You were very sure. Quite adamant, and very convincing. Also, if I may say so, a bit scary.'

'Right, but I was sure? Will be sure? This is the only way

272

this could be done? It has to happen this way?'

'That's what you said. You told me it was written.'

And that was the point where I realised what was happening, why I was there. Time, a dimension that I understand much better now and yet will never not be an enigma to me, seemed to stand still. The next second stretched out. I saw everything in front of me and it all fell into place.

'Written?' I asked. 'Written where?'

I knew the answer to the question. Of course I did.

'In a book,' said Venn. 'The Book of Keyes, you called it. You said it was an old book, from before the Dissolution, from before…'

She clamped her hand over her mouth. As well she should have. I didn't know what the Dissolution was. It hadn't happened yet. She needed to be careful with that kind of loose talk. Universes have been destroyed for less.

Fortunately, she said it to the one person who didn't need protecting from the strictures of the Time Protocol. More pieces stacked up, made patterns in front of me. The scope of reality presented itself to me, and I was awestruck.

'He must have said I'd be coming,' I said.

I realised I had always been destined to do this, always meant to come here on this day, and to meet Venn and… I was getting ahead of myself. It was hard not to when so much was unlocking and emerging. I closed my eyes briefly and breathed as everything settled in my mind and I adjusted to the plan.

'No,' admitted Venn. 'No, this is a complete surprise. I had no idea that you were coming. I presume that you always knew?'

I thought that was probably true. It felt like the sort of thing that I was going to do.

'I guess,' I said. 'It's lucky you were here.'

'I guess,' Venn echoed.

She ground her teeth again. I got the distinct impression that she didn't believe that anything that was happening was down to chance.

That was smart on her part. I was here for a reason, a reason that, somehow, I had always known even though I'd only just found out about it.

'So he didn't give you any instructions?' I checked. 'This isn't part of the plan?'

'No,' she confirmed. 'Would you like to suggest a course of action?'

Also smart. I did want to suggest a course of action. I knew exactly what I needed to do next.

'I've come looking for the Book of Keyes,' I said. 'It sounds like you know who I need to speak to about that. I think I need you to take me to see… well, me.'

CHAPTER 43

HAEZLE

The urgency with which the stranger, James, ushered her out of Guardian Whiteley's office and back into the Library shocked Haezle. She didn't recall him asking her to go with him, but she also didn't feel that she had much of a choice.

He hadn't dragged her, or pushed her, or touched her in any way, but she felt swept up by the torrent of him raging forward, dragged along by the current of his panic. She bobbed along in his wake.

'Where are we going?'

She knew the answer. It couldn't be anywhere else. They were going back to the Catacombs.

'You can't leave them on their own.' James was shouting over his shoulder, but his words echoed up into the high roof of the Library, bouncing back from each hard, stone surface. Pretty much every Reader looked up from their studies and paid attention to the two of them hurrying down the main aisle. A not insignificant number tutted.

Haezle scowled at everybody. It wasn't her fault that this was happening. This wasn't what she had come back for.

Phil Oddy

'I absolutely can leave them on their own. I did leave them on their own,' she protested. 'I'm not going back…'

James stopped in his tracks, spinning on his heel to face her. Haezle almost ran into him but stopped herself in time, ending up standing uncomfortably close, staring upwards into his strong, intelligent eyes.

She took a step back. She was breathless from the brisk striding across the library. It wouldn't do to let him think there was any other reason.

'They can't find the book without you, Haezle. You have to help them,' he pleaded.

'I don't see why I have to. It's their problem, not mine.'

'What happened? You're the Reader. You're the one who will… who's meant to unlock the book's secrets. Why don't you care that it's gone?'

'Maybe it's all bullshit. Maybe there's no wisdom in those symbols and squiggles. Maybe it's all a stupid game, a power trip for stuffy old monks like Onu Lek and… whatever that Estrel guy is. He's an idiot, I can tell you that much.'

James pulled a face. It looked almost like pity. Haezle did not like that face. She did not appreciate that face and was going to turn against Sergey James very quickly if he insisted on pulling it.

'You're right,' he sighed. 'He is an idiot. A total idiot. The only reason he's here, the only reason he still exists and isn't a wisp of memory floating through the void between time, is to recover the Book of Keyes. And if he hasn't convinced you to help him, then I don't know what the point of him…'

James tailed off.

'Can you hear that?' he asked.

Now he mentioned it, Haezle could hear something. It had started off faintly, but had been growing in volume and intensity for the last few minutes. It was nagging at the edge of

276

her attention, demanding that she notice.

She was noticing now. It sounded like a crowd of people. Angry people.

The doors of the library burst open and someone rushed through. As he turned to push them closed again, Haezle recognised him. It was the Authority Cadet she'd met the previous day.

Sim. Sim? Was that his name?

It seemed like weeks ago. A lot had happened, and she hadn't slept, but it had only been the day before.

He leaned his back against the doors, as if bracing ready for them to be pushed from the other side. Looking around, he disregarded all the Readers who, although their attention was no longer on their books, did not even try to get up from their stools to help.

His attention settled on Haezle and James. Haezle thought she sensed a small jolt of recognition from Sergey, like he knew this man and was surprised to see him. Perhaps she'd imagined it. She'd seen nothing the other way.

'Help me barricade this!' Sim shouted across the Library.

Ordinarily this would have prompted a chorus of shushes from the assembled Readers. Haezle thought she felt the burning desire to do so, from some of them, heavy in the air. It was almost a reflex. She didn't blame them. For a moment, she wanted to do it herself.

Instead, she ran across to her own bench, which was empty because of her not being at work and because of the lack of a meaningful text for her to study. She pushed it with all of her strength, but it didn't budge.

'Are you going to help?' she cried out to anyone.

James quickly joined her. The bench was heavy, which made it an ideal barricade, but they were going to need more people. She didn't hold out much hope. Readers were a passive bunch. It was going to be almost impossible to get it to the door.

'Well, this is different,' said a voice in her ear.

Haezle turned to see the pale, soft, grinning face of Isaak to her right. Her heart leaped.

'We have to move it,' she whispered, not so much an instruction, more a wish that she was trying to manifest.

The bench jumped forward suddenly, the force of the pushing overcoming the friction for a moment, before its legs caught again and they juddered to a painful halt. They pushed again. Wooden legs bent and creaked. There was the sound of fibres tearing. Haezle had visions of the bench collapsing and the three of them falling face first on top.

Then, with a jolting bounce that caused it to dig into her ribs, the bench lurched forward again. Now more Readers joined them, and now it was moving, feet screeching on the floor as they careered towards the door.

Sim jumped out of the way and the bench crashed into place with a reassuring thud, just before several loud bangs from the other side could be heard. There was a suggestion that the doors were about to bow inwards, but the barricade held firm and they stayed closed.

All of them - Haezle, Sim, James, Isaak and the other Readers, leaned back against the bench, chests heaving as they gulped in air. No one spoke.

The background noise grew steadily. More voices added to the crowd that they could hear was building outside. There were several thuds, at irregular intervals, but nothing that threatened the integrity of the door. They sounded like missiles launched from the mob, rather than concerted efforts to get inside.

'What the hell is going on?' asked James, eventually.

'Lunatics,' said Sim. 'Fanatics. I don't know what's riled

them up, but it's something to do with an eclipse. Is there due to be an eclipse?'

Haezle's heart thudded in her chest.

"The eclipse is the end."

Is this the end?

'Oh wow,' said Isaak. 'I... I think there might be.'

This was news to Haezle. She knew Isaak studied the charts - he thought that the Book of Moors might have an astronomical element to it - but he hadn't mentioned an upcoming eclipse. Given what she kept seeing that morning, she definitely would have remembered. It definitely would have been something that Isaak wouldn't have been able to shut up about.

Isaak turned to Haezle.

'It was yesterday, after you'd gone to see Onu Lek about the...' Isaak dropped his voice to a whisper and Haezle remembered that she'd asked him not to talk about her concerns regarding the Book of Keyes. '...problem you were having. With your book.'

'It's OK,' she said, glancing at James. 'I don't think that's a secret anymore.'

Isaak looked surprised, as well he should. A secret of the Citadel, let alone of the Library, was not something that would normally be shared with an outsider. Haezle could see him sizing Sergey James up, wondering who exactly he might be.

She wouldn't be able to help him, she was none the wiser herself.

'Right, OK,' he said, not entirely convincingly. 'So, yeah. I saw something. In the Book of Stay. It was...'

Isaak wasn't the Reader for the Book of Stay. He looked guilty, but there wasn't time to find out what had happened, however much Haezle would have loved to know.

He dug around in a pocket and pulled out what looked to

be a napkin. It was scrunched up into a ball and had something stuck to it that might have been a boiled sweet, although it was mostly coated in fluff.

'It looked like this.' He unscrunched the ball. 'Urgh, what's… never mind… The moment I saw it, I knew. I felt what it meant. You know, when that happens, how it punches you in the guts?'

Haezle didn't know, but her approach to reading was more logical and less based on feeling than Isaak's was. She glanced down at the crumpled napkin in Isaak's hand. Her heart pounded against her ribcage so hard it hurt. It was the same symbol.

Estrel's symbol. From the Echo. From inside the time loop. The stupid, ill-conceived attempt to fix a future that seemed destined to happen whatever they tried. If Trinity was doomed to tear itself apart, it seemed improbable that stopping one woman's actions on one particular day would prevent it. It had to be more complicated than that.

'Where did you get this?' She snatched it from him. 'What kind of…'

'I drew it!' he protested. 'It's what I saw in the book. I needed a copy because I'm not sure I understood all of it. There's this sword, and the jewel, but… It's an omen of an eclipse, I'm sure it is. That's why I went to check the charts. I wanted to understand when it might be coming. I was sure it would be soon, but I didn't know how soon…'

'Show me that,' growled Sim, leaning over Haezle's shoulder.

'Do you recognise it?' Haezle wasn't sure what led her to ask that question. Maybe it was something in his tone, but she wasn't surprised when he answered in the affirmative.

'They're appearing all over the city,' he said. 'That's what all of this is about.'

'All of what?' asked Haezle. 'The mob? How is that related? What does this mean?'

'It's a kind of symbol. There's a gang, or an organisation or a... something. I don't really know what it is yet. They're called the Clippers. The Clippers of the Black Night. There's graffiti. Slogans.'

'"The eclipse is the end?"' asked Haezle.

Again, she wasn't sure why she was so certain. This time, however, Sim didn't immediately agree.

'The end? No, that's not... "The eclipse is the beginning", that's what it says.'

'The eclipse is the beginning,' Haezle murmured, under her breath. 'The eclipse is the end...'

Estrel was from the future. His message was from another time. A time that hadn't happened yet.

Perhaps it wasn't talking about this eclipse. Eclipses were cyclical things. Estrel's message could have come from the end of the cycle. A cycle that would begin...

'Isaak, what did the charts say?'

'What?'

'What did the charts tell you? When is the eclipse?'

'Well, today, that's what I've been trying to tell you. It's today. In fact...'

Haezle looked up to the top windows of the Library. It was midmorning. The sun would have been bright and high in the sky by now and, whilst there was never a lot of light flooding in through those narrow slits, it was definitely dim.

If anything, there was less light than there had been when she'd entered the Library.

'It's now, isn't it?'

'Yes. Yes, it is. I think that's why it's getting so dark.'

'And why the mob is getting louder?' asked James.

It was true. It wasn't just the volume of shouts. There was

chanting, and the sound of missiles striking the door had increased in both frequency and intensity.

The voices swelled to a roar, and the door bowed, testing their barricade.

Haezle, Sim, James and Isaak all looked at each other.

'It's not going to hold,' said Sim, reaching to his belt. 'We need to get out of here.'

He withdrew a gun which, as he turned, he pointed at the door, taking a step back.

'The Catacombs,' said James. 'There's nowhere else to go.'

Haezle wasn't sure how wise that was. The Catacombs were vast and sprawling, with multiple exit points. But they were also narrow and caving in and prone to developing dead ends without notice.

It would be very easy to get trapped in the Catacombs. But Sergey was right, there wasn't anywhere else to go.

They abandoned the barricade and ran.

CHAPTER 44

LAGRANGE

Haezle's friend, Isaak, doesn't come with us. He shows us to the hole in the ground, with the ladder that drops into the darkness, and he leaves us to it. He seems to think that he'll be safe if he stays in the library. He seems to think the mob is only chasing me.

I mean, they *are* chasing me. He also has a point that he makes repeatedly, that disappearing into a hole in the ground, into a labyrinth of underground corridors, may not be the best plan to evade them. But I'm not so certain that he'll be as safe as he thinks in his precious library. They don't seem like a very focused group. They've already engaged in a lot of unnecessary smashing.

I guess you can't smash a book. But I don't think they'd think twice about smashing Readers. Then setting fire to everything.

The other reason we're ignoring his advice is the certainty that Haezle has that she needs to locate some guy named Lek. I think I recall the name. I think she talked about him yesterday. *Wow, was that only yesterday?* He's the monk who found the book she's reading. *Compiled* the book she's reading. He seems to have gone AWOL in the Catacombs. She *seems* pretty pissed off at him.

It's this other guy who has convinced her she needs to find him. He's dressed weirdly. I can't quite put my finger on what it is. Every garment is, in and of itself, completely acceptable, if a little flamboyant for my taste. But, put together, he looks out of place, like someone from another time. Not one I can identify. Not one that I think has ever happened.

He's also looking at me funny. It's been mostly glances, but he doesn't seem to be able to stop checking me out. Even now, as I'm standing in the half-dark, waiting at the bottom of the ladder while he follows Haezle down, I can see him dart a look in my direction.

In different circumstances, this wouldn't be unwelcome attention. Don't get me wrong. There's something about this guy, James, a comfortable energy between us, like we've known each other a while. He seems familiar, but in more than a *"I recognise your face"* way. But this isn't the time.

Haezle takes a step back from the bottom of the ladder to give him some space. I stay where I am, so she has to squeeze behind me in the narrow passage. She looks at me with a puzzled expression, but I say nothing.

James drops off the ladder a couple of rungs early, landing with bent knees. He springs up and spins around, almost jumping about to face me. He smiles. It's a confusing smile, with what seems to be a fair amount of genuine warmth behind it.

'Perfect,' he sighs. 'I haven't had a chance to introduce myself yet. Sergey James.'

He sticks out his hand. I have to unfold my arms to take it.

'I'm…' I begin, gruffly.

'...Simeon Lagrange!' he beams. 'Indeed you are. You are,

may I say, looking incredibly well. So fresh faced. So... not grey.'

I don't look incredibly well; I look normally well, and I don't know what he would know about it, anyway. He's actually quite irritating when he opens his mouth. I conclude that I definitely do not know this man.

'You know who I am, then?' is all I actually say.

'I do, oh yes, I definitely do!' He pumps my hand a few more times before letting go. 'Although, I guess in another sense, no, I don't. You're not like the man I know. It's not just how you look. You're a different man...'

'I've changed? When did we meet?'

It's possible that I do know him. From the Academy? From school? That might explain things. Perhaps he's got more irritating as he's got older?

'We haven't. Not yet, not from your perspective. You're not like the man I know because you haven't had a chance to become him yet. Oh, it's good to see you...'

He takes a step towards me and raises his arms, as if he's going to hug me, before thinking better of it. My face remains impassive throughout, which is exactly what I want to communicate. A determined lack of emotion in the face of over-familiarity. He's not just irritating. He's possibly insane.

'Can we get a move on?' asks Haezle. 'We're meant to be finding Lek. And escaping from the mob.'

Everything is still quiet at the top of the ladder. As far as I can tell, there isn't an imminent danger from the mob, and whilst we don't want to hang around and lose any head start we might gain, I have questions.

'Who in The Creator's name are you?'

James pauses. He seems to be doing some sort of calculation. His face is screwed into a puzzled expression.

'I'm... OK... this is going to get complicated, but I'm a

colleague,' he says, apparently deciding that whatever he was worried about doesn't matter. 'From the future. I travelled back in time.'

I'm nonplussed. I don't know how to process this. I look around and stare at Haezle, but she seems fine with it.

'You…'

'No, don't say anything. Haezle's right, there isn't time. You're going to find this difficult, but I just want you to hear me for now. You don't need to trust me, you don't need to believe me. I'll just tell you what's going on and then we'll get on with escaping. OK?'

'OK,' I manage to splutter.

'Right, so in the future… about thirty years, I think, we work together. You're actually my boss, you're a Senior Oficier in the Black Knight Division and I'm one of your Juniors…'

I mouth the words "Black Night"…

'…not "Black Night", though,' he says, confusingly. 'It's with a "K", in the future. I don't know what's happening here, but this "Black Night" was never a thing. Not unless it's been forgotten or suppressed or something. And the Clippers? They're just a death cult. They're… nothing. Something's changed. None of this happened before. But Lek warned me about things like this. That's why he sent me back…'

'He sent you back too?' Haezle cuts in.

'Of course, he sent more than one of us. He always needs a backup plan…'

He looks me straight in the eyes.

'I came back for you, Oficier Lagrange. I came back to help you. Or protect you or… I'm not completely sure of the specifics, but Lek was very persuasive and absolutely adamant that this was about you. I wouldn't have… but you don't need to know about that…'

He trails off, his eyes a little glassy, his voice catching in his throat. Whatever he had to do to get back here had affected him deeply. He did that for me.

He also called me "Oficier". It's hard not to warm to that.

'This whole Black Knight confusion. The possibility that you're being chased by the very gang of criminals it will be your mission to bring down? That only convinces me he was right.'

'Are you sure you should be telling him this?' asked Haezle. 'Don't you have to be careful about cause and effect, or something?'

'It's Simeon Lagrange,' said James. 'It's hard enough to persuade him to do anything. Nothing less than the truth is going to cut it.'

Despite myself, I'm coming round, although I'm uncertain that I'm not losing my mind at this point. None of it stands up to scrutiny, none of it withstands a rational interrogation. But I think I agree that this is what we need to do.

No, I don't agree, that's too logical. I *believe* that this is what we need to do. I feel it in my heart. In my gut.

'So what…?' I begin to say.

There is the unmistakable sound of the library door being blown off its hinges by a colossal explosion. The floor of the passage we are standing in shudders. Dust and dirt cascade from the ceiling.

Then there is silence. We need to run.

CHAPTER 45

ESTREL

Despite my reservations about meeting them because of the non-zero chance of accidentally ending reality, it was reassuring to be in Clar's company. They brought a sense of calm, and of all things being possible. Situations that seemed dark and hopeless suddenly seemed less so once you talked them through with Clar.

Obviously, I couldn't really do that, but they brought the aura, anyway. I felt better while they sat and waited for me to finish my drink. I felt better while we rode the miniTram back uptown.

We sat next to each other, but were no chattier than during my ride down with Mouse. I didn't mind. It was late, and I'd had a few beers and I was worried that, if I started talking, I'd let my mouth run away with me and say things that it really wasn't a good idea to say.

But Clar made it OK. We sat in a pleasant, comfortable silence to the Crossing Arch and then we walked in single file across the plaza to their building.

It's not that nothing was said. There were directions and

acknowledgements and agreements, but it wasn't a conversation. I couldn't recall us talking about anything, not until I sat down at their kitchen table and they offered me a beer.

I didn't really think another beer was a great idea but, faced with the prospect of being impolite, I accepted. Clar went to the cupboard and pulled out a box of cereal, from which they extracted a bottle. They evidently caught my expression of confusion.

'I have a friend who has a problem,' they explained. 'I try to hide the alcohol. I'm trying to help them, as far as I can.'

'Does it work?'

Clar pulled out a second bottle. I didn't think there was much cereal in that box.

'No. Not even a bit. He's knows I'm trying to help, though. Maybe that's as much as I can do. Someone has to look out for him. I worry he's given up on himself.'

It wasn't the same, but I thought of Lek. It was hard to think of him as being Lek. His life had taken such a different path to the one I was familiar with. But maybe that was what he needed. Someone to look out for him, someone to be there even when he'd given up.

I had a momentary flash that maybe that was why I was here. Maybe Lek, my Lek, future Lek, seemingly omniscient Lek, knew what had happened here, and he'd sent me back to do something, to be here at least.

If that was the case, then I'd failed at the first hurdle. Some warning would have been nice. He'd attacked me. What was I supposed to do?

I hadn't been sent back to save Lek. I'd been sent back to help him, sure, but to help him stop Evie Chaguartay. A feat that was well beyond us in the current situation.

I couldn't save Trinity. I couldn't save Lek. I was going to do what was within my control, and that was to save Mouse.

So for the time being I was just going to accept a beer, listen to the list of house rules I was sure I was about to be briefed on by Clar, get my head down and sleep until morning. Then I would go to Mouse and persuade her to leave. That was how long I had to figure out how.

Clar sat down opposite me and took a long pull on their beer. They were staring at me intently. This felt way too serious for a discussion about quiet hours and bathroom times.

'You're new,' they said, eventually. 'You're not one I've met before, are you?'

I was not expecting that on any level. Did they really just say what I thought I heard? I couldn't have. I was twitchy, worried about doing something wrong. They just meant that we hadn't met before.

'We've…?' I thought it was worth checking, though.

'Well, of course, you've met me. I know we have a history from your perspective, but as far as your travels are concerned… This is a first for you, isn't it?'

No. I was wrong. They meant exactly what I thought they'd meant. This changed everything, I thought. But I needed to be cautious.

'This is… unexpected. What do you know? Do you understand what's going on?'

'I don't know I'd go that far.' Clar sat back, regarded me a little less intensely, although no less thoroughly. 'I've met you before. In the past. My past, but definitely your future. You're young. You're much younger than the last time.'

'I…'

I wasn't particularly young. Forty was coming up on the rails, faster than I would have wanted, if I still cared about that sort of thing.

'It makes sense,' continued Clar. 'We're getting close now,

aren't we? It can only be a few years away.'

Something crept down my spine, cold, spiky. It caused me to shudder visibly. Clar was talking about the time loop. Maybe it didn't matter, because it was Clar, and Clar was trustworthy, and a friend.

But no one was supposed to know about that. There was no way for anyone to know about that. Even Venn didn't think it was possible yet. No one had thought about using her theories to change the course of time. The events that we wanted to change hadn't happened yet.

'What can you tell me about what's going on?'

'Only what you've told me yourself,' shrugged Clar. 'This sort of thing isn't in the Archives. There's no one I can interview. There's…'

I don't know where it came from, but at that moment I saw the way out. I needed confirmation that the version, or versions, of me that had apparently been stomping all over my past knew what they were doing. I needed to know that they were real. I also needed information. I thought I could get all three with Clar's help.

'You can interview me.'

'I can? I didn't think you knew anything. You just asked me to explain it to you.'

'I've got time,' I said. I was reaching, making things up on the spot, but if this didn't work, I'd know soon enough. 'You meet me again in my future. I can do research. I can figure it out. I can tell you.'

'You can, but I can't go back and ask you. I…'

A strange look passed across Clar's face. They stared up above my head, their eyes flicking right to left, right to left repeatedly.

'What's happening?'

'I… I'm remembering something. Something I did, a

conversation I had. Months ago, but also... It's a paradox. It's a paradox that's playing out because, for as long as Evie White's Continuity machine exists, the paradox can't do any harm. Not to the world, anyway. Just to us. This one isn't dangerous, though.'

'How do you know? Who told you that?'

Clar adjusted their gaze and looked me straight in the eye.

'You did, Estrel. The last time I met you, you sat me down and told me I had to interview you. And then you proceeded to talk for half an hour straight, so I'm not sure you understand what an interview actually is. But you told me a lot. You told me how this would feel.'

'How does it feel?'

'Like I've suddenly woken up from a dream. Like everything I thought was real wasn't quite right and now I'm seeing things clearly. I feel relieved, and I feel anxious, and I feel confused how I could ever have mistaken that other place for reality. But I know it was real. Until a minute ago, it was real. You changed things.'

'I tried to. Seems like it worked?'

'You don't know?'

'It hasn't changed for me. It's still in my future. But now I know one thing I need to tell you when I get there. You just told me what you need to know, not to be completely freaked out by that experience.'

'Is that really how it works? How did I know to tell you?'

'You were living it. You just told me what you felt. It was easy. We created that knowledge.'

'Is that really how it works?' Clar asked, again.

'We're finding that out,' I grinned.

'You told me a lot.' Clar rubbed their temples, screwed up their eyes against the sharp pain of sudden, unexpected information rushing unbidden into their hippocampus.

'You've got a lot of research to do.'

'Or,' I said, 'you can just tell me what you know?'

Clar eyes grew wide as realisation dawned.

'And then you'll know?'

'And then I can tell you.'

'OK. Give me a moment. It's difficult. Not like a normal memory…'

Clar screwed up their face again, took another gulp of beer, swallowed it hard.

'…because it isn't a normal memory,' they said.

They spoke slowly and carefully. I got the impression of thoughts whirling, concepts forming as they spoke. I wanted to ask a thousand questions, but I knew that this moment was crucial. I couldn't afford to screw this up. This might be bigger than me.

'A memory isn't you thinking about something that happened,' Clar said.

They continued to speak slowly, with a toneless detachment that suggested these weren't their words. I realised I was speaking with myself, in a sense, across time. I shivered.

'A memory is you thinking about the last time you thought about what happened. And I've never thought about this before. So it's like it's happening right now. At the same time, I've been thinking about this for weeks. I've been playing this over and over, rehearsing what I'm going to say, how I'm going to say it…'

They winced, drank more beer. I put down my bottle on the table and pushed it across to them. It seemed like they were going to need it more than me.

'It's a lot. So don't interrupt. You were adamant that I should tell you that. I'm going to tell you everything I know - which is everything you need to know - so I'm either about to answer what you want to know, or I'm never going to be able to tell you. You'll have questions, but you're never going to fill in those gaps.'

I stayed silent. Not just because I'd just told myself off across time. The toll this seemed to be taking on Clar was difficult to watch.

'The first thing you need to know is that we only have one universe, Estrel. We only have one reality. Others exist, an infinite number, probably, but there's only one where you and I can exist and it's this one. Anything that jeopardises that reality is incredibly, unspeakably dangerous, which is why - whilst it's always been theoretically possible - time travel has been technically beyond anyone's reach. Until Venn found a loophole, and Lek used you to exploit it…'

'The time loop?' I asked.

I couldn't help myself. Clar grimaced at my interjection. I resolved not to do it again.

'Yes. The time loop. You contained any reality ending paradoxes you created within their own pocket timeline. If you broke everything, killed the universe, you got a do over, a second chance. Or a third, or a fourth. It was brilliant. But it was costly. You carved off enough alternate timelines that they almost broke everything, anyway. Each new timeline became a sliver, a shard so delicate that they risked being blown away in a gust of temporal wind…'

Clar stopped there and shook their head, as if trying to clear something from their mind. They picked up my bottle of beer and took another swig.

'That was weird. Those were your words. You got poetic there. But you seemed different. You sounded like someone else… someone…'

They trailed off.

'Lek,' I said, despite my earlier resolution.

'Who?' asked Clar, which was weird, because they'd only just mentioned him.

Another shiver. Clar picked up where they'd left off.

'When one of you managed, against all the odds, to do it, to end the loop, it did what it was supposed to. The universe poured all its energy into that one timeline, and reality was fixed. But those other timelines didn't die. If you knew where to look, and you looked hard enough, you could see that something wasn't right, that the ruptures you'd created hadn't healed properly. Someone who was interested enough, and clever enough, could pick away at that scar tissue on the fringes of reality and figure out what you'd done. And that's just what happened. Now, you're going to guess that it was…'

'Evie Chaguartay,' I concluded, right on cue. 'Because I managed to close the loop without killing her.'

Clar nodded, swigged, carried on. The words were tumbling out now, faster, more fluid. It was like they'd stopped thinking and were now just hearing and repeating. I couldn't imagine the turmoil that must be happening inside their head.

'Close enough. She soon found out about it. And as the primary victim of your meddling, she was not happy. She also had different ideas. That's how Continuity came about, and that changed everything. Now the paradoxes don't matter. Except that anything is now possible, and that's not natural. Everything is heating up, and the universe is going to end, anyway. So she's taking a different approach. She's trying to go back to the beginning and start again. She wants to reset reality, to put things on a different path, one of her own design. There was only one person stopping her. The… the man with the book…'

'Lek,' I said again.

'Find it,' Clar said, urgently, a fire igniting behind their eyes. 'The book is lost again and you have to find it.'

'Why?' I asked. Screw the not asking questions thing. Everything Clar had said sounded like impending doom and their solution - my solution, I guess, if I thought about it - was to find a book? 'Quasi-spiritual mumbo jumbo? How's that going to help?'

'The Book of Keyes isn't like that,' replied Clar, not reacting to my scorn. They were still reciting words from memory. 'The Book of Keyes is different. There's a reason it disappears, there's a reason it changes. Every time she does something, it finds a way. It holds the key. It will always hold the key. The keys...'

Clar slumped forward, their head crashing to the table, knocking the empty bottles to the floor. It was silent in the kitchen. I took a deep breath.

That same shiver shot up my spine again. This time it solidified into something substantial - a determination, a resolve. I knew what I had to do.

It was her. Evie Chaguartay was what had happened to Lek. And now she was headed back to the beginning of time to reboot the universe in her own image? What, exactly, was I meant to do with this information, other than despair? What could I possibly do in the face of this power, so much greater than anything I understood? Find the Book of Keyes, apparently.

I eased Clar's arm under their head, cushioning it from the hard surface of the table. I didn't know how to find a mystical book. It had eluded Lek for decades. I wasn't going to look for a book.

I was going to seize the day. If the universe was about to be reset, particularly if the universe was about to end, then everything I knew was about to be lost. I couldn't bear that, not without making the most of what I had, of what I'd found.

I quietly shuffled out of Clar's flat, down the stairs and back out onto the street. I was exhausted. I was a little bit drunk, but I was determined.

I was going to find Mouse.

CHAPTER 46

CANON

They had stopped some time ago, but Canon wasn't sure how long it had been. His mind was a maelstrom of emotion, fragments of thought, and blind panic. He hadn't said anything to Estrel, but this didn't seem to concern his travelling companion.

Canon suspected that the earlier sympathy he thought he'd detected hadn't been real. It had probably been a ruse to get him to open up and reveal who he really was. Perhaps Estrel was a psychopath.

Perhaps he used to be nicer. It sounded like he'd taken a long time to get to the point he was at now. Maybe he hadn't always been that bitter, or hard, or cruel. It didn't really matter. What mattered was what happened now.

He'd been told he wasn't real. Canon didn't know what that meant, but he felt real enough. He was thinking thoughts, feeling discomfort. He was there, at that moment, with agency. He could do something.

Estrel had said that he needed Canon for whatever he had planned. But Canon didn't have to just accept that.

Apparently, he was a story. *The* story. And stories have power.

He wasn't sure that Estrel was doing the right thing. He understood his motivations; if love was a powerful force, then, coupled with grief, Estrel was going to be hard to stop. But he thought he had to try. He'd been tasked with protecting the elephant, which he'd spectacularly failed to do...

...tasked by someone I've never met, without my knowledge or consent...

Canon pushed that thought away. It wasn't helpful. He was trapped in a situation of his own making - even if he hadn't intended to make it - but without enough information to make an informed decision. He had to trust something, someone. All he had was his gut.

Who can you trust if you can't trust yourself? Who indeed? Canon suspected that he shouldn't probe that question too hard, in case the answer turned out to be "no one".

Canon looked around the carriage and realised that Estrel was no longer there. He hadn't noticed him leave and did not know how long he'd been gone for, but the coach's door was hanging open. Beyond it was darkness, and the possibility of escape.

Canon scrambled for the door, crossed the threshold of the carriage and felt the cool, fresh air. His foot hit the step, and he almost fell as his ankle turned over, but he used his momentum to shift his weight to the other foot, which he planted firmly enough on the ground that he didn't actually fall. His knee jarred, and he struggled to regain the breath that was knocked out of him, but he was upright. In a moment, he was running.

A shot rang out. Canon felt something whistle by his ear and, before he had time to decide if he should stop or keep running, his feet had ceased moving. He waited for a second shot.

It never came. He didn't know if that was because he'd stopped but, just in case, he put his hands in the air and slowly turned around.

The hooded coach driver was pointing a gun at him, at a distance of about twenty metres, which was all the ground he'd covered in his scramble. It was a less impressive getaway than he'd hoped.

He dropped his hands; it was clear to anyone watching that he wasn't going to try to run again.

'Nice try,' said Estrel, stepping out from around the back of the coach.

He was holding a lamp, which cast eerie shadows around them. Canon realised that they were standing at the bottom of a steep slope. He'd started to run along the bottom, but if his random choice of direction had been any different, he would have found himself either trying to scramble uphill, or stumbling off the edge of a cliff, down a ravine that he couldn't see the bottom of.

It had been pointless to even try to run. The coach driver could have saved themselves a bullet.

Estrel leaned into the coach and heaved out the box. He held it in front of him while he walked up to Canon.

'Here. I think you should carry this. It's only appropriate.'

Canon took the box without a word and followed his two companions as they climbed the hill in front of them.

At the top were a tree and a woman. The woman stood beneath the broad branches, as if she was sheltering from rain that wasn't falling, until the group got close enough for her to see Estrel's face by the light of his lamp. She took several steps towards them as they made their final ascent.

Up close, Canon could see that she was wearing similar hooded robes to the coach driver. Except her hood was down. Her sharp features were vaguely familiar, but Canon couldn't tell from where, or when. He wondered if her hair, pulled severely back, was different, or whether the heavy robes were a distraction, but he was sure he knew her from somewhere. Another life, of which he had no actual memory. Except in flashes, like the flecks of fire in her eyes.

He felt the ache of everything he'd lost. Except, had he? Was there ever anything else? Did he have another story, or was that just as much of a fiction as the ship? Was this, now, here, on this hill, any more real? It didn't feel like it. How would he tell?

The woman stepped close to Canon until he could see the lamplight reflected in her eyes. They caught him, holding him still. Beads of sweat pricked his forehead.

'Is this him?'

Her voice was like ice. Canon felt the fear freeze on his skin.

'It's him,' said another voice.

It wasn't Estrel. If Canon had been forced to say, he would have sworn that it was the woman in front of him, only she hadn't moved her lips. Over her shoulder, he saw the coach driver move into view and remove their hood.

It was the same woman. Same pointed features, same fire-flecked eyes. A twin, or a doppelgänger, or...

Canon thought about the stories Estrel had told him in the coach. About travelling in time. This was the same woman from another time. He was certain.

'It's in there.'

She nodded towards Canon. He proffered the box. He didn't know what else to do. With a mocking smile, the first woman took it from him.

'You will be released soon,' she said.

Canon felt that this was supposed to be a reassurance. He didn't like what was happening here. He didn't understand it and he wasn't reassured.

'Do we need him, still?' asked Estrel with a sneer.

The woman turned sharply to face him.

'Of course we don't need him, but he deserves to be here. He told such a good story and one should always respect the story. You, on the other hand, are entirely dispensable now...'

The shot came from the other woman, the one who Canon had been thinking of as the coach driver up until then. She kept the gun hidden beneath the folds of her cloak, but he assumed it was the same one she'd pointed at him earlier.

'Thank The Creator,' she said.

Canon heard it clearly. Her voice was like the other woman's voice, but carried a crackle and spark in place of the rough drawl of her companion - a younger version of the same vocal chords.

'What... Who *are* you?'

The woman had said that Canon deserved to be there, but that had been a brutal moment. He didn't know if he was safe, or if she'd merely meant that he deserved to live for the time being.

The woman turned back to him, from staring at the prone bundle of Estrel's corpse. She smiled. It wasn't pleasant.

'My name is Evie Chaguartay. I expect that Estrel here mentioned me at some point. Thank you, I suppose I should say, for protecting my elephant. You may not have realised it, you may not have meant to, but you've played your part excellently.'

Canon felt about as much like a pawn as it was possible to feel. He'd done nothing deliberate, nothing with purpose, but apparently he'd been in service to a man he'd never met and, in doing so, pleased his sworn enemy.

'I don't understand,' he confessed. 'I don't know what is happening. I don't know which side I'm meant to be on.'

'I suppose not.' This time some genuine delight broke out

across her eyes as she laughed, even if only for a moment. 'I don't suppose it matters much, anyway. But, like I said, you've earned your place here…'

'And Estrel hasn't?'

There was a fight in Canon's tone, which surprised him. He had no love for Estrel, who, it seemed, had used his good nature and friendship against him, manipulating Canon for his own ends. But the injustice of his abrupt despatch left an unpleasant taste.

'Estrel has outlived his usefulness,' replied Evie, the coldness returning. 'And he wouldn't be able to handle what's coming. The war that's coming. There are many, many versions of him who will be lined up against us. There are only a few who we've persuaded over to our side. Every single one of those Estrel Becks has started out on a mission to kill me, or my sister here. There are more of us, of course, just as there are more of him, but nowhere near as many. At some point, one of them should have been able to fulfil their mission. We shouldn't exist, we should have lost long ago…'

'He couldn't do to me what I just did to him,' said the second Evie Chaguartay. 'How do you think he'd cope with having to kill another version of himself?'

There was a cold, cruel logic to what they said, Canon had to admit.

'And me?' he asked. 'Do I have a role in this war as well?'

'Maybe,' said the older woman. 'We will never run out of uses for stories. But for now, we need a myth. You are here at the moment of creation…'

She placed the box on the ground, and then turned and spread her arms wide, as if gathering up the valley beyond and holding it to her. Dawn was breaking. The sky was already lighter, and the sun was about to break from behind the distant mountain peaks.

Canon realised that this view was familiar, the wide basin exposed to the sea on one side, the crags and mountains beyond. He'd seen it before. He'd described it before. He'd told stories of this place.

He looked down the steep slope ahead of them, how it dropped to their left into a narrow pass between hills. The Armpit, they called it. Something was missing, though. There should be a city down there.

'Is this Trinity?'

He knew, the moment he said it, that he was right. This was Trinity. They were standing at the top of the Northern Exposure; there was the shore of the Middle Sea. The peaks of the Proctean Mountains towered in front of them. All that was missing was the city.

'It will be,' whispered the younger woman. 'And this time it will be different… What's keeping her?'

She turned to her double, who was still gazing out across the valley in awe.

From behind them, Canon could hear a high-pitched sound, a ringing in the air that nagged at the edge of his hearing. They were bathed in a pale blue light that brought an icy gloom to the breaking dawn.

From the canopy of the tree, the light was shining down. In that shower of blue stood another hooded woman. Canon didn't even need her to remove her hood.

'There are three of you now?'

'Perfect, we are ready!' declared the senior Evie, turning back to greet the new arrival. 'Welcome sister.'

She took a step forward and nudged Canon in a way that he thought was probably meant to be playful. She wasn't pulling it off.

'You see. A new creation myth. Three sisters. A trinity. It's like it was meant to be. Like this was what always happened.'

Canon's mouth dropped open. He wasn't sure that was right, but he wasn't sure that it was wrong, either. What did he know about the founding of Trinity? Nothing, except the story that Estrel had told him about the wise men and the tree. And here was a tree…

The Tree had been killed, had the life squeezed from it. If these women were trying to change that, was it truly a bad thing? Just because it had always happened that way before…

Is it bad to change what happened, if what happened was bad?

'Where have you been?' asked the second Evie, the one who had been driving the coach.

'I had to deal with someone,' snarled the new arrival. 'It didn't go entirely to plan, but I fixed it. We don't have a lot of time to lose. Do you have it?'

Canon blinked, squinting against the sun, which was suddenly high in the sky. He raised his hand to shield his eyes. How had so much time passed? Was that her doing, or his?

'The elephant, yes, we…' began the first Evie, indicating the box on the ground.

The Evie under the tree strode forward with purpose, swinging her leg so that she caught the box fully with the top of her foot, locking her ankle and propelling it into the air.

It barely passed below the edge of the cliff before it exploded.

Canon watched as a dark cloud rose from the smoking remnants of the box. It drifted through the air, slowly thickening, growing in substance. It fizzed and sparked with a dark, pulsing energy. Canon could feel it creeping across his skin, smell and taste it in the morning air.

Canon lowered his hand. The cloud seemed to draw light from the overhead sun, sucking it in to make itself more complete. Already the sunlight was less intense than it had been. Shadows were fading, merging back into an early dusk.

Canon looked into the three faces of the woman in front of him. They were transfixed.

'Wh-what is this?' he asked.

The eldest Evie Chaguartay turned to him. Her smile was severe, lacking in warmth or humour, stretching her face into a mask of malevolent glee.

'This? This is where it ends. Right at the beginning. We're fixing things. Fixing a path, fixing the future. Everything will happen, from here, the way it should. No more battles, no need for war.'

The cloud took on a shape, a recognisable shape. Canon still didn't understand why - what it signified or, really, what it was for - but the outline of an elephant, a shape darker than the most unreachable part of the night, hovered in the air in front of him.

'This…' Evie Chaguartay threw her arms upwards. '…is Victory!'

The elephant shot into the sky, blocking out the sun.

CHAPTER 47

LEK

Venn took me through the Catacombs - the parts that hadn't been converted in the building of Research - to my rooms. They were very familiar to me. I had moved into Onu Castor's quarters.

'Onu Castor vanished,' I explained to myself, 'on the first night of your Trial.'

It's a strange thing to come face to face with a future version of yourself. That should be obvious, but it's worth mentioning that you never get used to it.

I thought I would. I thought that, as time went on and I became more accustomed to the phenomenon, that the novelty would wear off. But it never has. That uncanny feeling of watching someone so familiar, close up, with no filter of distance or memory.

Imagine hearing your own voice, recorded or echoed back at you, and how strange that sounds when you only ever get to hear it vibrated back through your own skull. It's like that, but so much more intense. You never get to hear in real time the way your voice sounds to everyone else. On the other hand, you regularly see your own reflection and you think you have a sense of what you look like, how others perceive you.

But your reflection is narrow and flattened and inverted. You are a completely different person than the guide image you use to adjust your hair, or to avoid cutting off your own ear when shaving. To see yourself acting, wholly and independently, unencumbered by any memory of the original event, every extra wrinkle etched individually by time? That is a truly strange experience.

I had come to meet what, to me at the time, was a very senior version of myself. From my current viewpoint, he was still relatively young, although "relatively" is a word that has lost a lot of meaning subsequently.

'When I returned from the Trial, he was gone,' he continued. 'I suspect he left due to his own actions, but whether or not they were intentional, I will never know. I tried to recreate the conditions, to go looking for him. I was never successful.'

The older man sucked on a long pipe, which I recognised as also belonging, originally, to Onu Castor. It was unclear to me if this was part of trying to recreate the conditions of his disappearance.

From my perspective, I can confirm that it was not. Onu Castor also left the recipe for his tobacco blend and it is delicious. I always thought I'd like to take up pipe smoking. I had the excuse that I was doing it in his honour.

'The blue light? What does it do?'

As I spoke the words, I knew the answer.

'It allows travel between places that can't be found through usual means. Along timelines, outside reality… It brought you here.'

I hadn't done it alone. I certainly hadn't done it by getting drunk.

'There was a man I met. He was Keyes. I thought he had a hand in this…'

'His name wasn't Keyes,' my older self laughed. 'I think he was making fun of you. That man's name was Estrel Beck. He's a comrade of mine. Probably a friend. He gets about a lot. It's easier for him…'

And suddenly that made sense to me, too. It was easier for him because there were so many versions of him out there. Every jump back, every time loop he'd lived through, had created a new version, an alternate iteration. Now they'd been freed from the loop, because of an unforeseen consequence of Evie Chaguartay's meddling, and they were working hard to stop her from making things any worse.

'How do I know these things? Now, as we're talking, I know things I never knew before, without you having to tell me.'

'We can share our knowledge along the timeline. Things that you will know become things you do know. Experiences you will have, people you will meet - all of that will become available to you. At the moment, it's a little piecemeal, I'm sure you've realised, but in time you'll get better at it. And then time will mean somewhat less to you.'

'And you have this insight?'

'Well, when it comes to you, I have memories. But yes, I can see a lot more. One day, everything will fall into place. It's a magnificent gift from the universe. And a terrible curse.'

I nodded in agreement. I wasn't sure I was ready for it. But it was true that at no point along my journey to date had I felt ready for any of it. That hadn't been enough to stop it from happening to me.

'Do you have the pages that he gave you?' asked my older self.

I rummaged in the folds of my robes and extracted the

rolled bundle from an inside pocket.

'I didn't understand them, but then I don't think I'm supposed to. I'm not a Reader.'

'It's not in code. Check it again.'

Confused, I unrolled the paper. There was nothing written on them, they were completely blank.

My older self chuckled.

'I think that was Estrel's idea of a joke. He knows the traditions, he thinks they're ridiculous. *"Why can't you just write down what you think, and let people read it normally?"* is what he would say. He's not wrong. It would be a far more efficient way to convey knowledge. But when has religion ever been about efficiently conveying knowledge? Why deliver facts when a cryptic parable will do, eh? Why write down the secrets to the universe when a vague, coded notation will keep everyone guessing for hundreds of years? If we unlocked all the secrets just like that, where would be the reward? For the Brotherhood, there would be none. They wouldn't need you anymore.'

I noted the use of the second person pronoun.

'"You"? You're not part of the Brotherhood any more?'

We were in the Citadel. My older self was wearing robes, albeit they were a shade of blue, not the traditional saffron. I wondered if there had been a splinter, a parting of the ways. I wondered which route I had taken.

'It's not quite that simple…'

He dodged the question. It wasn't helpful for me to find out about the Dissolution this early.

'…but no. Much has changed. Including my take on what might be useful information to pass on. *This…*'

The older version of me reached into his own robes and withdrew a small, leather-bound book. The cover was marked with patterns, waves of colour that intersected and seem to pulse as the light moved across the front and back. It was beautiful. I knew immediately what it was.

'This is the Book of Keyes,' he confirmed. 'This is what you're looking for. It is not, I should add, authored by anyone by that name. As far as I know, a man named Keyes does not exist. I can't tell you why the book is called what it is, but that is its name. It has always been its name...'

He handed over the book, and I flicked through the pages. There were a lot more than ten. Despite what I had said to myself, the contents still seemed vague and confusing, and not actual words as I recognised them.

'I don't understand,' I said. 'I still can't understand it. I thought...'

'The contents are not words, but nor are they obtuse code, or - worse - meaningless nonsense. These are carefully calculated mathematical equations, devised by my esteemed friend Venn, who brought you to see me here. They are difficult to understand now, for anyone who is not Venn, but they contain the complete realisation of her theories. Given time, and the right Reader, they can be unlocked and then they can be used. Hopefully, rather earlier than we have been able to do so in our version of the timeline.'

There were too many questions at this point. I didn't know what order to ask them in. Fortunately, that much was obvious. My silence, open-mouthed and wide-eyed, was interpreted as an invitation to explain.

'This isn't how I remember things, Lek,' my older self told me. 'When I undertook the Trial, I did many of the things you did. I got lost. I wandered aimlessly around the Catacombs, from tunnel to tunnel until I found a door. But I found many doors. I went to many places. I brought back the original Book of Keyes.'

He reached out and put his hands on my shoulders,

holding me in place as he fixed me with his stare.

'I was reluctant, just like you were, Lek. I was scared, just like you were, even if neither of us admitted it. But I passed through that wine cellar without taking a bottle. I barely remember it in my own timeline. You were making a mess of things. I needed Estrel to intervene or you would never have made it to the end of the Trial. We needed to make sure you brought back the text that you needed. That everyone needed. We needed you to find the right portal, and we needed you to come here.'

'You're changing things. Isn't that incredibly dangerous?'

'It is, but these are incredibly dangerous times. I have an awareness of what happens to me in the future. You do, too. You've been experiencing it through this conversation. It's a feature of how enmeshed into the fabric of time we have been able to become. But increasingly I'm seeing evidence that there are gaps, branches in time that I can't see. Worse, sometimes I see things from the past, or that should be in the present, that haven't happened, or happened differently in my recollection. I recently discovered why, and it means that you can no longer fulfil your destiny with vague notions of philosophical truth. You need hard facts.'

He pointed at the Book of Keyes in my hand.

'They are in there.'

This wasn't the satisfactory answer I was looking for.

'But why can't you just tell me what I need to do to fix things? Why give me a book of equations that I can't understand? Nor can anyone else. At least for an unspecified period of time, until the "right" Reader comes along. How will I know who they are?'

'It has to be this way. I can't tell you directly. We're messing with things too much already. We're up against a powerful opponent. We need to make sure that the damage we do is less than the damage she does, otherwise all we're doing is making things worse. I've given you all I can. The rest is up to you. Hopefully, when the time is right, you can use this to stop her.'

'Her? Who? Evie Chaguartay?'

I looked at my own horrified face.

'You shouldn't know that name. Venn was wrong to tell you too much. You will meet her, and she will be just a child. I warn you now, because I know what you're thinking. You cannot solve things that way.'

Of course I knew what I was thinking. I was going to live through the rise of Evie Chaguartay. I sounded like I would know who she was from childhood. Why couldn't I just kill her before she wreaked any havoc? It was at least as good a plan as putting a man into an infinite time loop until he became an assassin.

'Could you really kill a child? Could you really hold them responsible for the deeds of the person they have not yet become?'

'Maybe I don't have to kill her. Maybe I can coach her, mentor her, prevent her from…'

'She will know, and she will stop you. This is the only way.'

I reached out and placed my hand on the book. There was a silence between us.

I blinked, and my older self was gone. I was back in Onu Castor's room, his effects scattered across the rug, a pipe still smouldering in the stand beside his chair...

CHAPTER 48

EVIE

'Ah, you're here. I think you have something for me…?'

The voice came from behind Lek's shoulder. It was a young woman's voice. He turned, still crouched on his knees, not knowing who he expected to see.

She wore a long hood and a cape that wrapped around her, hiding any distinguishing features.

'Who are you?'

'You don't need to know that. Give me the book.'

She took a step towards him and reached out her hand, as if she expected him to hand it over. Lek pulled the book back, hiding it behind his back.

She withdrew her hand as the other shot out, a knife grasped in its palm. She plunged it into Lek's shoulder.

Pain shot through him and his grip loosened, the book falling to the floor. Lek clutched at his shoulder with the other hand, tried to turn towards the book, but he only got halfway up before he lost his strength and staggered sideways.

The woman was quick. She was already crouching over the book by the time Lek righted himself. She scooped it up and hid it in the folds of her cloak.

'You failed,' she sneered. 'Your Trial is incomplete. Your place in the Brotherhood is gone.'

Lek opened his mouth to protest, to ask a question, to say something. Nothing came out except a low groan of pain, expressed through a single word.

'You…' he breathed.

The woman grinned.

'Yes, me. You knew, didn't you? You knew that someone was manipulating you, trying to rewrite your history. I tried to tell your story, tried to put you off course, but you knew, and you wrested back control for a while. Even then, it took two of you to do it. You're on your own now. You're weak, and I'm taking over. You think you've got this figured out; you think you have a plan, but I understand more than you will ever know. Now I have the book, and I will write the ending.'

She opened the Book of Keyes, and a bright blue light spread from its pages. It grew quickly, intensifying until it blinded Lek and he had to close his eyes and turn his head away.

Then it was gone. He could feel that it was gone, as the warmth flowed back into his legs and his fingers and his cheeks.

Lek opened his eyes. It was no surprise to find that the woman was gone, too.

CHAPTER 49

HAEZLE

They stood, frozen in the immediate aftermath of the explosion, as the floor shuddered, whilst dust and dirt cascaded from the ceiling. Then there was silence. They stared at each other, openmouthed; Haezle at James, James at Sim, Sim at Haezle.

'That was an explosion?' It wasn't really a question. Haezle was in no doubt about what they'd just heard. She just couldn't believe it. 'Where did they get explosives from? Administration controls explosives. They're only for use in construction...'

'I think they'd be more use in destruction,' quipped James.

Haezle gave him a top grade withering stare. It wasn't the time.

'I mean Administration keeps a tight grip on the supply of explosives. They're imported under their supervision, only released for pre-approved construction projects. *Before* they get to the constructive part.'

'Welcome to the whiff of corruption,' said James. 'It sure smells like home.'

'I am familiar with the concept, and indeed the practise, of corruption,' snapped Haezle. 'It's just… Administration is one of the three Offices. If they've been infiltrated, then what hope do we have?'

'Sure smells like home,' James reiterated.

'I hate to break up the political banter,' called Sim, from the end of the corridor. 'But I think we should be moving. Or hiding. Definitely not standing around bemoaning the state of the city.'

'It's speeding up…' James trailed off.

'What?' asked Haezle.

'I mean, it gets worse. It really does. There's a long downward spiral coming for Trinity. But this isn't part of it. There was an eclipse. But, as we've already agreed to disagree on, it's not Black Night, it's Black Knights. And they don't emerge until after Chaguartay wins the election. It's all happening too fast.'

'Still standing around talking. Still not running,' said Sim.

Haezle ignored him.

'Chaguartay wins the election? Do you come from some kind of doom dimension? I don't know much about time travel, but could you have crossed into a parallel universe?'

'I don't know. I don't think so. But I don't know. I didn't choose to do this, remember? I was sent on a mission.'

'Just like Estrel,' pondered Haezle. 'By the same guy, as well.'

'The only guy who's likely to be able to explain any of this. We need to find Lek.'

'I don't know that will help. There's something up with him. I'm not sure he's going to explain anything. He's not himself. He wasn't a lot of use to Estrel, either. Estrel was getting quite frustrated with him.'

'He's our only hope…'

Haezle thought it best not to point out how little hope that, personally, gave her.

'Well, if we're going to find him, we need to go down.'

Sim made a strangled noise, which gave a very clear indication of what he thought of that plan.

'I know I've been advocating that we move, but isn't "down" a dangerous direction to go? The deeper we are, the more likely we are to find our way blocked off. It would be easy to corner us...'

'I don't see what choice we have.'

Haezle wholeheartedly agreed that this was a terrible plan, but she also agreed that they needed to find Onu Lek. They definitely needed to find him before yet another of his time travelling missionaries turned up to manipulate history in some vague and convoluted way.

'Well, if that's where we're going, can we hurry up and go there?' asked Sim. 'Which way?'

Haezle glanced up and down the stone passageway. It kinked up ahead, and part of the ceiling had fallen in. The resulting hole looked like a lowercase "h", which was why it had registered with her earlier. She spun around and pointed into the darkness.

'It's down here, I think,' she said. 'Around this corner. Come on!'

They ran, turned the corner, and scuttled down some steps. Haezle recognised the wooden A-frame acting as a prop to part of the ceiling that looked sketchier than all the rest and raced off down that fork of the tunnel.

'You suddenly seem to know where you're going,' observed Sim, breathy from the effort it was taking to keep up with what had become a bit of a sprint.

'I do, don't I?'

'How is that happening?'

'It just kind of came to me. Memory is funny like that.'

It wasn't a satisfactory answer. It was only partially true. Haezle didn't want to admit it, but she thought she knew what was happening here, and it wasn't down to her remembering the way.

They emerged into a large hall, what might once have been a reception room, or a dining room, before it dropped from ground level and crashed into the subbasement. The floor was cracked from corner to corner, with one side a metre and a half higher than the other.

Haezle skidded to a halt. She remembered this place. But there were dozens of passageways leading off it. Above each one was an elaborately carved wooden cornice of different designs.

'Which way now?' asked James, spinning on the spot, taking in the number of options.

'I don't know,' replied Haezle, but she wasn't defeated. 'I'm just figuring that out…'

She cast her eye along the row of ornamental decorations, just below the ceiling line. There were animal faces - a dog, an owl, a frog - a moon, a leaf, what might have been a potato, and some more abstract patterns.

'This one,' she declared, eventually hopping over the crack in the floor and disappearing down the darkest passage.

Sim glanced up as he and James followed her through. The cornice bore a simple swirl, starting in the middle and radiating out for a turn and a half. It looked like a letter "e".

'Are we just following things that look like letters spelling out your name?' he asked over Haezle's shoulders.

Haezle winced. She'd hoped they wouldn't notice. She hadn't done it on purpose. It was only when she was trying to figure out which passage to take from the hall and triggered the memory of the swirl that she'd confirmed to herself what she was doing. It was what she, Lek and Estrel had done earlier, without even being conscious of it.

'Yes, I think we are,' she sighed, twisting through the first of a series of switchbacks that she couldn't see from the right perspective but almost certainly were in the shape of a "z".

'Is that… some kind of coincidence or…?'

'It's some kind of coincidence,' she asserted. It had to be some kind of coincidence. It had to be chance.

It couldn't be some kind of mystical alignment. It certainly couldn't be destiny. Haezle didn't believe in those things.

There was another possibility. Until very recently, she would not have included it in her list of rational possibilities, because it would have seemed to be anything but. Things had changed.

She slowed down to a walk. It seemed likely that the mob following them would be delayed by the sheer number of choices before them in the hall. At a minimum, they would have had to split into smaller groups to cover all bases. Haezle was confident they could hold their own, even if it came to a confrontation, now.

She looked over the other shoulder.

'Was it you? The trail? My name?'

James shook his head as slowed to fall in step beside her.

'Not me. Why would I have done this?'

'Someone has done it. Someone laid this trail, someone wanted me to follow it. Someone who knew I'd need it.'

'A time traveller.'

'I don't mind if it was you. At least you're on my side. There's a genuine possibility that, if we're being led somewhere, it's into a trap.'

'I don't think it's a trap. Honestly. This wasn't me, I didn't lay this trail for you, but I meant what I said earlier. They can't find the book without you. You don't even really need them.

It's you, Haezle. You're meant to find it. I think this is someone trying to help you out.'

Haezle sighed. This wasn't what she wanted. She didn't want help. She wanted to be done with this nonsense. She wanted to be safe, back in the Commons. *Well, safer, back in the Commons.*

'Lek's going to regret helping me find him again,' she muttered. 'If this is all him, I do not appreciate the way he's going about this.'

'OK, well we can also be on the lookout then. For traps, and also, I guess, for something that looks like an "l"?'

'I think this is the "l",' said Haezle.

They were walking down a very long, very straight, stone-flagged corridor. The light was dim. She wasn't sure where it was coming from, but up ahead was completely dark.

'Possibly also the trap?' asked Sim, peering into the gloom. 'I can't actually see where we're going.'

'It's OK,' said Haezle. 'I recognise this.'

She took a step forward and then stopped in the darkness.

'How can you recognise it if you can't see it?' asked Sim.

Haezle couldn't explain what she meant. She didn't understand it herself, not in ways that she could put into words. But this felt familiar. There was something in the way their footsteps had echoed to a halt, something in the way the dust tasted as it coated her tongue when she breathed in.

There was something in the way the air moved, a warm gust coming up from below. Haezle understood where that was coming from. She knew where they were.

'There are steps here,' she said, shuffling forward in the dark. 'Be careful. When I was here before, there was a shaft of light coming through up there.'

She reached up and ran her finger along a crack in the low ceiling.

'It must go up to ground level,' she said. 'It must have been a streetlight. They won't be on right now, because it's the middle of the day, and there's no sunlight because of the eclipse.'

'So we go down?' asked James.

'Yes, we go down,' she agreed, as her fingers reached a stone carving, another abstract shape. The same one they followed from the hall.

'"e",' whispered Haezle, stepping off into the darkness.

CHAPTER 50

LAGRANGE

There's a wine cellar at the bottom of the steps. I smell it before I see it. It hits me before I get to the bottom.

I see Haezle and James ahead of me recoil and put their hands to their faces, trying to filter out some of the wave of stale air that wafts up from below, tainted with the sour tang of wine consumed too fast and sweated back out again.

The cellar itself looks like it has been the scene of significant partying. The rack is half empty. There are bottles strewn about. Some of them are broken, some of those apparently whilst still full of their contents, which pool in deep red puddles around the jagged shards of glass.

Three of the bottles are lined up against the far wall, their contents paler and cloudier than the wine in the others. I don't need to get close to know that they're full of piss. There's a small pool of vomit over on that side, too.

There are only two people here, though, which means this has been a superlative bender, if they've got through that much wine between them. I was under the impression it had only been a few hours since Haezle had left them.

It's remarkable they're still conscious, although they're slumped against each other for support, bottles held loose and listless in their hands. The older man's eyes roll as he peers at us. He seems to struggle to focus. I'm not, frankly, surprised.

'Oh, for…'

Haezle swoops in and shakes the younger man, who may not have been as awake as I thought. He splutters and groans, resisting, but Haezle is persistent.

'Estrel!' she coos. 'Wake up Estrel!'

'What?' Estrel grumbles, stiffly struggling into a more upright position.

He stretches his shoulders and digs his elbow into who I assume, by a process of elimination, to be Onu Lek in the ear. These two do not look to me to be in the middle of an important quest.

'Haezle!' exclaims Lek. 'You're a sight for sore eyes. I think we might just be saved…'

He turns to Estrel as he says this. Estrel stares back at him blankly.

'The book…' Lek hisses. 'She's brought the book. This is not our Haezle. She's come from a different timeline, she's…'

'No,' says Haezle. 'No, that's not what's happening. I have come from the Library…'

Haezle points upwards.

'Right up there. No time travel, no multiple selves tripping over each other. Apparently what you're doing… what you're *meant* to be doing, is important. I thought, once I discovered that the fate of reality was in your hands, that I might have left you in the lurch somewhat. I thought it might be a burden to carry. I thought you were pursuing a noble cause…'

'This isn't what it looks like,' begins Lek. 'I was just trying to…'

'This isn't what it looks like? It isn't two useless men getting drunk, avoiding their responsibilities and failing to live up to even the very low expectations that they, themselves, have set?'

'It is a bit like that,' admits Estrel. 'Lek said this was how it happened last time, that it all started with him getting very drunk, and then this man appeared and...'

'You're supposed to be searching for enlightenment. You're only going to find what you're looking for, and you're only looking for what you already know. You should be looking for what you need.'

'And what, exactly, is it we need?' demands Estrel, exasperation humming in every word. 'Honestly, if you have the slightest clue, you need to tell us. Because this guy sure as hell doesn't have an idea that's worth anything...'

'I don't know that's altogether fair...' begins Lek.

'Lek Benwar,' Estrel begins. '...'

And then everything changes. It's like a giant iron bell has been dropped on the stone cold floor. One cacophonous clang rings out and echoes around the enclosed space. Everyone's ears are numbed by the violent auditory impact. Silence falls.

Lek sits back suddenly and eyes Estrel.

'It was you,' he says. 'No one calls me that. No one has called me that in decades. Lek Benwar is... I am not Lek Benwar.'

Estrel says nothing. He stares back at Onu Lek. Lek gasps.

'But you... You're him. You're Keyes...'

'Wait, what?' James pipes up.

If I were him, I wouldn't get involved. I'm not getting involved. I'm listening. There are noises echoing down the passageway above, floating down the stairwell. They're getting closer.

I should say something. But there's something happening here. Something that I don't understand, something that I don't think I could ever understand, but something that feels important.

I don't need to understand it. Unfortunately, no one else down here seems to understand it either, and they really need to. Quickly.

'Why?' says Haezle to the pair of men at her feet, failing to hide her frustration. 'Why aren't you better at this?'

'Better at what?'

Estrel scrambles up.

'I don't know what you expect from us. But you're not shouting at the right guy. I have no idea what I'm doing here, not anymore. I don't know why he sent me back. I don't know what I'm supposed to do here. I don't know why he thinks I'm Keyes. I don't know - most of all, I don't know - why this particular version of Lek is as clueless as he seems to be. I don't…'

'You know nothing. I get it. You know nothing and it would seem that he knows nothing either. That's my problem, if I'm completely honest. This guy…' Haezle flings her arm behind her, furiously, to point at James without looking at him. '…seems to think that the universe is in danger, that its continued existence depends on finding a book, and that I am the one who is going to have to find it. But I don't know anything either. I could do with some help here. Which leaves me with just one question. There are, apparently, many versions of both of you, travelling the timeline, trapping yourselves in loops, writing and rewriting in the name of goodness and justice and love. I have one reality. I have one time. It's here, and it's now. It matters to me. This is all that matters to me. So what did I do to deserve you two, the worst possible versions out of all the possible versions of you two? How are you going to help me? You couldn't even…'

'It's not supposed to be like this,' says James.

Haezle stops in her tracks. Lek finally, unsteadily, makes it to his feet.

'What do you mean?' asks Estrel.

I would have asked the same thing, but I don't expect to understand the answer, so I don't. Those noises are getting closer. I should say something about that. It feels like people still have things to work through. I don't think I could get a consensus on where we should go at this moment.

We need a plan, though. If we wait here much longer, we're going to get cut off. We have two ways up, and several potential choices if we make it to the top of either of them. But we don't have much time to do that, and if we don't, there will be only one choice.

Maybe we don't need a plan. I eye up the staircase leading downwards, which looks old and unstable and unreliable. It might be all we've got. I wonder where it goes. What's underneath a cellar?

James is explaining something. I wasn't listening. I swear he said that he'd died. It's about as likely as anything else anyone has said.

'…was that all for nothing?' he asks, pained. 'Really?'

'Something changed,' says Lek.

'Now he has an answer!' cries Haezle. 'Finally, we're going to find out what the fuck is going on! What great wisdom do you have for us, Lek?'

I think that's the first time I've heard her refer to him without his honorific. She's really pissed off.

'Something changed,' says Lek, again. 'I've changed. I lost something… something I used to have. Lost it so much I almost forgot I ever had it. I'm sorry, my dear…'

Lek says this directly to Haezle. She seems to accept the sentiment, even if I see her visibly bristle at being referred to as "my dear".

'I used to be able to see things that hadn't happened, not to me. Not yet. I had a connection that spanned timelines, crossed dimensions… It's gone.'

'Gone?'

It's Estrel that asks, but I can see the same question on Haezle and James's lips.

'Gone,' repeated Lek. 'Something happened. Something was broken. It's affecting me. Maybe it's affecting all of us. It's cut me off from other versions of myself, past and future. Maybe it happened very recently, and there are still younger versions out there who can help. But if that's not right, if the thing that is lost was lost long ago, back in the past, then it could be affecting many more of us. It could be affecting all of us, in which case…'

'Everyone is doomed?' ask James.

'Everyone, everything, everywhere. All at the same time.'

'Shit.'

'Indeed. If this is a war, then we might have lost a long time ago and never even realised it.'

Silence engulfs the group again, the mood sombre and thoughtful. But we don't have time for that. Everyone can hear it now. There's a mob coming, and they're closer than even I realised.

'The stairs!' I shout, putting the only plan in town into action.

I run down, pointing to the rickety staircase as I go. Estrel moves first. Haezle isn't far behind. She drags Lek along with her.

But James isn't turning. He's looking past me, over my shoulder. I turn to see what he's looking for as a shot rings out.

I don't see who fired it, but it must have come from the steps behind me. They were even closer than I thought. As adrenaline sucks the flow of time from the room, as everything grinds to a slow crawl, at least for me, I see James leap forward, his arms outstretched.

He catches me full in the chest, knocking me off balance. I fall backwards and hit the floor hard, but without a bullet hole tearing me back to front.

I let out a cry as I see James fall forward into the same spot I've just vacated, fully in the bullet's path.

But Lek is there. He is already mid-dive when I realise that he's anticipated everything. Far from being a confused old man, he seems to know exactly what's going on at this moment. He's coming at James from the perfect angle to knock him out of the way and to leave all three of us unscathed.

For a moment, I think that maybe the whole thing has been a trick, a long con, all part of a strategy, too clever for the mere mortals that surround this mysterious and confusing monk to comprehend. Maybe, far from everything being doomed, maybe he's got this.

And then he's not there anymore. Suddenly, without warning, he fades from view, losing substance, dissolving until nothing is left but motes floating in the air.

He never makes contact with James. James does not get knocked out of the way. The bullet slams into his chest with an explosion of crimson.

Somebody screams. It might have been me.

CHAPTER 51

ESTREL

Crossing the plaza, the light was already creeping in, grey and drowsy, for the next morning. I tried not to think about how long I'd been going for without a proper rest. Lying unconscious in an alleyway didn't count, I didn't think.

I didn't know where to look for Mouse other than Eamer's, where she was probably done, or home, where she would head, eventually. How long that would take was an unknown variable, but I had no way of finding out what other assignments she might have had around Trinity that morning. I didn't, couldn't, wouldn't have kept tabs on her when we were together. Going home and waiting was a normal tactic. She always came home eventually. I just had to hope that it was in time.

It was about twenty minutes' walk between Clar's flat and Mouse's place, but the steps were programmed into my feet. I could have made it there with my eyes shut. I didn't need to think about where I was going. I had other things I needed to think about.

I'd had two messages from myself in the future. One quite

substantial one, delivered by Clar, which told me that the continuation of our universe depended on me finding the Book of Keyes. One delivered via Fricker, which told me to consider what Continuity meant to me.

I didn't know in what order those messages had been passed on. One of them must trump the other, and I was choosing to believe that Fricker's came second. I was also trying to ignore the fact that this was likely because I preferred the sound of that mission over the first one.

If I knew I'd already given one brief message to Fricker, why wouldn't I tell Clar to tell me that my later, more detailed instructions nullified that previous vague hint? If the message to Fricker had come second, it would make much more sense. It was short; it was vague. It was probably all I could relay to Fricker to remember.

He was much less plugged in to the general time-travelling-reality-crisis. He wouldn't have understood if I'd tried to explain. It might have been dangerous to explain too much to him. That made sense. That was logical. That was why I felt it was the course of action that I needed to take. It wasn't just because it was the one I was emotionally drawn to. It meant I could stop lying to Mouse.

I ignored the fact that the message was given to Fricker who I had, at best, a working relationship with and not Clar, one of my most trusted friends. It was easier to imagine extenuating circumstances than to acknowledge that there was little logic to my choices.

It wasn't like it was easier this way. I had no idea how to persuade Mouse of something she found hard to believe, even when I thought it was obvious and logical. I was, actually, irrefutably, her time traveller soulmate, but I didn't expect her to readily accept that…

'Estrel? Estrel, wake up…'

Mouse's voice cut through my thoughts. I didn't know where I was, but lifting my head caused a draught of cold air to flood into the cocoon I'd created, curled up on the hard stone. A ridge dug into my back, something scratched the back of my head. Brickwork.

I was huddled on Mouse's front steps. I couldn't have been there very long because the light wasn't much different from when I'd left Clar's. Unless I'd been asleep here all day and it was dusk already.

I peered up into Mouse's concerned face as she took hold of my arm to pull me to my feet. I got up with a creak and a groan, stumbling as the blood returned to my tingling legs.

'What time is it?' I groaned.

Mouse gave me one of her looks.

'How long have you…? Oh, right, yeah. The sky. It's nearly midday. The eclipse has started. There's an angry mob on the rampage. Let's get inside before they find us.'

That sounded like a good idea, so I let myself be led inside. Once we were through the door, Mouse let go of my sleeve and let me follow her in a more normal fashion. She went to the kitchen, so I did too.

'Sit,' she said, as I crossed the threshold.

I did as I was told.

Mouse was filling the kettle at the sink, her back to me so I couldn't see her face. I knew that tone, though. There were things she wanted to talk about. She meant business.

She flicked the switch and turned to me, leaning back on the work surface. The way she looked at me, there something different there. Not something I'd seen before, not what I was used to seeing when she looked at me. But there was something more than the last time we were here.

More than when she'd sent me to Clar. I wondered what had happened whilst I'd been elsewhere.

We said nothing. The kettle boiled. Mouse turned away and filled some mugs with water. She brought them across to the table. Tea bags bobbed at the surface.

'Here you go,' she said. 'I'm not even going to pretend I have any milk. I've got this, though…'

Mouse pulled a short, squat bottle from the inside pocket of her waistcoat. She waggled it in front of my face.

'What's that?'

'It's Talking Brandy.'

'How's that different from normal brandy?'

Mouse grinned and poured a generous measure into my mug.

'It's very similar. Only if you drink this, you have to talk. And you're going to drink, Estrel.'

I nodded to show that I understood. Of course I understood. I was familiar with the concept of Talking Brandy. It had played a significant role in us getting together in the first place.

I did, of course, wonder if that was what this was. Us getting together. I thought I was allowed that moment of hope.

I knew it wasn't, though. I plucked at the edge of the tea bag, inflated with steam, with my fingertips, scooping it out of the mug and dunking it a few times to wash out as much of the brandy as possible.

'What are we talking about?'

'About you, Estrel. About you and why you're here. And about why you're so interested in me.'

I swallowed hard. The moment of hope was proving hard to kill.

'What about me?'

I wanted to tell her all about me. I wanted to tell her my life story. I wanted to tell her my hopes, my dreams. I wanted to tell her how I felt. I wanted to tell her how I felt about her.

I couldn't be trusted in this situation. I needed her to ask me questions. Only then would I know what was safe to say.

'Estrel, are you a time traveller?'

That wasn't what I expected to hear in the slightest. I reeled. 'What? I...'

'I don't know. There's something about you, Estrel. I feel like I know you, but I also know, with certainty, that we've never met before. I feel you know *me*, and that doesn't creep me out like it should. I don't know if it's something you did or something you said - and, to be honest, even if it wasn't, I couldn't tell you what it was but...'

'I mean, I'm new in town...'

This was permission to tell the truth. I was a time traveller. We did know each other. I ached to tell her all of it, confess everything, but in the moment of my unmasking I panicked.

The rationale was twisted, confused, but I felt it deep within me. I'd been lying to her. It was by omission, but I'd been lying to her and the thought of having to admit that scared me more than the risk of her not knowing the truth.

'It's not just that, though, is it, Estrel? You don't belong here.'

'I...' I didn't know what to say.

'My father was a time traveller,' she said.

This was sudden, and out of the blue. She'd spoken about her mother before; she died giving birth to Mouse. Her final words had been to name her daughter. She'd never spoken about her father. I'd assumed she knew nothing about him.

She'd been raised by the Devoted, the newly established order in the Citadel, at the insistence of Lek, for whom Mouse's mother had worked. Between them, her "uncle" Sim Lagrange who, in my personal timeline, I'd accidentally shot a few days ago, and several unsuitable but unavoidable influences from the shadier side of Trinity's streets, Mouse's identity had been forged. Her parents had very little to do with it.

I didn't think she'd known or cared. And now it seemed she'd known all along.

'You never said…' The words slipped out before I knew what I was saying.

Mouse grinned.

'I knew it!' she cried. 'I thought you'd put up more of a fight, Estrel. That was too easy. My daddy was a policeman, so I'm told. An Authority Oficier, if you can believe that. But he travelled back in time and fell in love with my mum. I think he's around here now, in Trinity. He wouldn't be much older than I am. But I could never bring myself to look him up. I was worried that he'd be disappointed in his little girl…'

She looked a little wistful as she sipped her brandy-laced tea.

'He went back to save Sim's life,' she said. 'Sim has always said that's what drives him. That someone would go to all that trouble to sacrifice themselves for him must mean that what he is doing is important.'

This was a mess. I knew what Simeon Lagrange's life meant in the end. His death had kick-started Continuity. It was what had brought me here. It was what was threatening to end the universe.

'I don't think you're a policeman, though, Estrel. You don't seem the type. You're a bit more… Well… What are you?'

It was a good question. I stared down at my mug. This really was a mess. I only knew one way out of this kind of mess, a mess that I had largely created with my lies, even if I hadn't meant to. I took a deep breath.

The words formed on my lips. I looked up into Mouse's eyes. But Mouse wasn't there anymore. A haze persisted, a vague suggestion of a shape that had once been the woman I loved. Motes floating in the air.

My breath caught in my throat, metamorphosed into a sob as the realisation dawned. I didn't know how, or why, but Mouse was gone.

I would never see her again. I could feel the gap between her existence and my reality already. It was growing, getting further away. Every memory I had of her suddenly felt weaker, more distant.

The fluorescent overhead light flickered and went out. I sat in darkness, in silence. On my own. More alone than I had ever been.

It looks like you've finished reading ECLIPSE...

Thank you!

I really hope you enjoyed it, and if you did it would be great if you could leave a review somewhere... Amazon, Goodreads, Social Media, just tell a friend - any of those would be fantastic and make all the difference for me, struggling little indie author that I am.

Next, if you'd like to stay up to date with what I'm writing and when you can read it, pop along to https://philoddy.com where you can find links to my own socials, and you can sign up for my monthly newsletter.

Finally, there are other books I've written and contributed to, so if you're not sure what to read next, check out:

ENTANGLEMENT SERIES

PHASE I:

Echoes

Entrapment

Eclipse

Enlightenment (coming late 2025)

PHASE II:

Exodus (coming 2026)

Welcome To Trinity (companion novella)

FOR CHILDREN

The Man In The Moon

AS CONTRIBUTOR

Royston and District Writers' Circle 40th Anniversary Anthology

There Are Many Ways Of Getting Lost: The Royston Writers' Circle Lockdown Anthology

About the Author

Phil Oddy lives in North Hertfordshire and writes stories about how to cope in a confusing world, cleverly disguised as sci-fi/fantasy adventures. Find his website at https://philoddy.com - everything he's currently up to should be on there.

He is happily married with two sons, and has promised everyone lavish gifts if he ever writes a bestseller, so if you've bought one of his books then they all thank you.

Despite a long and successful career as an IT analyst in both the public and private sectors, writing is something he seems to be unable to prevent himself doing which means that by encouraging him you're either feeding an addiction or providing therapy. You can pick which.

When his fingers are too tired to carry on typing, Phil likes to relax by reading something by David Mitchell (either one is fine) or binge-watching Drag Race.

Acknowledgements

There are some people who I need to thank for helping craft the version of Eclipse that you are holding.

First of all, thank you to Alex Oddy who, over the course of a fairly long walk, helped me figure out that my initial plans for what was "Enlightenment" were far too vast and sprawling and were, in fact, two books. From that conversation Eclipse (and its somewhat catastrophic ending) was born. Alex came up with the title, as well.

Thank you to Mark Stay, whose advice and guidance is always welcome and incredibly helpful. When I thought I'd bitten off more than I could chew, his response to questions like "how many POVs is too many POVs" gave me the perspective I needed. (Note, there is – of course - no definitive answer to this question, so if you think this book has too many POVs that's my fault, not Mark's).

Thank you to the marvellous Julie Dore who, despite me always seeming to send her one of my books just before she's due to go on holiday, unfailingly gives me exactly the feedback I need. Whether it's an enthusiastic reaction to something I was worried about landing, or a gentle spotlight shone on my blind spots, these books would be far poorer without her help.

Finally, starting out on my writing career I've been lucky to have many cheerleaders amongst friends, family and colleagues. But most of all I'm lucky to have three people whose support and trust I value the most. To Susan, Sam and Alex (again): thank you for being the people you are and being part of the family we've created. I couldn't do this without you.